CITY

OF

TREES

CITY

OF

SHADOWS

CITY

OF

TREES

CITY

OF

SHADOWS

RACHEL L. ERTASSI

ARCHWAY
PUBLISHING

Archway Publishing books may be ordered through booksellers or by contacting:

Archway Publishing
1663 Liberty Drive
Bloomington, IN 47403
www.archwaypublishing.com
844-669-3957

ISBN: 978-1-6657-3233-8 (sc)
ISBN: 978-1-6657-3232-1 (hc)
ISBN: 978-1-6657-3234-5 (e)

Library of Congress Control Number: 2022919629

Print information available on the last page.

Archway Publishing rev. date: 12/23/2022

Dedicated to many, as this is my first book.

To Shawna, Renee, and Lauren
for the support.

To the diabetic community,
you deserve more representation.

And to the people of Sacramento,
a story set in our city.

As of early 2022, insulin is the sixth most expensive liquid in the world, climbing up to $26,400 per liter.

If milk cost the same as insulin, an 8oz glass of milk at the diner would cost $5,819.

—Gupta, 2022, *Science ABC*

PROLOGUE

They call it the City of Trees. The Sacramento State campus alone
has over 400 species. The leaves change into miraculous shades
of gold and red in the fall and brilliant greens in the spring and
summer. In November, leaves fall fluttering to the ground; and
in March, the petals of white blossoming flowers rain down from
the trees like snow.

However, beneath the canopy of trees lays a dark secret. Each tree
in the city casts a long shadow. And in the shadows lurks something evil. Something dark, violent, and insatiable.

INTRO

The moon illuminated the dark riverbank of Discovery Park. It was bold, big, and bright tonight. Enough that the sky painted the city below in a blue hue and looked itself like a navy watercolor. The river lapped at the sandy beach shore. During the day the park was often full of life, children playing in the water, families out on boats; men could be seen across the way fishing in isolated spots. Tonight, the air stank of death.

The dull lapping against the shore pulled blood from the sand that swirled into the water, tinting it red. A coyote approached the water cautiously and sniffed the red pool of blood. Unimpressed, the coyote trotted off, past a body lying face down on the beach. The water continued to pull the puddle of blood into the river with each soft wave. The moon sparkled brightly above the red river water, which shined brighter and more exaggerated by alternating red and blue as the lights from a patrol car approached the scene.

CHAPTER 1

VERA

She would forever be in school. She sighed and tapped her pencil on the desk. She didn't mind it though. School was something she was good at. She had been doing it for so long that it was ingrained in her personality. She was a student. And she was a good student.

Professor Wong slid her graded exam onto her desk- 68 percent. *Fuck.* Well, sometimes she was a good student. She slid the papers into her bag, not bothering to take out a binder to organize them. She felt the papers crumple as she jammed them against something else, probably her water bottle at the bottom of her backpack.

Whatever.

Vera hiked her backpack onto her shoulder and headed out of the classroom into the cool dusk air. She looked around campus. It was eerily quiet at Sac State. Friday night in the spring though, so that made sense. Nobody took Friday classes if they could help it, much less a Friday evening class. Even less than that during spring semester. As the weather warmed, students stayed out late in the sun drinking and socializing. Still, it was evening and the quiet made Vera feel unnerved. She balled her keys into her fist, *just in case*, and headed to the parking structure.

The breeze had picked up a little as she approached the parking structure by the school gym. It was the furthest from her class, clear across campus, but it usually had parking spots. She shifted the weight of her backpack as she pressed the button for the elevator. Vera checked the time. 5:45p.m. She raised her eyes as the doors opened and watched a startled couple peel their lips apart from each other, embarrassed. The girl giggled as she adjusted her shirt as they exited together. Vera rolled her eyes.

That should be me. I need to get back out there.

She stepped into the elevator, smelling an overwhelming amount of *Acqua di Gio* lingering in the air. It reminded her of Nathan. He used to wear it when they went on dates. She could still smell it on her clothes when she got back into her dorm room after they would mess around. Sometimes she would smell him before she saw him. She would be working on homework in the library and smell *Acqua di Gio* creeping up behind her and smile when she felt his arms wrap around her waist.

And then the smell turned sour when she smelled it in her dorm room on days she had not seen him. She began to smell it on her roommate. Turned out he was fucking her too. *Classic.*

They had dated for only a few months, but her roommate was blonde and beautiful. A Sac State *Hornets* dancer. So naturally, when she introduced him to her friends, he was struck by her roommate's blatant and *in your face* Barbie beauty. Vera liked to think men were attracted to her intelligence, but at eighteen, not a chance.

She pretended that she didn't notice the affair at first. He was great in bed, he was handsome, he made her laugh. If she thought *really* hard about it she could pretend he was a good guy too. But of course, nothing young lasts. For Vera anyway, that was just her luck. She took the breakup hard. Hit the bottle hard. Tanked a semester, pulled herself back up, got a new roommate and moved off campus after her first year. She dove into her academics in year two, and year three, and now in year four... But it had been a while since she had been pushed into an elevator wall and felt up by someone wearing *Acqua di Gio.*

I need a beer.

Vera walked to her car in the mostly empty parking lot. The few cars that were in it were on the first floor and had just arrived as eager Friday night gym goers. Most of the students were off campus by now. Vera started her Fridays late in the day, so she had to park at the top of the structure where there were still spots when she arrived. She made her way to her car and was immediately struck by a white streak on her left bumper that crept up the side of her back door.

"Oh you've got to be kidding me."

I really need a beer.

Someone had hit the side of her poor Civic with their car leaving a swipe of white paint across her door. Her car was nothing special, a silver 1996 Honda Civic, all manual. Manual windows, locks, transmission. She had a wheel lock to protect it from getting stolen from the parking lot, since Civics are one of the most easily-stolen cars in the world. Her friend had warned her before she moved to Sacramento for school that you could steal a Civic by jamming a screwdriver into the ignition and drive with it sticking out like that. She doubted that was true but was unwilling to put her baby at risk since she had paid for it herself.

At least they left a note... Vera reached over the windshield and pulled it loose from behind the wiper. It was written on a *Gordito Burrito* receipt.

"My Bad."

Vera crumpled it up furiously and threw the note into the street. She jammed her keys into the lock and let herself into her car, allowing her head to fall onto the steering wheel. She stared at her hands and collected her thoughts.

These parking spots are too fucking small.

After a few minutes, she accepted defeat and jimmied her wheel lock off so that she could drive down the street to the nearby pub where she worked part-time, for that beer.

CHAPTER 2

VERA

The gravel made a satisfying groan under her tires as Vera pulled into the parking lot of Mosaic Brew Pub. It was still early for a Friday night at Mosaic, but a steady flow of customers trickled in and out with their beers. Mosaic was one of the only places in Sac where you could get a stein of beer on tap, and that was kind of the appeal. The beer was good, but the customers were really here to take stein pictures for their social media.

Recently, Mosaic had blown up on Instagram because a local influencer had taken a few pictures with the steins in front of the pubs ivy fence and tagged the location.

Mosaic had a cute, rustic, pub vibe, while being trendy and chic. Something that hard-core brewers in the area resented about the pub, but that from the business-end of things was making it very successful, since chic was in. Ivy crawled up the brick walls and along the fence lining the outdoor patio. String lights illuminated the seating area like fireflies and occasionally there would be live music and corn hole on Saturdays.

The inside of the pub had dark walls covered in paintings of hops in different sizes and varieties. A large glass window allowed the customers to look into the brew house and wave at the brewer, who might wave back, depending on his mood. The owner was considering getting a roll-up door like some of the more popular breweries, but he would have to knock out a brick wall to do so. Because of this major construction setback, he had more recently been leaning toward just getting a dart board for the pub instead.

Vera strolled in and planted herself at the mostly empty bar. Aside from herself, there were no other patrons at the bar- other than a young couple a few stools away jabbering about their classes together. Vera caught a whiff of *Acqua di Gio* and rolled her eyes.

"Need a beer, Ver?" Sam walked up to her with a rag in his hands, drying a stein that was giving off warm steam from the wash.

"More like two," Vera retorted with a groan as she rolled her neck. Sam smiled. He had a nice smile. He was about her age, maybe a few years older, and he went to Sac State too. Before they started working together she had seen him on campus a few times around *Mendocino Hall*- the School of Arts building. Although she thought he was an economics major so that didn't exactly add up. Maybe he had a girlfriend who was studying in Mendocino.

Sam poured her a stein of their West Coast IPA. Vera liked her beer strong and bitter, same as her coffee. Although, she didn't used to. When she started drinking she started like most people do, with light or fruity drinks. The first wine she liked was a Moscato that tasted like apple juice. But now she liked her wine dark and bitter. She joked that she was jaded by life. She liked things with a bitter edge.

"Did you see we have a new hazy on tap?" Sam asked.

"You know I don't like that shit Sam. It messes up my blood sugar," Vera said after a long pull from her stein.

"See, that doesn't make sense to me. The West Coast and the Northeast are brewed with about the same amount of sugar," Sam argued.

"I don't know what to tell you, man. The hazy ones taste a lot sweeter, and they make my blood sugar high. Plus, I like my beer hoppier than that."

"Whatever, I'll bring you a sample." Sam winked. Vera rolled her eyes but tasted the sample when he brought it over.

"Yep, that's a hazy." She smiled. But it wasn't bad. All of the beer Mosaic brewed was good. Sam walked away to continue putting glasses on the hooks and shelves as Vera checked her app on her watch that displayed her blood sugar level. A perfect 120 mg/dL. She felt a small amount of pride and cheers'd herself silently. Vera had been type 1 diabetic for fifteen years. Totally insulin dependent and totally healthy for the most part, as long as she took her injections.

Sam strolled back when he noticed that her glass was looking light.

"Thirsty tonight?" He grinned.

Vera looked at her glass, she had almost finished her stein and had only been sitting for a few minutes.

"Someone side-swiped my car today..." She sighed heavily. Sam frowned.

"In the school parking lot over by the gym," Vera continued.

"Those spots are too tight. I've had my car swiped there too." Sam cleared her empty glass. "Another?"

Vera nodded. "Bring me the session though, please."

Mosaic had a killer session IPA. Sam returned with a fresh pour and leaned into the counter.

Damn he's cute.

The thought surprised her. Vera put her hair behind her ear.

Where is this coming from? Must be the cologne at the end of the bar playing with my emotions...

"Think you could do me a favor and cover my shift tomorrow? I have a date." Sam grinned at her.

"Why did you set a date for a day you had work?" Vera teased.

"Come on, Vera, please? I know you don't have plans."

That was true, but annoying that he presumed so. He was looking less cute by the second.

"Fine," Vera sighed, "But buy me this round."

Sam flashed her a smile and walked away to adjust the calendar. Vera sipped her second beer and turned around on her stool to face the other customers. It had started to fill up a little since she had arrived. She could see through the window that a food truck was setting up outside and Vera decided to go see who was here tonight. She left her beer, confident that Sam would keep an eye on it, and went out to the truck.

Not your Mama's Meatballs sat waiting for her. She walked over to check the menu display. Meatballs, turkey meatballs, vegan meatballs, spaghetti and meatballs, meatball sub, meatballs and polenta… She pulled out her wallet and ordered a sub, then headed back inside with a pager.

When she returned, someone was sitting at the stool next to hers. She rolled her eyes because nearly the whole bar was still open. She sat down at her seat and took a swig from her beer, eyeing the newcomer suspiciously and hoping that he would get the hint and scoot a couple seats down. He noticed her looking and smiled.

"I'm Aaron."

Great. Now I have to make conversation.

For a moment, Vera considered pretending that she didn't hear him, but it wasn't busy enough or loud enough for that. She forced a polite smile after her long day.

"Vera."

"What are you drinking Vera?"

"The session. It's pretty good."

Sam walked over in that moment, another steaming glass in hand from another load of dishes that he was drying. Aaron ordered a session without asking about any other beers.

Great. Looks like I've made a friend.

Vera turned and assessed him quickly. He was actually pretty good looking. Sandy hair, sandy eyes, sandy-golden skin. Kind of a generally tan person all around. He looked like he played water polo or something. He was in excellent shape, based on the way his clothes were fitting. He smiled at her with his teeth, and that was what got her. Great smile.

Sure, what the hell.

They made relaxed conversation and when his friends arrived Vera found herself a little disappointed to be losing his company suddenly.

"Well, it was nice to meet you. Mind if I get your number?" Aaron asked as he was standing to leave. Vera blushed and gave him her number. It had been a while since someone had asked. As he walked away her pager buzzed, indicating that her food was ready. She picked it up from the truck and ate in a hurry at the bar, eager to get out of there. She was feeling a bit shy now that she and Aaron had interacted and he would be sitting only a few tables away with his friends, while she sat alone at the bar.

She reached into her bag to get her insulin after she finished eating. Vera still used syringes and a vial. They were cheaper. She set up her syringe and slyly gave herself a quick injection in her stomach. She replaced the cap and looked up, making eye contact with a woman across the bar. The woman shot her a dirty look, shaking her head. Vera felt herself shrink a little, wanting to explain that she was taking insulin and nobody in their right mind would *shoot up* drugs on a bar stool in a busy pub in East Sac.

Whatever, fuck her.

Vera grabbed her bag and left after settling up with Sam.

CHAPTER 3

VERA

Vera tossed her bag aside as she walked into her apartment. Her roommates Grace and Shanice were sitting in the living room on the couch watching trash TV and getting high. Shanice held up her bong offering it to Vera as she passed and Vera shook her head politely.

Vera tried smoking in high school and she really wanted to like it because all of her friends liked it so much. She wanted to fit in and be *normal*, but the sensation of being high reminded her of what it felt like to have low blood sugar. Disoriented, confused, dizzy, out of control; she found herself checking her blood sugar over and over again, forgetting the number, or thinking that maybe she was low and if she ate something she could make the feeling go away. But her blood sugar was always fine, and the feeling remained. She just had to wait for the high to wear off;

anxious, and feeling falsely low and off equilibrium. Thankfully, Vera never felt that way when she drank. She just stuck to her beers.

"How was class?" Grace asked.

"*Shitty,* I got a D on that test," Vera said as she walked into the kitchen to grab a *Corona.*

"*Oooooooh,*" the roommates groaned together on the couch.

"And then," Vera popped her beer open, "I went to my car and someone had side-swiped me and left a note that said 'My Bad.'"

"*Ooooooooh noooo,*" they groaned in unison, louder. Vera walked into the living room and stood with her beer, watching the TV. They were all quiet for a moment and a haze of smoke floated in front of the TV as Grace exhaled. Shanice scrolled through Tinder and Grace scrolled through Instagram during the commercials. Vera looked over Shanice's shoulder at her Tinder account, considering that maybe she should make one for herself.

"That guy is cute," She suggested.

"Nah, he has weird hair," Shanice retorted. The next photo was of a girl in a bikini on a boat. Shanice dated both men and women. She swiped left a few times before settling on a guy with a sharp jaw and blue eyes to swipe right on. Vera watched her swipe a while longer, and then walked herself upstairs after it became apparent that Shanice and Grace were lost to their highs and had become absorbed in their phones.

Before bed, bolstered by her encounter at the pub and her rage against her lasting memories with *Acqua di Gio,* Vera downloaded Tinder and made herself an account.

CHAPTER 4

UNKNOWN

It was a windy night. He laid in bed and listened to the trees sway outside. He heard a flurry of branches crack and break as a gust of wind blew them clean off a tree and into the street. That crack. He closed his eyes and tried to relive the moment. The last crack he heard, followed by a piercing, guttural, scream.

A gust of wind shook the house and a high-pitched whir of air rushed past his window. He thought of the way the boy's hand had cracked first, when he tried to defend himself. His hand shattered as if he had taken a bat to a wine glass. *Too easy.* The crack wasn't loud like his leg was. That thick, satisfying break, like the larger branches being torn off a tree outside, not like the small snaps of twigs rapping at the window now. The wind died down and it was silent for a moment. The silence was what he liked the best. The snaps, the screams, the gasp, and then… silence. Then nothing but his footsteps as he padded away from a limp, broken body.

CHAPTER 5

VERA

Vera woke slowly and rubbed her eyes roughly as she stretched out in her bed. She had the strangest dream. She was walking through a field and it was full of fog. She looked up at the soft orange sky as the sun set. She walked through the tall wet grass, feeling her socks begin to fill with cold, dampness, as her shoes became wet in the field. She was uncomfortable with soggy feet. She looked past the field and saw an opening to a highway.

Vera picked up her pace and pushed through the tall, thick grass, with some difficulty. When she arrived at the edge of the grass, she noticed that the road was totally silent and empty. She looked around. She was utterly alone. In front of her was a banged up little stand that looked like it would sell lemonade. She walked up to it carefully and assessed it. She felt tired from pushing through the grass. She looked at her hands and they were shaking. She was exhausted and weak.

The stand was covered in candy bars. Large ones, small ones, old vintage things that she had not seen anywhere other than novelty stores. Vera looked around for the person selling the candy but saw nobody. She felt dizzy. She reached for a chocolate bar and peeled back the wrapper. She ate it quickly, frantically, as if she had not eaten in years. Then she had another, and another, and another, until she was surrounded by trash and candy wrappers. Vera's hands were sticky with chocolate. Guiltily, she looked down at the mess she had made. She caught sight of her hands and gasped. They were sticky with blood. Deep cherry red stained her skin. The shock of the blood woke her up.

Her eyes fluttered open and she stared at the ceiling, disoriented. Vera pushed herself up with her elbows and reached for her cellphone to check her blood sugar levels on her glucose monitoring app. Vera had a continuous glucose monitor inserted in her leg, high on her thigh in the fatty part. It looked like a band-aid with a little plastic piece. It was easy to insert and easy to remove, and there was a small wire under her skin that read the levels of sugar that circulated in her blood.

As a diabetic, those levels fluctuate more greatly than people who did not have the illness. It was a balancing act that she had been doing for years. A little like riding a rollercoaster. Her blood sugar would go up, and she would take insulin. Then it would go down, and she would need sugar to balance it. The body needs to reach equilibrium, something that is easier said than done when dealing with a chronic illness.

The little plastic piece on the device read the numbers from the wire under her skin and sent it to the app on her phone via bluetooth. Medical technology has come a long way thankfully. When she was diagnosed, she never would have dreamed of having something so convenient. Albeit expensive...

Her blood sugar was low. The app read 65 mg/dL. Normal

range for someone with diabetes runs about *90-160* mg/DL. For someone without diabetes, it runs roughly *80-100*.

She knew it was going to be low. For one thing, she could feel it. The disorientation, the drowsiness, she felt uneasy, a little like the room was spinning, almost hung over. *Nothing* was worse than waking up with a hangover and low blood sugar. Today however, it was just symptoms of the low blood sugar that was making her feel this way.

Aside from feeling it physically, Vera knew she was low before she woke up because she had that strange dream. She found it fascinating that her body would try to tell her that her sugar levels were off through her dreams. Before she had been diagnosed, she had recurrent nightmares about blood. And when she was low, she often had disturbingly vivid dreams about sugar or food. In these dreams she would gorge herself, indulging in anything she could get her hands on as if she were starving. It's all about survival. The mind is a marvelous thing.

Vera swung her legs out of bed and reached for a juice box. She kept a little pack under her bed. Grace teased her about them. She thought Vera looked like a child drinking her little apple juice with the straw. Vera took a moment to drink her juice and allow her body to reset before getting out of bed.

Once she was up, she dragged her feet to the window to open her blinds and let in some light. It was a beautiful day. The sun cascaded through the leaves of the tree by her window, casting lacy shadows into her room. A lovely Saturday. The weather had been warming up nicely after the wet winter that they had in Sacramento. It rained much more than usual, which meant snow for Tahoe. The local ski bums were ecstatic.

For Sacramento though, it meant mud, and flooding. The river was much higher than it had been in years. But again, the local fish and boat bums were ecstatic about that. And with the weather warming up, college students had been talking about doing a float down the river with tubes.

Vera had always thought that the river was pretty gross. It was muddy and dark. She had heard rumors of needles at the bottom from drug users who camped by the river banks under freeways. She would not be participating in the river float. Nevertheless, the river was nice to look at, and a fun place for a picnic before the weather got unbearably hot.

Vera ran her fingers down her long beige curtains and admired the warmth from the flooding in sunlight. She decided that she would ride her bike to a nearby coffee shop and do some homework outside. Once her blood sugar was back to normal and she felt up to it of course.

After a cup of coffee and the time it took to get dressed, Vera felt ready to tackle the day. She pulled her red beach-cruiser from the side yard and stuffed her schoolbooks into the front basket. She set out down L street on the midtown grid, keeping to the one-way roads with the least amount of traffic. She had not decided which shop she wanted to go to and allowed her bike to lead the way. She smiled as the breeze kissed her cheeks and occasional loose green leaves fluttered down from the trees. The air was crisp and fresh in the spring.

She swerved her bike through the field of broken tree branches, twigs, and other mild debris. It had been a very windy night and midtown showed the beating it had taken. She turned a corner and bumped up the sidewalk to park her bike at her final destination. Her cruiser had taken her to *Old Soul*, a cute coffee house on H street. It had two locations, one on L, not far from her house, and the one on H. Vera decided as she rode that she wanted to check out a different side of town.

She parked her bike and headed inside with her books. After ordering a latte, she found a table outside in the shade and set up her study station. She decided to study for the class she performed poorly in, Federal Tax Procedures. She would be damned if she got another D in Professor Wong's class. Motivated, she sipped her drink from the rim, disrupting the perfect leaf that had been made with the foam, and dove into her chapter.

"Vera?"

A familiar voice called. She turned. Sam's tall figure stood behind her holding a scone and an iced tea.

"Hey Sam." She smiled.

"Fancy seeing you here," he chirped. "Mind if I sit?"

"No, go ahead."

He dragged out a chair from the patio set with a screech of metal legs on the pavement and took a seat.

"What are you working on?" He asked as he sipped from his glass.

"Tax procedures. I nearly failed my last test."

"So unlike you." Sam said with a *tsk*.

"I agree!" Vera laughed.

"Well don't mind me, I just came here to get some air because it is so nice today. I brought a book." Sam said, holding up a novel. Vera angled her head to try and read the cover.

"What is it?" She asked.

"*The Whisper Man,* by Alex North. A thriller," he said dramatically.

"I see… well, if it's any good you'll have to let me borrow it after."

"Sure thing," he said, cracking it open.

Vera continued to work in silence, sipping her latte and taking notes as Sam sipped his tea and flipped pages. Vera rolled her neck and took a moment to look around as she drank more of her coffee.

A butterfly fluttered toward them and turned sharply before getting too close. It had miraculous yellow and black wings that flapped gently as it glided through the air. She smiled and turned back to her textbook. After a while longer, Sam stood to leave. Vera checked the time and was surprised to see that she had been there almost an hour and a half already. She glanced at her empty mug, wondering if she should get another.

"You out of here?" She asked, looking up.

"Yeah, I have some other stuff I need to get done before my date tonight. You're still good to cover my shift at Mosaic, right?"

"Yeah. I'll be there with bells on." Vera said sarcastically.

"It's good money" He shrugged with a smile. "Thanks again. See you later," he said as he headed out.

"Bye Sam!" Vera called after him.

He was right though. It was good money. And Vera enjoyed the work. She smiled and turned back to her textbook.

CHAPTER 6
UNKNOWN

A nother restless night. He stared at the ceiling and sighed. The man sat up in bed and looked out the window. He had work to do. He stood and dressed himself. It was late morning, nearly afternoon, but it was a Saturday so that didn't matter and his work was not time sensitive. More than anything, it was sensitive to his sanity. The windy night made him yearn for violence. He had to get out of the house.

Despite having people in his life, he was lonely, constantly. He felt that he had trouble connecting with people and that nobody seemed to understand him. His victims saw him in his purest form. He felt like releasing himself tonight. He was caged inside the body of a man who only let his monster out every so often. Tonight, was the night. He was sure of it. He just had to make it through the day.

CHAPTER 7

VERA

Vera never usually struggled with numbers. Numbers were consistent and easy to understand. They were also a huge part of her major in school so she had a significant amount of practice with numbers and calculations. Maybe it was a beer going to her head. Vera had a stein of the Mosaic pilsner as she was closing up. She counted the drawer once more to confirm the amount and divvy out tips.

Vera heard a rustle and looked up. She kept still, only moving her eyes as she peered around the pub and listened. Again, rustling and then a soft bang, as if something had been knocked over outside. The pub was dead silent. Vera had cut the music when she started counting the drawer because she kept losing track. She set the money down and listened. *Nothing.*

She went back to counting the 20s. *20, 40, 60, 80, 100, 120-* BANG, a loud clatter in the brew house. She shut the drawer and wandered into the back pushed by her fear, curiosity, and adrenaline.

Vera flicked on the lights and the overhead bulb sputtered and glowed dimly. It was on its last breath; normally it lit up the room brightly. Probably something that she should change but she was exhausted and wanted to go home, especially after the added fear of the mystery noises. She would change the bulb during her next shift. The brew house looked still, *calm*. There was no sound save for the soft bubble of one of the tanks fermenting.

She heard a door close suddenly and made her way back up to the front. A man stood at the bar, dressed in a dark hoodie and jeans. He looked disheveled, desperate, unwell. He looked like someone she would not be able to talk to with rational conversation.

"I'm sorry, but we are closed for the evening," Vera said without moving from her position by the door to the brew house.

The man looked up. He looked tired, as though he had been up for days. He said nothing. She held her ground, unsure if she should advance toward him or stay completely still like a decorative statue of the pub. The man looked away, out the window, and then back at Vera. He reached into his pocket and fished around.

Vera watched him and quickly assessed her surroundings. It was nearly 11:00p.m. She was alone. Her keys were in her purse, about four feet away to the right. There were glass cups and mugs to her left. The cash drawer was closed. There was a phone charger on the counter. There was a jar of pens next to where she kept the signed receipts. There was a fishbowl full of tips that she had not counted yet.

Her thoughts were interrupted by a small flash of light when she realized he had drawn a cigarette from his pocket and proceeded to light it in the pub in front of her.

"Sir, you can't smoke in here... and we are closed. You have to leave."

He ignored her. Suddenly, Vera felt her fear dissipate. She felt angry and protective of the pub.

"Hey, you have to leave. Go now or I'll call the police."

He looked up. This caught his attention. With his cigarette dangling from his lips, he mumbled in a raspy voice *"Call them."*

Vera stared, perplexed.

Suddenly he lunged over the bar. Vera jumped back, stunned.

This isn't happening!

The man grabbed at the register drawer, lifted it, and threw it onto the ground trying to break it. The register smacked the ground hard, with a loud BANG, but did not bust open. Instead, one of the sides dented inward and the gray paint scuffed badly. He picked it up and threw it down again, mangling it further, but the register would not open.

Furiously he snatched it off the ground and threw it at the wall behind Vera. She ducked down reflexively and it struck the wall violently above her directly where her head had been. A split second after smashing into the wall, the register came down onto Vera with a hard thud.

It struck her skull with such force that she saw stars. Pain split through her, rattling her teeth as she clenched them together so hard that she thought they might break. Heat spread through her body like a poison coming down from where she was hit on her scalp, causing her to break out in a full body sweat from the pain. She was sure she had been nailed by a corner of the register box.

She opened her eyes and through her blurry vision, she made out coins and bills scattered across the floor and the shape of the man charging at her like a child after bursting open a piñata. He was frantic, manically grabbing for the cash.

Vera bolted up with a sudden surge of adrenaline and darted away from the scene. She stumbled as she stood and fell back down, landing hard on her hands. She got to her feet again as quickly as she could and rushed out of the pub and into the gravel parking lot to call 911.

She took in a sharp breath of night air to steady herself, only to realize she left not just her phone, but her purse and car keys inside the pub. She felt her eyes sting with tears from fear, but shock and adrenaline forced her legs to carry her back inside before she could stop them. She wasn't thinking, she was just moving, taking the situation second by second.

Inside she heard shuffling on the floor as the robber collected bills, although she could not see him. Vera was frozen in place.

Move.

She willed herself. Carefully, she made her way to the bar and peered over the counter to try and catch sight of him. He was gone. Her eyes darted around the room trying to locate him. She hadn't heard him move from the floor. Her head was pounding from the strike by the register.

Vera scanned the counter for her purse and spotted it exactly where she had left it. She took soft steps toward the other end of the bar to grab it when a clatter from inside the brewhouse stopped her in her tracks.

She peered through the window into the brew house. The window displayed the lit-up tanks where the customers would see their brewer working during the day. In place of their brewer stood the man, bashing the tanks with a wrench that he had taken out of their pub tool kit.

BANG BANG BANG!

He beat on the tanks as if he was trying to break them open. He brought it down hard over and over, quickly, like a man frantically trying to hammer in nails.

"What the hell??" Vera said, her voice louder than she had meant it to be.

He wouldn't be able to hear her through the glass window, but suddenly, as if he sensed her presence, he turned around and looked her dead in the eye. Vera ran for her purse and the man threw the wrench at the glass window as if he were pitching a baseball and then darted away. The window made a loud bursting sound as the tempered glass shattered into small pieces all over the pub floor.

Oh, my boss is going to be so mad.

Vera thought as she cursed herself for covering stupid Sam's shift so he could have his stupid date.

Vera grabbed her purse and spun around to leave. The glow of her iPhone caught her attention as she was about to run. It had fallen off of the bar top and was on the floor just outside of the snow field of broken glass. She crunched over the glass quickly to grab it when a stein came flying at her, missed by an inch, and shattered on the floor.

She looked up, startled, and saw that the man had snuck out from the brew house and was behind the bar throwing the glassware. He threw another. This one broke against the wall next to her causing a shard of glass to ricochet and nick her outstretched hand. Blood dripped down the tips of her fingers. She backed up as he advanced. Behind her were the restrooms. She turned on a heel and bolted in, locking the door behind her, terrified.

With her back against the door, she saw her reflection in the mirror across from her. Her first thought was *Carrie* but brunette. Blood poured down from the top of her head where the register had struck her and trickled onto her forehead and face. Her bangs were caked red and plastered down. She ran her hands over her cheeks to try to wipe the blood, but found that she just smeared it, making her face look pink. Frightened by her reflection, she looked away.

I have to get out of here.

The only thing in the bathroom that she could lift was the lid to the tank on the back of the toilet. She picked it up and turned to open the door. As she turned the handle, she heard the yell and laugh of Ozzy Osborne's *Crazy Train* as it poured out of the speakers. He had turned on the music.

Fuck, so much for yelling for help.

Vera stepped out into the pub and looked around. Her phone was still on the floor outside the field of glass. The quick pace of the music was making her anxious. Vera held the ceramic top of the toilet tank tightly for protection as she crunched on the glass toward her phone.

The man had relocated again. She saw that he was no longer behind the bar. There was a blind spot between her and her phone and she was sure he was hiding there for her.

She gripped her weapon, swung her arms back, and stepped forward, swinging the heavy cover at the same time. The weight of the toilet cover pulled her forward as it connected with nothing and glided through the air. She scanned the room, confused, and then felt him grab her from behind. They lost balance and fell to the floor; the ceramic lid smashed to pieces as it hit the ground.

Vera pushed up quickly on her hands and tried to wriggle from his grasp around her waist. She brought her fists down against his head and managed to free herself. On her hands and knees, she reached for her phone, but dirty, blood-stained fingers snatched it up before she could reach it. She looked up, face to face with the thief as he grinned a horrible, crooked smile at her before giving her a swift fist to the face.

Vera fell backward in pain, clutching her cheekbone where he struck her, holding pressure on it to stop the throb and keep the room from spinning.

She felt him jump onto her and rain additional blows at her body. She cried out as Ozzy played into the main course. *"I'M GOIN OFF THE RAILS ON A CRAZY TRAIN..."*

She put up her arms to block the punches from hitting her in her face but felt the weight of his fists forced her arms back toward her, *hard*, crushing her nose. Vera tasted blood and smelled the stink of the man on top of her. His weight lifted and she took the opportunity to get to her feet and stumble away.

Without wasting any time, she lunged for the counter and grabbed the fishbowl of tips, swinging it hard toward the man. He jumped back and dodged the first swing, but as she brought her arm back with the bowl on the second swing, she knocked him on the side of the head with it, using all of her strength.

The bowl broke against his skull and the cash erupted out of it, fluttering through the air. He fell to the ground with a yelp, dropping her phone and cracking the screen. Vera snatched it up and ran out the door with her purse.

Breathing hard, she slowed her pace in the parking lot as she unlocked her car and called 911. She put 911 on speaker and opened a text to her boss and Sam to let them know what had happened. After a few minutes she saw the man dart out of the pub, trailing bills fluttering behind him as they fell from his pockets while he ran.

Vera told the police what she was seeing and had been advised to stay where she was and that a patrol car would be there momentarily. Soon red and blue lights flashed in her rear view mirror and the gravel crunched as the car pulled into the Mosaic parking lot. Vera felt a wave of relief and burst into tears in the driver's seat.

Vera pulled into the parking lot of her midtown apartment complex. She got lucky and found a parking spot quickly, probably because it was a Saturday night, and everyone was out. She took a deep, shaky breath before opening her door to get out of the car and pleaded silently that Grace and Shanice were not sitting on the couch smoking again.

She couldn't handle the questions right now. She needed to compose herself and unpack what had just happened before she could tell them about it as if it were "just a crazy story." It was still too real, and it hurt too much. *Physically* as well as emotionally.

When the police had arrived at the scene, an ambulance followed. The paramedics helped her into the back of the truck and examined her carefully. She had been a mess, caked with so much blood from her head injury that the paramedics thought she might have a gushing wound. They were surprised to see that the injury was relatively small, and she would not need stitches; she was "*just a bleeder.*"

She was alert, coherent, and had not lost consciousness or vomited after being struck by the register. The paramedics told her that it was unlikely that she had a concussion. Overall, she had emerged nearly unscathed. Minor head injury, despite the bleeding, minor cut to her hand and a few nicks from glass of the broken window, and some bruises. More than anything, she had been scared.

Vera unlocked her front door cautiously and released a breath when she found the living room empty and the lights off.

The girls must be out tonight.

Vera proceeded upstairs and went straight to the bathroom to turn on the shower. She stripped off her beer covered work clothes, drenched in her sweat, dirt, and dried blood. She turned to face the mirror.

Her chocolate hair was matted like a rat's nest against the back of her head and her bangs stuck out at unnatural angles. She looked like shit. A few strands pressed to her cheek, dried by blood from her nose when she bashed it in the scuffle on the floor. It didn't look crooked though, and she was sure it was not broken. The bleeding had mostly stopped when she stuffed almost all of the *Taco Bell* napkins she had in her glove box into her nostrils before the ambulance assisted her.

Vera had refused a ride to the hospital, claiming that she would take herself if she felt worse. She couldn't afford the cost of the ambulance ride. The paramedics did their best to persuade her, but she was adamant that she needed to go home.

Vera leaned into the mirror to get a closer look. Her cheek had swollen up and was looking like it would leave a nasty bruise. Vera looked down at her pale chest and torso to examine her other bruises. Her head pounded. She tilted her chin down to examine the top of her scalp where she had been struck by the register. Dark dried blood pasted her hair down. She touched it gingerly and winced at the pain, feeling a lump under her fingers. She licked her lips and noticed that her bottom lip had a small cut as well that started to bleed as she wet it.

Vera washed her hands and took out her contacts, thanking herself silently for not wearing her glasses to work that day. She pulled back her shower curtain and stepped inside, letting the water run over her body before tilting her head in to wet her hair. She could feel all of her wounds reopening as the dried blood washed away. It stung and she had to fight the instinct to pull away from the water.

She washed out her cuts and did her best to untangle the matted mess of hair she was dealing with. The water ran a bubbly red orange as her blood washed down the drain. She checked that her continuous glucose monitor was still attached to her skin so that she could read her blood sugars. Miraculously, it had suffered no damage because she had it inserted on her upper thigh. Vera finished up and dried off for bed.

In bed, she found herself unable to sleep and decided to swipe through Tinder to kill time. After several disappointing swipes to the left, Vera came across a photo of the man she had met in Mosaic on Friday after class, *Aaron*. He was wearing an Oakland A's baseball cap and standing outside of the stadium. She swiped right and he messaged her a few seconds later, "Hello stranger."

CHAPTER 8

UNKNOWN

I t was cool outside, but not cold. A perfect evening for a late night walk. He locked up and wandered down the street not thinking about where he would go. He just allowed his legs to carry him forward a few blocks before turning one way or another, only mildly aware of what direction he was going. He knew the city well enough that he never got lost. He could walk down the street blindfolded for hours, take off his blind fold, and get himself home easily.

The air was light, and the city was quiet for a Saturday night. Granted, he was near East Sac and most of the energy would be in deep midtown. Maybe he would go that way, however the thought of interacting with drunken college kids was off putting. Last time he had been in midtown over the weekend every few feet someone was fighting. Alcohol made people so stupid. He took a swig of Pendleton from his flask and replaced the cap as he crossed the street.

He walked down toward the light rail, behind the *7-11*. It was late now; the streets in the area were relatively quiet. A soft breeze blew the protective plastic around a construction site nearby. A man sat in the dirt next to the construction site, fumbling with wads of crumpled cash with his grubby hands.

He walked up to the man and looked down at him. Panicked, the grubby man shouted at him to leave, trying to hide the money that he had spread all around himself to count. He tossed dirt and spit at him to shoo away the newcomer.

The man pulled out his flask and took a long swig. The grubby man looked at him concerned. He continued to pull from his Pendleton, draining what was left of the flask. He released a refreshed breath after he had finished. He felt the heat of the whisky as it passed through his chest, stoking the fire that had been burning for a few days now.

The grubby man changed his tune, feeling threatened, and backed away carefully, as if he could do so without being noticed. The man followed him casually until he was close enough to touch him. He closed his fist around his empty flask and brought it down hard on his victim's head.

The grubby man wailed, and his attacker liked it. In the distance the light rail approached the station, but nobody got off and nobody got on. It was a still Saturday night. Once the man had battered his grubby victim to the point that he was no longer screaming, he withdrew a small knife from his pocket and stabbed at him frantically.

Blood rushed out of the wounds and poured down his victim, soaking his dirty clothing. The grubby man coughed and burbled blood from his mouth, his crooked teeth coated red. The man considered slitting his throat for a moment, but that felt too final. He wanted this to last. He stuck his knife into the grubby man's thigh one last time to ensure that he wouldn't try to walk away, and blood flooded out from his femoral artery, pooling around him. Silence followed shortly after that, as the gurgling and gasping ceased.

The man looked at his empty blood-covered flask and shook his head, disappointed that he could not have a drink after that. Although, he didn't need one. The rush of blood lust gave him such a high, and the quick intake of whisky prior to his attack made him feel warm and pleasantly dizzy. He returned the flask into his pocket and headed back to the house to shower.

CHAPTER 9

VERA

Vera slept like a rock when she finally managed to fall asleep, so much so that she didn't dream. She just shut her eyes and woke up into a new day.

Oh good, I'm still alive...

Vera thought when she opened her eyes. She hoisted herself up on her elbows, sighing when she felt her muscles cry out at the movement.

Barely alive.

She looked at her clock. It was after 2:00p.m. She had slept late, but she felt that it was well deserved after the night she had. She reached around for her remote control with her eyes shut and found it tangled in the covers after some searching. She powered on her TV and propped herself up with pillows.

I'm not doing fucking anything today, she thought.

Vera flipped mindlessly though channels while she scrolled mindlessly through the apps on her phone at the same time. She set down the remote, leaving it on a commercial that she had landed on, when she noticed that her mom had called her five times and her boss had called her twice. She had a few texts from Sam as well. Vera rubbed her temples and decided that she was not ready to talk about last night. She addressed a notification on Tinder instead.

Aaron had messaged her again. They talked for a little while last night before Vera had been tired enough to go to sleep. He was straight to the point and had asked to see her. She told him that she would consider it, doing her best to flirt after the night she had. But at the time it was a welcomed distraction. She could pretend that the attack was a dream and that it had not happened at all.

Today he had messaged her to follow up on "their date." Vera was tired and didn't feel like talking to anyone. She typed out *sure*. And left it at that. They would meet on Tuesday evening.

Why not?

Vera picked up the remote to continue channel surfing for something better. The commercial that she had stopped on rolled into the news and she would have preferred to watch a cartoon or something. She pointed the remote at the TV but let her finger hover above the channel button when she saw what was on.

The news ticker at the bottom of the screen read:

Murder by Sac State has Students Terrified.

An Asian American news woman with beautiful glossy black hair was holding a microphone to a scruffy looking 7-11 employee as he explained what had happened.

"Yeah, I went outside to have a cigarette on my break when I saw the body by the construction site," he said in a gruff voice.

"It was awful. One of the bloodiest things I have ever seen in real life."

The employee scratched his head and looked at the camera. He looked like he was about 60 years old, balding, with a bushy salt and pepper beard covered the scowl on his pale face. You could see all of his emotion expressed in his eyes, he was scared. The screen cut to a clip of the yellow caution tape around the back of the 7-11, continuing into a construction site and chain link fence. The camera zoomed in on the blood-stained cement. There were red and brown crumpled bills all over the ground, as well as some dried into the blood. They almost looked like fallen leaves in the winter, but it was spring, and the red stained cement ruined the illusion.

"Law enforcement officers are thinking that this is a robbery gone wrong, looking at the way the scene is littered with money. Sacramento State students that live in the area are reporting that they are scared to walk to campus after seeing such a gruesome crime scene," the news woman narrated in the background of the clip.

The screen jumped to a pair of college girls looking at the camera nervously.

"We live right over there…" One of the girls pointed behind where they were standing. "It's scary to think that this happened right next to our apartment. I walk to this 7-11 *like*, every day."

The other girl nodded. "Yeah, we were here *like*, yesterday evening too, probably *like* right before it happened."

The camera cut back to the beautiful reporter outside of the 7-11.

"Okay, it sounds like we have some footage that has just been released to us." She held her hand to her earpiece.

Just before showing the images the TV screen flashed a warning of graphic content in big bold letters. The screen showed a poor-quality video that looked like it had been taken with a cell phone. The red and blue lights of a police car flashed in the background, illuminating a pool of fresh blood in alternating shades.

Vera was reminded of the movie *Nightcrawler*, when Jake

Gyllenhaal raced to crime scenes to get gruesome footage of the accidents and sold them to news teams to boost viewer ratings based on shock value. She wondered where this footage came from and was surprised that they were allowed to show something so graphic on TV, even with a warning.

The video zoomed in on the ground, but an officer's legs were blocking the view of the body beyond the victim's legs. He stepped aside suddenly and Vera felt her stomach lurch.

It was the man from Mosaic.

Vera sat straight up in bed, her heart racing. He was killed? Was that shortly after he attacked her? It must have been; she had been attacked last night and they were just finding his body.

The news clip was poor quality but graphic, and although his face had been blurred, Vera knew it was him. She couldn't get the crystal-clear image of him out of her head as he stood in front of her, lighting his cigarette.

"No way...," Vera whispered to herself.

She reached for her phone to check her texts and missed calls. Sam had texted her apologizing for what she had been through, saying he should not have asked her to cover that shift for him. The texts were from last night, nothing today about the death of the man who had robbed them.

She had a voicemail from her boss, checking on her, asking if she was feeling okay, if she needed anything, but again nothing about the death of the thief.

They don't know... Of course they don't know; nobody saw him but me. Nobody knows about this. What do I do with this information? Do I go to the police? He is already dead...

"I need some coffee." Vera groaned and pulled herself out of bed, stepping carefully on to the floor.

Before she went out to face her roommates, she went into her bathroom to splash some water onto her face. She looked up into the mirror. She looked much better than she did last night, aside from her very visible bruising. Shanice and Grace would see it and ask what had happened and she would have to relive the night as she told them.

Fuck it, no time like the present.

She patted her face dry with a towel and walked back into her room, pausing to watch her TV screen again. The same clip from before had been put back up, showing the police officer's legs and then, the man lying dead on the pavement.

Well, Vera thought to herself, *at least they found him.*

CHAPTER 10
GINA

Dr. Garcia, PhD.

Mondays were the worst for Gina Garcia. She almost always had a new client starting in addition to her normal case load and some days she had a few. Today she had only one new client to see, and the case was after lunch, so at least she could get through the morning and make sure she had the proper paperwork before they arrived. She had a light lunch, not wanting to be sluggish after a big meal, and an iced coffee to help her get through the second half of her day.

Mark Langdon, 32 years old, arrived early and waited quietly in the lobby for her to come retrieve him at 1:00p.m. Dr. Garcia didn't make a habit of bringing her clients back early, as she normally wanted to finish up her treatment notes from her previous session. She allowed herself to slurp the last bits of coffee from her cup, making sure to get between the ice cubes, and tossed it into the trash before collecting Mark and bringing him into her office.

Her objective impression was that he appeared tidy, clean

cut, well groomed. He had showered and his hair was still wet. He smelled like lavender soap. Mark wore a plain navy crewneck sweatshirt and well-fitting black denim pants with casual brown leather sneakers. She knew nothing about his case yet. He took a seat on the soft gray couch in her office and gave her some background.

Mr. Langdon grew up in the Midwest, Kansas. His father was abusive, both physically and sexually. His mother was absent emotionally throughout the years of abuse. She worked long hours and drank through most of the evenings. Mark suspected that she struggled with depression, but she never saw a therapist of her own or worked through any of her problems.

Once when he was sixteen, he skipped school and wandered around town. He went to the park and was jumped by a group of older high school kids and beaten badly. Mark made his way home after that, arriving with a black eye and split lip. Nothing he couldn't handle since his dad had gifted him with a shiner a few times a month. He went to the bathroom to wash up and saw a trail of blood down the hallway into the kitchen. His mother had slit her wrists and was pale on the floor. He called 911 and saved her life. She never forgave him for it. Two years later, she left in the night, leaving Mark with his father in their small home. She even took the dog.

Mark, knowing he had to get out of that house, picked up any work he could find. He worked as a line cook in a small restaurant, a dish washer in another, and he eventually started delivering packages for UPS until he scraped together enough money to move to Sacramento. He now worked as a manager of a higher end chain restaurant in Carmichael.

He complained of anhedonia, insomnia, and nightmares when he did manage to get to sleep. He struggled to maintain a relationship and perform sexually after the years of sexual abuse he endured from his father. Despite it all he fantasized about living what he believed was a *normal life*. He wanted to meet a woman, settle down, have children that wouldn't be fucked up like he was. He was proud of the job he had secured and felt that it was his only constant in life.

He was well-spoken and charming, but Dr. Garcia could see the cracks in his confidence and felt insecurity emanate from him. He had seen a therapist before but didn't feel it was a good fit. He seemed comfortable in her office, but it was only the first appointment.

When their hour was up, Dr. Garcia thanked him for sharing so much today and set up their follow up appointment for Wednesday. He left the office with a looming cloud over him, as many of her clients did after unpacking so much of their trauma. She typed up her note and compartmentalized the sadness she felt for him as she set up for her next appointment.

CHAPTER 11

VERA

Vera always struggled to find parking on this side of town. She drove down Castro Way looking for a spot without any luck. She went a little further down and managed to find a spot around the corner on 27th street. She locked her car and decided against the wheel lock, since she wouldn't be gone for very long and this was a relatively nice area. She made her way down the street toward Franklin Boulevard.

Vera went casual with her outfit, a white tee that she tied up in a little knot above the edge of her high waisted blue jeans and her checkered Vans. She wore her glasses today. She thought that they gave her a charming elegance, and she wore her hair in a loose bun with wavy pieces of hair to frame her face. She thought that she looked okay; it wasn't a formal date anyway, just ice cream.

Vera made sure to cake on the foundation to cover her bruises before she left the house though. She felt like she was treading a fine line between looking like a victim of abuse and looking like a clown. Shanice said that she looked fine though and Shanice was honest to a fault.

The line at *Gunther's Ice Cream* went down the street and she contemplated if she wanted to stand alone in it or if she should text him and see how far away he was, when she saw his truck pull up and snag a spot right in front.

How did I miss that?

Aaron climbed out of his red GMC. Vera guessed it was a 2007, but she didn't know much about cars, nor did she really care. A red truck was a red truck in her mind. It looked nicer than her piece of shit car though. He smiled at her when he saw her crossing the street toward him.

"Hey," he said lazily.

He was wearing almost the same thing he wore at the pub the Friday she had first met him. Khaki pants and a black Sac State hoodie with green lettering.

"What's up?" He smiled.

Vera felt a little timid, she had not been on a date in such a long time that she was embarrassingly rusty.

It's not a date though, it's just ice cream.

She stepped closer to him and they walked together in stride toward the back of the line. She smelled his cologne.

Fucking Acqua di Gio. Is that the only cologne in this whole city???

They made light conversation in line. Boring stuff. *What's your major? How do you like it? Are you from Sacramento? What do you do for fun? Have you ever been to Low Brau? Blah blah blah.* But he was cute, he looked like he had gotten a haircut since she last saw him, and he wore cologne, so maybe he was interested in her.

When they finally got inside the shop Vera perused the menu. She had a mean sweet tooth for a diabetic, ironically enough. She settled on a scoop of marble fudge and a scoop of banana ice cream. Aaron got plain chocolate. He started talking about the work he had been doing on his truck as they sat down at a table outside and Vera found her mind wandering.

She looked up at the neon Gunther's sign. The sun was setting behind it and the sky was a soft orange. The playful character tossing a scoop of ice cream from the spoon over to the cone in a perfect arc was *picturesque* in the golden lighting.

She thought about her childhood experiences with ice cream in grade school. Once they had an ice cream social at her after school care program. The kids all lined up for a scoop of vanilla ice cream and then walked the length of the picnic tables outside adding M&M's, rainbow sprinkles, fudge, caramel sauce, whipped cream, cherries… and then the children, high on sugar, would run around the playground like wild animals laughing and screaming.

Vera waited in line with her friends, giddy with excitement and riding the wave of energy among the other ten-year-olds. When she got to the front the teacher gave her a look of disapproval and walked inside to the kitchen. She returned with an orange and handed it to Vera. The kids around her laughed openly.

"But I want ice cream like the others…" Vera protested softly.

"You can't have ice cream. You're *a diabetic*." The teacher lectured. She spat the word as if she were calling her *"a"* stray, placing an A in front of the word diabetic, in an almost objectifying manner. Vera surged with frustration.

I know I'm diabetic. I can have ice cream. I just have to take insulin, which I am going to have to do for this stupid orange anyway.

She opened her mouth in dispute, but the staff wouldn't have it. She openly outcasted Vera in front of her peers and scolded her into submission. Vera dragged her feet all the way to a bench by the lawn and plopped down. She dug at the peel of her orange, getting the pith deep under her fingernails and watching the sticky juice dry out her hands. Nobody sat with her. They all shoveled ice cream into their mouths and went back for seconds, then to the playground. She sat on the bench with her orange and quietly watched the others play.

Vera tuned back into her conversation with Aaron just as he had started to change the subject.

"Yeah, it's pretty fun, we meet on Thursdays usually, which is great because nobody on the team has a Friday class so we all just get hammered after."

"What?" Vera was embarrassed that she hadn't been paying attention. Aaron licked ice cream off of his lips.

"The kickball league. You should come watch a game. It's fun, and we all go out after."

"Oh, yeah that sounds fun. Every Thursday?"

"Yeah, we usually will bring beer and hangout in the bleachers, pregame the game, and then go out and drink more around downtown after. It's at Roosevelt Park. We sometimes go to that bar *Coin-Op* after. It just depends on what the team wants to do." He wiped ice cream from his chin.

"A couple of the guys I was with at Mosaic the other day are on the team. It's a cool crowd."

"Okay, cool, I'll try to make it." Vera smiled. It did sound fun.

After their ice cream they walked a few blocks through the neighborhood together and he took her hand as he walked her toward her car. He laughed a little when he saw it, and Vera was glad that she didn't put her wheel lock on to add to the trashy aesthetic her transportation gave off. She smiled shyly. He said goodbye and went in for a kiss, which surprised her since she barely knew him.

I guess this is how Tinder works.

She let him give her a big wet kiss and felt herself blush.

"See you Thursday," he said with a wink, and he turned and headed up the street toward his truck.

CHAPTER 12
GINA

Mark Langdon was quiet today in Dr. Garcia's office. She smiled at him from behind her desk. He looked away. She referred to her chart notes from last time he had been in. He met a woman last Saturday at the midtown farmer's market. She owned a booth that sold homemade jams. He had started a garden in his backyard and was growing jalapeño peppers and was intrigued by a strawberry jalapeño jam she was handing out as a sample.

Gina Garcia scratched at the back of her neck politely. The tag on her blouse was itchy. She spruced herself up in a yellow floral button down with loose sleeves. She read somewhere that yellow made people look more friendly and thought that it might help her build rapport with one of her more difficult patients and get them to share today. Worth a shot, right? She was running out of options. She tucked her short blonde hair behind her ears and noted the time.

"Well, Mark, it looks like our time is up for today. I will see you again on Friday. Does 10:30a still work okay for you?"

Mark gave her a curt nod and stood to leave. Hopefully she would find out what was bothering him on Friday once he had some time to process it.

CHAPTER 13

VERA

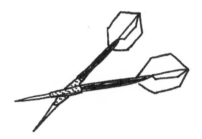

Thursday rolled around and Vera found herself looking forward to seeing Aaron again. She contemplated what she would wear to the game instead of paying attention to her finance lecture. Her eyes glazed over, looking through Dr. Granucci's PowerPoint instead of at it. The numbers blurred in her peripherals.

Vera was snapped back to reality by the sound of her classmate sitting directly in front of her responding to a question Dr. Granucci had posed to the class. Vera glanced up at the clock. Only a few more minutes. The class began to shuffle papers and zip up bags as the red clock hand ticked into 3:00p.m. Vera rose with her bag slung over her shoulder and made her way toward the door, shuffling along with the other students as they flowed out into the walkway.

The students moved through the building like salmon downstream, all headed for the door outside. It seemed that nobody was taking afternoon classes and Thursday was pretty much wrapped up for *Tahoe Hall*. Vera shielded her eyes from the sun as she walked out into the busy campus courtyard. She moved toward her parking structure and saw Sam headed in her direction from the parking lot away from his car.

"Hey!" Vera chirped.

"Oh, hey Ver!" Sam matched her energy.

"You headed to class?"

"Yeah, unfortunately. I am actually headed to the library first to kill some time. I don't have class until 4:30p.m."

"Ugh, why would you do that to yourself?" Vera teased.

"The classes are all so impacted, and this is the only one I could get into. And you are not one to talk!" He laughed, "At least I don't have a 3-hour class on a Friday."

"Fair enough." Vera rolled her eyes.

"What are you getting into tonight?" Sam asked. He shifted his weight from one foot to the other.

"I'm going to this kickball thing downtown."

"Oh, for the social sport league? I did softball with that group last year. You'll have fun." He smiled. "Well, I've gotta get to the library. I'll see ya around!" He waved over his shoulder while he walked through the trees.

"Later Sam!" Vera called after him. She was starting to feel excited about the kickball game. *It will be fun.*

———

Vera walked from her apartment in midtown to Roosevelt Park quickly. She had a beer at her place as she got ready, sipping from it as she tried on shirts and shoes and different pairs of glasses. She ultimately settled on black jeans, Converse, a black V-neck tank top that did wonders for her chest, and her dark blue denim jacket with the white fleece collar. She wore contacts instead of glasses and brushed her bangs so that they landed just right. She grabbed another beer as she headed out the door to calm her nerves and drank it as she walked.

By the time she had arrived at the park, the game had already started. Vera saw some bleacher seating and walked shyly over to a group of strangers in matching red t-shirts after tossing her empty can into a trash bin nearby. Vera stuffed her hands into her pockets and slipped onto the edge seat of the bench. She scanned the crowd for Aaron. He was in the game and up to kick. Aaron wore a blue shirt that matched the crowd on the opposite bleachers and Vera realized that she was sitting with the wrong team. *Shit.* She stood to leave but stopped to watch him play.

Aaron gave the ball a swift and hard kick and sprinted through the bases, making it to third. He was fast. He wore black athletic shorts and had the strong legs of someone who bikes everywhere that others might drive.

He put his hands on his waist and laughed at something a teammate called over to him. Vera shifted uncomfortably and hoped that he wouldn't notice that she sat in the wrong area. He of course saw her in that moment, seated in the wrong area, and waved. Vera felt her cheeks turn pink and tried to laugh it off as she made her way to the blue team bleachers.

By the time she had arrived at his team's side, Aaron had made it to home base and was walking off to join the others by the ice chest.

"Hey," he said breathlessly.

"Hi." Vera gave him a nervous smile.

"Beer?" He asked, extending a *Coors Light*. She took the cold can in her hands, the mountains were blue. She cracked it with a hiss and took a swig. Aaron gave her an up and down glance as he cracked open his beer and drank it with a smile. He introduced her to a few people and left her with the girlfriend of another player who was there to watch. *Alison.*

It was both of their first time at a kickball match and they made a game out of watching the players. They drank if the blue team caught the ball to get a member of the opposite team out. They drank whenever Aaron was up, they drank whenever Alison's boyfriend Phillip was up. They drank when someone got a home run, regardless of the team. By the end of the game, they were a little drunk. The blue team won by two points and the whole team cracked a beer and chugged it to celebrate.

Vera was giddy from the beer and the energy of the team. She and Alison had really hit it off and linked arms as they walked with the team to their next stop, *Streets Pub n Grub*, formerly known as Streets of London. It bore no resemblance to a London pub, but Vera had liked the name better and was disappointed when they changed it.

It was a bit of a walk, but arm in arm, Vera and Alison strode in-step on a mission for a pint. Vera was having so much fun with Alison, she nearly forgot about Aaron. She looked back over her shoulder and saw him chatting with a few of the boys from the other team while the crowd from the kickball league walked as if they were on a pub crawl.

Aaron wiped sweat from his forehead and caught her eye with a wink. Vera admired his confidence. They were basically strangers but he seemed so sure that they would hit it off. She found herself leaning into that idea and allowed herself to have fun with the thought that maybe it would all work out well for them.

Once they had arrived at *Streets*, they filed inside and crowded the bar. Alison ordered four beers and managed to carry three of them in a triangle with her hands while Vera carried the last glass. Alison insisted that she could do all four glasses herself, fueled by liquid confidence, but Vera had a distinct premonition of the fourth pint shattering on the floor if she had let her try, so she took the liberty of carrying her own.

Aaron and Alison's boyfriend were not friends, just teammates, so Alison went outside to sit with Philip and left Vera to find Aaron after handing off the other beer to her. She found him occupying the dart board in the front of the pub and went to join him. He threw with confidence but lacked accuracy. Vera chuckled as she handed off his glass and he threw a dart right into the brick behind the board. She took one from his hand and gave it a swift toss at the board, hitting a triple 16. She gave him a teasing smile and the game was on.

By the time it was neck and neck, Aaron proposed that they raise the stakes. Loser buys the next round, and if he hit a bullseye in his last throw, Vera would have to give him a kiss. She rolled her eyes.

"Do we have a deal?" He asked enthusiastically.

"Sure," Vera laughed.

As if he were hustling her the whole time, he tossed all 3 darts into the bullseye one by one and smiled.

"Is that three kisses?"

"Not a chance," Vera laughed again, shocked by the outcome. She left him at the board to buy 2 more beers at the bar. When she returned, she stood on her toes to reach him, and gave him the kiss she had agreed to.

He leaned into it and kissed her back, turning one into two, and two into three. When they separated, he smiled and drank from his beer.

"Rematch?" She asked.

"Actually, I have a dart board at my place around the corner if you want to head over there after these beers and let someone else play here?"

Vera considered this.

Of course he has a dart board. How else would he have nailed those last three bullseyes with such accuracy?

The thought made her laugh. She was having fun and decided that *yes*, she would like to continue their night. They sat at a table to finish their beers and set out into the street to walk to his apartment once they were done. Vera waved goodbye to Alison as she passed her on the patio on her way out.

CHAPTER 14
VERA

The walk to Aaron's apartment took all of ten minutes as they strolled quickly in-step with each other down the sidewalk and up the stairs to his door. His roommates were both out for the night so instead of indulging themselves in another round of darts, they indulged in each other. As soon as they shut the front door, he kissed her and they fumbled down the hall and into his bedroom.

Is this really going to happen??

Aaron grabbed a fistful of her hair and opened his mouth into hers. She was giddy, and she wanted to be closer to him, as close as she could get. Aaron slid his hand up her shirt and cupped her breast. Their weight gave out beneath them as neither wanted to stand any longer and they both toppled onto his bed.

With her arms around his neck, Vera rotated her weight and rolled herself on top of him. They kissed frantically until she peeled herself away to yank off her shirt and he quickly did the same. Her head spun as he kissed her neck and slid his hands into her jeans. They kissed deeply, and after another minute, he shimmied her pants down and pulled them off of her one leg at a time. He slid himself under the covers and into her lap, kissing her thighs slowly.

Vera couldn't believe this was finally happening, she hadn't had sex in so long. She threw her hands over her head and stared at the ceiling, feeling dizzy with lust. Really dizzy. *Oh no. Too* dizzy. *Fuck.*

She looked at her Apple Watch on her wrist and saw her blood sugar tanking. *58. Nooooo.* She began to feel disoriented. She sighed and tapped at his head under the covers to get him to stop. He ignored her.

"Hey..." She tried to find her breath, feeling her eyes roll around a little, less from pleasure now and more so from the sensation that the room might be spinning due to her low blood sugar. He didn't stop. She shimmied her legs a little, they felt so heavy.

"Aaron," she said weakly.

She checked her watch again, 52. It was dropping fast.

"Aaron..." She felt his fingers creeping around on her skin. *Aw fuck please don't do this to me.*

Vera kicked the blankets off and tried to sit up. He reached for her and pulled himself on top of her. She tried weakly to push him off.

"Stop Aaron."

He didn't stop. He kissed her neck and she felt herself being smothered under his weight. She was disoriented, confused, and weak. She started feeling nauseous from the sensation that the room was swaying. She tried to focus on sitting up. Aaron went for her lips and she turned her head away, trying to push him off once again.

He groaned and looked at her.

"What?" He snapped.

"My blood sugar is low. I don't feel well." She gasped.

"Just take a shot or something," he said, kissing her neck.

Her head buzzed with frustration.

Yeah, more insulin, that's exactly what I need. She thought sarcastically.

Sugar. Sugar is what I need. Immediately.

"Aaron, stop."

He sat up sharply and looked at her.

"Do you have any juice or anything?" Vera pleaded with her eyes, feeling embarrassed and humiliated to be doing this in front of someone who was nearly a stranger, especially because the only connection they really had was that they were about to have sex and she had put a halt to that.

He looked a little drunk and very frustrated. He didn't say anything. He put on his shirt and walked out of the room.

If I had a fucking dollar for every time diabetes ruined the mood…. I could pay for my insulin.

He returned with an *Oreo.* Just one.

Ugh, way to dig deep, pal.

He proceeded to grope her again and tried to pull her onto him.

"Aaron, stop."

He rolled her so that he was on top and held her down, trying to be sexy, but really scaring her because he wouldn't listen. She began to see block spots in the edges of her vision. Her watch beeped an alert at her that her blood sugar was reaching a dangerously low level. It read 42. She began to feel faint, and he continued to run his hands all over her. She felt helpless and vulnerable under his weight. She turned her face away from his, in a refusal to kiss him and tried again to sit up and catch her breath. He scoffed at her when she pushed him off with the little strength she had.

"Are you serious right now?" He spat at her.

Well, that escalated quickly.

"Just give me a second…" Vera said, reaching for the cookie.

She felt offended that he could be so upset with her for saying no, regardless of how sick she was. Her eyes stung with embarrassed tears. He seemed so nice earlier, but when Vera thought back on her evening, she spent most of her time with Alison. Aaron had really only been present at the bar when they played darts.

Vera shoved the cookie into her mouth and struggled with her shirt. She got dressed and let herself out while Aaron set up a video game. It was clear that he wasn't interested anymore. He didn't have any desire to be a "caretaker" although Vera would call that being patient, or kind, or just a decent person. Most people she knew were less judgmental of her in this situation. At least he stopped and didn't rape her.

I guess there's that, she thought, feeling that her bar was set pretty low for herself at that moment. He didn't say goodbye to her as she left.

Vera stumbled outside and across the street to the gas station, cursing herself for not having any glucose in her purse. She bought a *Coke* and sat outside on the curb drinking it under the lights by the gas pump. She wasn't quite up to walking home yet, feeling disoriented still, so she would just have to wait out the clock.

Vera sat there feeling sorry for herself and annoyed that she couldn't have a normal sexual encounter like her roommates probably had. Feeling extremely annoyed that she had to ask Aaron to stop more than once, however, she was grateful that she wasn't too low to advocate for herself. Hopefully, Aaron didn't make a habit of ignoring the first two "no's" he received from women. He probably wasn't used to being told no, although that was no fucking excuse. He would certainly not be getting another call from her.

Vera picked at the tab on her *Coke* can and looked up at the moon past the gas pumps. In her peripheral vision, she saw a man smoking a cigarette watching her. She pulled her denim jacket tightly around her and walked in the direction of her apartment.

She was relatively close to her place. She checked the time on her phone and then checked her glucose monitoring app to see what her blood sugar was. 10:45p.m. and *72 mg/dl*. At least it was starting to come up.

Aaron lived on J street, and Vera lived on L, not too far of a walk for her and she had sobered up a lot. She picked up her pace and checked over her shoulder out of cautious habit to make sure that she was not being followed.

The man from the gas station had stayed put, puffing away at his cigarette. She released a breath and continued forward. It was prime time to be out and Vera almost forgot it was a Thursday and that she had to be in class tomorrow.

At least it is an afternoon class…, she thought to herself.

She watched people as she walked. A couple was fighting on a corner near a crosswalk outside of a restaurant, shouting and making a scene. A homeless veteran was setting up a sleeping bag in the entrance of a church walkway, leaning against the large door for support. A group of college kids on electric scooters *zoomed* by and one of them threw an empty can of *White Claw* into the street laughing. Vera watched it tumble toward her. Mango. She was not a fan of the mango ones.

Vera looked up and bumped into a woman in very tall heels and a very short dress.

"Watch it," she sneered.

"Oh, excuse me, sorry…" Vera apologized, embarrassed. Her female friend in tight jeans and a red top responded.

"Don't mind her, she's being a bitch tonight."

"I'm sorry though, I wasn't looking where I was going." Vera continued.

"Well, look alive," the friend retorted.

"And heads up down there. Some guy has been following us for a few blocks," the girl in red cautioned as they made their way into another bar.

Vera looked around the street. It was hard to tell who might be following them. The streets were not particularly busy, but they were active with pedestrians making their way to their next destination. Vera picked up her pace, feeling hyper-alert after that warning and her encounter at Mosaic from the previous Saturday. She was not looking for another violent incident.

She was only about a block away from her house when she noticed a bar that she had never seen before. A little hole in the wall with stairs that led down and a neon sign that said *open*. Her apartment was around the corner and her curiosity got the best of her. She made her way down the steps.

The bar had unique emerald green wallpaper that gave the place the feel of a speakeasy and Vera had the sense that she had just stepped into one of midtown's hidden gems. The bar itself was small, lined with wooden stools and tall, dark mismatched chairs. There was a big gold-accented mirror on the back wall that made the tiny room feel much larger. A bartender was mixing cocktails and pouring what looked like a lemon drop for an elegant older woman who was waiting for her drink.

Vera looked to her right and saw a row of booths against the wall, each lined with a yellow-gold velvet and accenting bar tables with dark brown wood and gold claw feet. She felt a little under dressed, but nobody in here was formal by any means. It was the kind of bar you might wear heels with a casual outfit to dress it up just enough to look more mature. Vera looked down at her beer-stained converse and wished she were wearing boots or something that might help her fit in.

She headed toward the bar to ask if they had a restroom when she heard someone call her name.

"Hey! Ver!"

Vera spun around and saw Sam waving at her from a far booth seat in the back. She felt warmth spread through her at the sight of a friend after the night she had with Aaron. She made her way over to his table.

"What are you doing here?" Sam asked cheerfully.

"I was on my way home and I saw this place. I had no idea it was even here."

"Oh yeah, it's been here forever. I'm honestly *like* a regular here." He laughed. He gestured to the couple sitting across from him. "These are my friends Sanjay and Vince."

Sanjay gave a little wave and Vince extended his hand to Vera. She took it and introduced herself.

"Sit down!" Sam urged.

"I have class tomorrow. I can't stay long. I just wanted to take a look around. I'll have to come back here some time," Vera said as she scooted into the booth next to Sam.

"How was kickball?" Sam asked as he sipped what looked like a whisky drink.

"It was okay, I made a friend. Her name is Alison Green. Do you know her? She is dating some guy named Philip. I think they both go to Sac State."

"Hmm… The name is familiar but I would have to see her face, I dunno." Sam laughed. He seemed a little drunk.

"Well, she was nice. I had a good time." Vera decided to leave out the part about Aaron. She wasn't sure she wanted to see him again and she definitely didn't want to talk about it with Sam.

"What are you drinking?" She asked.

"An old fashioned. They make pretty good ones here."

"It looks pretty good. I've always wanted to try an old fashioned." Vera contemplated ordering one but thought better of it. She should go home and get to bed.

"Here, try it." Sam said passing the drink over to her.

Vera took it and looked into the glass. The curly orange peel was a nice touch. It swam in the copper-colored drink around a large spherical ice cube. It was a very pretty cocktail. She took a little taste from his glass.

"It's good," she said passing it back.

"You should try their Moscow mule. It's probably the best one in Sac." Sanjay said, holding up his cup.

"I don't know- *Bottle and Barlow* has a pretty good one," Vince argued.

"Are you kidding? This one is way better." The two got into a heated debate about bars and their top drinks on the menu. Sam turned to Vera.

"Hey, I'm really sorry about what happened at Mosaic the night you covered my shift," he said in a low voice.

Vera thought about the register coming down onto her head after it smacked the wall with a loud thud. She instinctively found herself reaching her hand up and patting the lump on her scalp softly. She glanced over at the bartender shaking drinks and noticed he had a fishbowl tip jar that looked like the one she had broken over the thief's head. She was transported back to the sound of shattering glass and the burst of dollar bills fluttering around the two of them as he fell to the ground.

"Yeah. That was... unfortunate..." She wasn't really sure what to say to him. "Did they fix the window that he threw the wrench through? I haven't been back since it happened."

"Not yet. I think there is someone coming in to fix it this week. Right now, we just have a big piece of wood up."

"Did you hear they found the guy? He ran out after I called the cops... He was found... I saw on the news."

"Did they? Where'd they pick him up?"

Vera cleared her throat. "He's dead. They found him about a mile away."

"What are you serious Vera?" Sam's eyes were wide, exaggerated by the fact that he had been drinking, but in genuine shock.

"Yeah, he was murdered. Isn't that insane? The police are saying it was a robbery gone wrong. I think someone tried to jump him because he had all of that cash or something..."

"That's wild. I can't believe that." He shook his head. "Hey, if you don't feel ready to go back yet and want any of your shifts covered, just let me know. I feel really bad that this happened." Sam put his hand on her shoulder. "Let me buy you an old fashioned.

You could probably use one after that weekend. I definitely owe you. That should have been me."

Vera appreciated how genuine he was trying to be, but she needed to get to bed and really didn't feel like drinking more tonight. Her mood had taken a dark turn.

"Thanks, Sam, but lets rain check that drink. I need to get home. I just wanted to stop in really quick and check out this little hole-in-the-wall."

"A *gem-in-the-wall* actually, but yeah definitely, next time." Sam smiled.

"It was nice to meet you both," Vera said to Sanjay and Vince across the bar. They had transitioned from Moscow mules to Irish coffees and were debating if *Fox and Goose* had a better Irish coffee than *The Porch*. They paused their conversation to say goodbye and Vera made her way to the restroom before she walked home.

The bathroom was a single stall unisex restroom with a gold doorknob. The door itself matched the wallpaper and Vera almost didn't see it. It was like a secret door into a closet-sized space. Inside, the wallpaper had the same curly, floral pattern, but it was all gold instead of green. A large oval-shaped mirror with gold trim hung from the wall. Vera caught a glimpse of her reflection. She looked tired. That *low* had really wiped her out. She had dark circles under her eyes and was ready for bed. She splashed some water on her face and dried it with a paper towel, wiping her makeup from under her eyes as it ran a little from the water.

The wallpaper in the bathroom gave her the feeling she was standing inside of a jewelry box. The kind with the ballerina that would spin in front of a tiny mirror when you opened it as it played a lullaby. She indulged herself with a twirl in front of the mirror above the sink, longing deeply for her bed after doing so. She was going to regret having gone out when it came time for class tomorrow. Vera grabbed her purse and exited the restroom, making her way to the steep staircase to the exit and then headed home in the dark.

CHAPTER 15

UNKNOWN

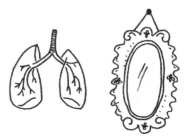

Some nights, he would have nightmares that he didn't understand. Tonight was a night plagued by a chaotic dreamscape. It took place in his childhood bedroom and the walls took deep breaths, in and out, in sync with his own. They bowed out and sucked in, squeezing his furniture and rattling the paintings that hung decorating the room. He tried to focus his breathing to keep it slow so that as the walls expanded the hanging mirror did not fall down and break. It had been a gift from his grandfather.

A gun shot rang somewhere in the house. The loud boom reverberated off the walls, causing the mirror to shutter. There was a piercing scream and another shot, then silence. He heard heavy footsteps climbing the creaking wooden stairs toward his room. His breath quickened. The walls expanded and compressed in sequence, faster and faster. He felt that if he didn't get his breathing under control, they might close in on him completely. He tried to focus on settling his breath through his tears. He heard the butt of the shot gun being dragged across the wooden floorboards, coming closer and closer.

He scanned the room for a way out, but there was no door, just four walls hyperventilating around him. If there was no door though, no one could get in, right? A shot rang and blew a hole through one of the walls. He clutched his chest, feeling as though it had pierced through his lungs. The walls shuttered and then, to his horror, blood began to pour into the room through the hole in the wall.

It quickly filled the room. He stood there, ankle deep, in warm, dark blood, desperate to take a satisfying breath, but feeling as though he were suffocating.

He awoke in a cold sweat and looked around his room. The walls were fixed in position. Outside a breeze blew the branches of a tree softly against his window with a gentle tapping. It was a dream. A grossly exaggerated one at that. He laid on his back and stared at the ceiling, focusing on his breathing. There was no blood pouring from the walls in his real memory of that night. There was no room without a door. But there was a gunshot, and there was a scream. He remembered that well and it rang in his memory like a siren.

CHAPTER 16

GINA

Gina stood to stretch her legs. It had been a long week and she had one more patient for the day. Howard Young. Mr. Young was a tough nut to crack. He was not receptive to most of her techniques to get him to share. He was struggling with major depression, schizotypal personality disorder, a new diagnosis of bipolar personality disorder and Gina suspected he had a touch of narcissism as well but she was not ready to add another diagnosis.

His family had pushed him into therapy. He had a few violent encounters with others, fights here and there, nothing too serious. However, he had once suffered from paranoid delusions so great that he locked himself in his house for weeks and injured a concerned neighbor who tried to check on him. The neighbor pressed charges because Young had broken her wrist. He pushed her hard when he saw her, and she fell, hands extended, landing on her wrist as she tried to catch herself. Her wrist was fractured badly. His sister, concerned with the decline in his mental health, talked him into therapy after the incident two years ago.

He had made some minor improvements. His psychometric scores were looking better. His PHQ9, which measured his depression levels, had reduced once he started taking medications; but he was still wary of people, experienced rigid thinking patterns and the occasional perceptual disturbance such as a mild auditory hallucination. He referred to it as his little voice. Gina always thought of the inner little voice that belonged to Danny from *The Shining*. "The little boy that lives in my mouth- Tony," he would say. While Young did not refer to the voice he heard by name as Danny did, and his voice was much less severe, Gina often wondered if one day she might have a *"REDRUM"* situation on her hands.

He was quiet now. Her yellow blouse from last visit had caught his attention and he told her that he liked it. He revealed that yellow was his favorite color and that the wallpaper in his childhood home had been yellow with flowers like her blouse. She was pleased by that, but after that piece of family trivia was disclosed, he went back to radio silence and stared at her top with such intensity that Dr. Garcia felt as though he was looking through it. It made her feel a little vulnerable, almost naked. Today she wore her usual black turtleneck and Young was unimpressed.

"How have things been going, Howard? Have you been looking for a job?"

He had recently been let go of his job at a local grocery store, Safeway. He had stopped showing up to work abruptly. When Gina had asked about it, he said he just didn't feel like it anymore. He also reported to her that he was feeling better, so he had stopped taking his SSRI medication, *Paxil*.

"No."

"Why not? With your experience at Safeway, I am sure you could pick one up quickly. Why don't we put that on your list of goals for this week? Just look into a few listings for things you may be interested in. You'll need a job. What about your Paxil? Did you start taking it again?"

"I gained too much weight on the Paxil and I don't need it anymore. I feel better. Plus, my doctor said she wants to start me on *Lithium* for bipolar or something. I guess I can't take them together, so I just stopped the Paxil because I want to take the other stuff." Young grunted.

He *had* gained a substantial amount of weight since his psychiatrist had started him on Paxil. Dr. Garcia made a note in her chart about his medication. He really shouldn't stop taking his antidepressants abruptly, she worried about withdrawal. She was not a physician though; she had her PhD in Psychology and worked with him solely as his therapist. It was not her expertise to tell him what to do with his medication. He would have to speak to his psychiatrist about that, and it sounded like maybe they had a plan. She prodded him about the job hunt a little more and sent him on his way at the end of their hour.

On his way out he turned and said, "By the way, I like your yellow shirt better."

She gave him a soft smile, regretting having worn it at all. This would become his new closing line at the end of each appointment.

CHAPTER 17
VERA

Vera parked her car and killed the engine. She squeezed her temples before getting out and heading inside to meet her sister for dinner after her Friday evening class. She hadn't told her about the incident at Mosaic yet, and it had been almost a week. She knew she would be pissed to find out so long after it had happened, but Vera didn't want to relive it and had brought herself to tell only a few people. She had told her mom. Maybe she could have her mom tell her sister. She would worry about that later. Vera took a deep breath and headed into the restaurant.

Char was sitting at a booth in the corner of the restaurant next to a window. She liked to people watch. Vera saw her as she walked up the sidewalk toward the door. She was reading the menu and twirling her long hair around her elegant fingers. She looked up and smiled at Vera when she walked in. She then stood and gave her a full body hug, swaying from side to side with her arms around her. Vera smiled back and sat down.

"I ordered you a beer. I hope that's okay." Char grinned.

"Always okay." Vera laughed.

The server brought a tray of drinks to the table and set down two glasses of water, two pints of *Singha,* and two small cups of sake. Char flashed Vera a wicked smile.

"I actually ordered us sake bombs." She laughed.

Vera rolled her eyes. This was totally on brand for her sister. They wasted no time dropping their tiny *ochoko* cups into their pints and chugging fast. Vera was much quicker than Char, but she knew that her sister just wanted to do it for the novelty and didn't actually care who drank faster. The server returned as they finished and collected their glasses.

"Could we get two more beers, please?" Char asked with her award-winning smile. The server returned her smile warmly and headed to the bar.

"So, what's up?" Vera asked.

"Hmmmm, not a whole lot..." Her sister dragged her sentence out, retracing her whole week in her head. "Oh! I took a new photo for my ID badge at work. It's much better than my first. *See?*"

She pulled her badge out of her purse and handed it to Vera across the table.

Sutter Medical Center
Charlotte Kowalski, PA-C
Urology

She was right. It was much better. Her hair was pulled back in a nice, glossy, low ponytail that looked professional in a warm way. Fashion is a fine line that women have to tread in most professions, especially medicine. They had to be perceived as competent, professional, calculated, without appearing hardened, cold, and mean. Pulling your hair back the wrong way could be the difference between looking put together and kind, and too sharp and bitchy. Charlotte nailed it. Light makeup, a baby blue button-down shirt, and the white coat with her name stitched into it that she praised as if it were made of gold.

Her old photo had caught her by surprise. Her hair was frizzy, her eyes were tired, and her smile was too wide as if she were being held for ransom. It made Vera laugh but she knew how much it meant to her sister to present herself professionally in her job, and that meant "the perfect ID picture" in addition to her work ethic, apparently.

She had only been a physician assistant for a few years, but *man*, she was proud. Her husband Conner was proud too. He was involved with medicine as well as an orthopedic surgeon at Sutter. They carpooled to work together. They were the perfect couple. It was enough to make you sick, but Vera was happy that her sister had someone who loved her as much as Conner did, and she appreciated what a good fit they were for each other.

Charlotte was six years older than Vera. Vera had followed her older sister out to Sacramento and gone to Sac State just like she did. She admired her, and it felt good to have an adult relationship with her as they had gotten older. Char and Conner had just started trying for their first child a few months ago. Vera crossed her fingers that it would be a boy. She wanted a nephew. So far though, no pregnancy.

"100 times better. Looks like you have been released from your captor," Vera teased.

"Ha- Ha," Charlotte said dryly, snatching back the ID card. "How's school going? You change your major again?"

Vera groaned. "No."

Charlotte gave her a look, urging her to go on. "And…?"

"And I don't know, school is fine. I got a D on a test a week or so ago, but it's whatever. I'll still pass the class. I don't want to talk about school."

The server returned with their beers and set them gently on the table.

"Are we ready to order?" He chirped.

Vera ordered *Pad See Ew* with beef and her sister ordered the yellow curry with chicken. The server smiled at them, mostly Char, and turned on a heel to send in their order. Vera sipped her beer.

"Okay then, well how is the pub?"

Vera coughed into her beer sending a splash onto the table and down her shirt.

"*Jeez* Vera, what the hell?"

"Sorry," she cleared her throat. "Um, it's fine. I don't want to talk about work either."

"Well damn, what do you want to talk about? How was your date last week?"

Fuck. I really have nothing to talk about tonight.

Vera sighed. She had to give Charlotte something, and she was her older sister, so she supposed this was someone to share it with and get it off her chest.

"Kind of crappy."

"Oh no, what happened?" She had Charlotte's full attention now.

"Well, we had that ice cream date at Gunther's and that was okay… and then he invited me to a game for his kickball league downtown on Thursday and that was really fun too. It was going well, and we went back to his place… and kind of started hooking up, and my blood sugar got *low*… and we had to stop. He just wasn't really cool about it." Vera felt color rush to her cheeks as she relived the moment. "It was just humiliating having this happen in front of someone who was basically a stranger. And he hasn't texted since. And I don't think he will. But I don't really want him to anyway."

"Oh Vera, I'm sorry."

"It's fine. We didn't have great chemistry anyway. I would have liked to have a normal sexual encounter though." Vera rolled her eyes. "It's been forever."

"Eh, well, screw him. You should date Sam anyway."

The Thai had arrived to the table and steam rose up from the plates, kissing Vera's glasses softly. She leaned back slightly to clear her fogged vision.

"Enough with the Sam thing," Vera groaned, allowing the groan to turn into a laugh.

Char had been trying to get Vera and Sam together since she set foot in Mosaic and saw him clearing tables. Char smiled slyly and rolled her eyes.

"On the subject of low blood sugar killing your sex drive though-"

Vera interrupted, "Um, that's not exactly how I would put it but-"

"Whatever, you know what I mean. The embarrassing part though, struggling to deal with the consequences of low blood sugar and feeling ashamed, etc, etc…" Char interrupted her in return, still trying to get her point across.

"Jeez Charlotte, get to the point." Vera teased but took slight offense to how nonchalantly her sister was talking about a real experience that she went through and had happen more often than she would like. Ashamed was a good way to put it. Not something she felt very casual about.

"The point is…," Charlotte snapped her chopsticks and picked up a steaming piece of curry-soaked potato, "that men deal with this too." She popped the potato into her mouth and then opened it wide and let it fall back out, mouthing *hot* to herself and taking a drink from her pint.

"Yeah, of course, low blood sugar doesn't discriminate by gender, Char. I don't get where you are going with this."

Char shook her head. "No, I mean, at work, we see it a lot in older diabetics. They can't *get it up* due to vascular disease from diabetes complications. It takes a huge toll on their self-esteem and self-worth." Char stirred her food and tried again with another potato. "All I'm saying is, diabetes has its role in sexual health that is not addressed by the public. So, while I can't relate, I hear you. And I am sure other people do too."

Vera considered this and picked up a wide noodle with her chopsticks.

She looked out the window and down the street and saw someone running by. She squinted her eyes to see better. It was not unusual to see a runner in midtown, not even at night, but what was unusual about this particular runner was that they were not dressed for exercise. She was wearing jeans and a coat, sprinting down the street. She was gone in a flash. Vera looked back at Charlotte to ask if she had seen her too and was startled by her sisters wide-eyed expression. Vera turned around to see that behind her a customer had collapsed to the ground and was seizing.

He looked to be in his 50's, salt and pepper hair, short gray beard, tee shirt and jeans, but thrashing and convulsing on the restaurant floor. His wife, Vera assumed, had turned him onto his side and was on the floor with him. When the seizure stopped, he did not wake. His wife was crying, scared, confused, frantic, as she shouted for someone to call an ambulance.

"Fuck," Charlotte said under her breath as she sprang into action. She rushed over to the man. The server was on the phone dialing for 911, desperate to get the man help and avoid a death on the floor of the Thai house. Charlotte assured the man's wife that she was a medical professional and that she was going to help him.

"Sir, can you hear me? Hello?" She shook him and patted at his chest. He did not wake. She checked his pulse, his breathing, her surroundings, and began CPR. His chest made an awful popping and crackling sound with the first deep compressions as Char put her weight into her hands, pumping his heart for him.

The cartilage in his ribs had crackled, startling his wife, and she cried out that Charlotte had broken his ribs.

"What is your name?" Charlotte asked in a breath.

"Joanne." She sobbed.

"Joanne, this is normal. The ribs make that sound when you start CPR on someone. I promise I know what I am doing." Charlotte looked around the restaurant at the concerned faces and customers recording her with their cell phones.

"Hey you! Go see if there is an AED here and bring it to me!" She shouted at a female server nearby.

The mousy red head darted into the back and returned with a green box for the automated external defibrillator. Charlotte pulled the man's T-shirt up to expose his bare chest. Luckily, he was relatively hairless. She turned on the AED and followed the instructions, placing the pads onto his chest and waiting for the device to analyze his heart rhythms.

"Shock advised, stand clear." The monotone voice from the AED stated before delivering a quick jolt to the man.

Vera stepped closer to the scene to see if she could do anything to help. She heard the whir of a siren and saw an ambulance pulling up to the front of the restaurant. Luckily, they were close to the hospital.

Charlotte had gone back to her compressions for the man and was counting out loud to keep track. A group of three paramedics burst through the door to relieve Charlotte and take over. Char backed up and watched them continue CPR. The man's wife, Joanne, was shaking with sobs. Mascara ran down her face as she said over and over, "We were just eating. I don't know what happened. He just fell over. We were just eating."

Vera looked at her sister. She admired her so much. Charlotte looked around the restaurant at the chaos. Her face had fallen flat. She shut her eyes and released a breath before returning to the table, sitting down, and finishing her dinner as the paramedics brought in a stretcher.

CHAPTER 18
GINA

D r. Garcia called Mark Langdon into her office for his appointment. He had canceled last minute on Friday the previous week, so she had not seen him since his day of radio silence in her office. He plopped himself down on her couch and bounced his right knee up and down impatiently but said nothing. He picked at his nail beds. He was quite fidgety today.

"How are you today, Mr. Langdon?"

He scowled at her. He was less put together than his last two appointments. She had noticed that on his first day he had put some effort into making a good first impression. Last week when he was giving her the silent treatment during their appointment, he arrived in a pair of joggers and the same navy-blue crew neck sweatshirt as the first day. Today, he wore gray sweatpants and a black pull-over hoodie. There was a dribble of toothpaste dried to the fabric just above the pocket of his sweatshirt.

At least he is brushing his teeth.

She gave him a few minutes to collect his thoughts. He continued to bounce his knee and stare out the window. She tried a more direct approach.

"Mark, you have been rather quiet during your last few sessions, and I noticed you canceled suddenly on Friday. Would you like to talk about what happened?"

He stopped bouncing his knee abruptly and looked sharply at her. She could see that he had not shaved his face in a few days. He looked startled, as if he wasn't sure how she had known this information, or as if he might have just been thinking about Friday and was unsure how she had read his mind.

He started bouncing his knee again and clapped his hands together. He sighed and shook his head, then chuckled to himself. She could see that it was not a friendly or fun chuckle, it was one of anger and disbelief.

"What a question. What happened? What's… wrong? Hmm. Well, for starters I am fucking miserable and these pills…" He took out a yellow prescription bottle of *Prozac* and shook it. The pills rattled loudly against the plastic. "These pills I am taking for my depression don't fucking work!" He stood and threw the bottle of pills at her, *hard.*

"Hey! Mr. Langdon, you can't throw things in here. If you are going to behave like this I can't see you today. Please take a deep breath."

"A deep breath??? Oh great! *'Take a deep breath, Mark'…*," he said, mocking her voice.

"Yeah, let's prescribe me deep breathing that will help! That will help me get my *life* under control."

He raised his voice. "Maybe that will make the woman at the

farmers market change her mind about going out with me! Maybe that will send my dead-beat mother back to whatever fucking rock she crawled out from under! Let's all TAKE A DEEP BREATH!" He was standing, shaking with anger, shouting, and pacing the room.

Gina sat still and maintained her poker face, although she realized she had started sweating into her green blouse.

She was one of the youngest clinicians in her office and relatively new to the practice, but she was so passionate about her work. She had only experienced a few client outbursts during her therapy appointments and found that if she could remain calm and make sure her patients knew that although they were out of control, she did not feel scared, they usually would calm down. Nevertheless, sometimes she would sweat when she was nervous.

"Your mother contacted you?" She asked surprised, realizing what he had just said. "Was this on Friday?"

"Yes," he said, dropping himself back onto the couch. "She reached out to me. I don't even know how she found me. She is in town, and I don't think I can stand to see her. I am trying to build a normal life. I wish I could cut out everyone who is attached to my old life."

He took a breath before continuing.

"She said she would like to talk to me. I don't know what it's about. But now she reaches out? Where was she when I needed her before? If she had been present maybe things would have been different. Maybe I wouldn't have…" He cut himself short. "Never mind."

"Go on, it's okay. Wouldn't have what?" Gina urged him softly.

"I *said* never mind."

Mark suffered from major depressive disorder, which often was accompanied by slow speech, slow movements, a lack of energy or motivation… but not always. For some people, their depression manifested as anger, especially when they felt backed into a corner. He was angry; that was for sure. He was also a new client of hers whom she had spent very little time with. He seemed nice enough on his first appointment, but Dr. Garcia knew very little about Mark thus far. She only knew what he had told her about his past during their first visit.

"What about the woman from the farmer's market? You asked her out?"

"Yeah, and that was a huge mistake. She said that I wasn't her type! How can someone be cruel like that? What does that even mean? She doesn't even know me! And neither does my mother! How dare they act as if they do! Nobody knows me!" Mark's face had turned beet red.

"I feel like I have been lit on fire. The anger is outrageous."

"Who are you angry with?" Gina posed the question gently.

"My fucking abusive dad! My worthless coward mother! And that bitch from the farmer's market! Everybody!" He was standing again, shouting. He picked up a vase of flowers and threw it at the wall, cracking the ceramic open and sending water and daisies all over the floor with the shards of vase. Gina's boyfriend had bought those for her to help brighten up her office when she had difficult days at work. *Ironic.*

"Mark. You have to leave. I can't allow you to throw things and become violent in my office. I am asking you to leave right now, otherwise I will have to call security." She kept her voice as calm as she could.

"You know what, fine. Fuck this place." Mark snatched the Prozac he had thrown at her off the floor and stormed out. He had a hell of a temper. Dr. Garcia released an unsteady breath and stood shakily to clean up the broken vase and flowers. She went to the front office to notify them that he was not allowed back in the building today.

By the time Gina had finished cleaning up the mess that Mr. Langdon had made, she had just enough time to make herself a cup of coffee before her next patient. The smell alone was enough to calm her down. She carried her mug back to her office and set it on her desk as she finished her notes from her session with Mark. His mother was in town. *Wow.* No wonder he had been acting so strangely. If she remembered correctly, she left when he was 16, *or was it 18?* Either way, it had been many years. And the woman from the jam booth at the farmer's market had rejected him. What had that interaction been? He seemed utterly humiliated when he spoke of it. She sighed and rubbed her temples.

On to the next.

Dr. Garcia rose to collect Mr. Young from the waiting area. He was seated in a far chair, long legs crossed in an unusual position where it looked like he had wrapped one around the other almost twice. He wore a red button-down dress shirt and had buttoned the buttons incorrectly so that they were all off by one, giving him the appearance that he was sitting at a sideways angle. His shirt was not quite long enough to cover his stomach, which bulged out from the bottom trim. He stood when he saw Dr. Garcia and adjusted his pants before walking with her into her office.

He took a seat on the couch and glanced at the small stain of wet office carpet near the wall where the vase had been broken.

"Good afternoon, Howard." Gina smiled.

Howard eyed the wet spot suspiciously. Then brought his attention to Gina's *"blouse of the day."* He clicked his tongue and shook his head.

"No more yellow blouse?"

Gina shook her head softly. "Not today, no."

"I see." Mr. Young said, scanning the office for other changes. "There were flowers in here before."

"Yes, they were knocked over by accident earlier. I will probably get another bouquet this week. Do you prefer any particular flowers that you would like to see in the office?"

Howard shrugged. "Your yellow shirt had nice blue and white flowers on it."

Dr. Garcia cleared her throat. "Yes, you mentioned that it reminded you of your childhood bedroom. Did it have white and blue flowers as well?"

"It did, yes."

Gina smiled and urged him to continue. "What else did you like about that room?"

"Well, it was my own room. I had a sister, but she had gotten older and moved out, so I got the flower room all to myself. I got a lot of hand-me-downs as a child. Hand-me-down bedroom and wallpaper, hand-me-down furniture as I got older, hand-me-down clothing, hand-me-down decorations…" His voice trailed off. "Quite a few hand-me-downs from my grandfather before he passed. These were his." He held up a foot and pointed to his very old leather shoe. It was in decent condition, but the leather was worn.

"Those are very nice. Have you looked at any job listings since we last spoke?"

Howard grunted and glanced back at the wet spot nervously. "Why is your floor wet?"

"We had a spill. I knocked the vase over, remember?"

"If you knocked the vase over the spill would be near the table. Why is the floor wet by the wall?"

Dr. Garcia made an attempt to redirect his attention.

"Have you seen your psychiatrist yet? About taking your new medication?"

"No."

"And you are still not taking the Paxil?"

"No."

"When are you scheduled to see her again?"

"Why is your floor wet?"

Gina was feeling impatient with his fixation on the wet carpet. Howard Young had been diagnosed with schizotypal personality disorder 14 months ago. He displayed some of the symptoms of criteria more so than others, but he had displayed them all at one point or another.

The suspicion of others and paranoid thoughts, misinterpreting conversations and intentions of others, peculiar mannerisms, style of dressing, way of speaking, peculiar thought processes; he had an unusual way of looking at the world. He had been called eccentric, but he had very severe social anxiety and distanced himself from others. He had very few friends, if any, although he was fond of his sister.

He experienced perceptual disturbances, as was mentioned with his tendency to hear voices, and he believed in the supernatural and paranormal activity in a way that was concerning to others. Most of which created distress in his everyday life, all of which were off-putting to a majority of the people he interacted with. Then of course, there was the incident of violence and isolation he had experienced before being put into therapy.

He had a tendency to create connections between things where there were none. He would find two very unrelated things and connect them with such devotion, that he became distressed when they were pointed out to be unrelated. With this tendency, he found himself experiencing a lot of paranoia and perceptions that people were after him.

"Mr. Young-"

"Howard," he interrupted.

"Howard…, the floor is wet because the vase was knocked over. I would like to talk to you about your job hunt. Have you looked at any job listings like we talked about?"

"I would like to talk about the vase."

"Alright. What are you thinking?"

"I don't understand how the vase could have been broken so far from the table if you knocked it over unless it were transported there and broken on the other side of the room. I am feeling very unsafe in this room, and I think that there are unsettled spirits who are feeling vengeful and shattered the glass over there." He pointed at the floor across the room.

"Howard, I had someone in here earlier become upset and

throw the vase. That is how it broke across the room. You are very safe in here," Gina assured him.

He scratched at his wrist. And began mumbling to himself.

Now you've done it Gina. What the hell were you thinking telling him you knocked it over. He is never going to be able to let go of the white lie you told.

Very suddenly Howard became angry. He jumped up and grabbed the coffee mug off Dr. Garcia's desk and threw it at the wall with all his strength, sending it into the same spot that Mark had thrown the vase. He threw it with such force that the mug hit the wall and burst into dozens of tiny pieces of white ceramic. Hot coffee dripped down the wall, leaving a large stain as it pooled on the floor, combining with the wet rug from the flower accident.

Gina jumped up out of impulse. He had caught her totally off guard.

"THIS ROOM IS UNSAFE!" He boomed at her.

"Howard, you are okay, take a deep breath with me. This room is safe. There is nothing paranormal in this office."

His mind raced as he made connections that weren't there. He concluded that the yellow shirt she had worn was a trap, and that too much of his mind had been exposed to the malevolent forces in the room. He became panicked and pushed Gina when she put her hand on his shoulder to try to help him relax. She had never seen him so worked up before.

"Howard, I understand that you are feeling scared right now." Dr. Garcia spoke to him in a steady voice, using slow sentences and clear words. He looked at her, his eyes wide with fear.

"What can I do for you?" She asked.

He released an unsteady breath and sat back down on the couch. "Someone has been following me recently," he said to the rug.

"Okay, let's talk about that. Are you up to talking more?" Gina asked gently. He nodded.

Howard had a complete meltdown during his session. He

told her about how he had been out the other night and a man followed him for several blocks. The man wore a dark purple windbreaker and a black cap, but he never saw his face. He told her about how he had been noticing broken glass more often, it was downtown as broken car windows, it was at the grocery store represented by broken bottles in the wine section, the broken vase, the broken mug, a broken shop window; these things were all happening on a timeline of broken objects. They were all connected. They were connected to the department stores that were selling ceramic plates and mugs and vases, and to *Home Depot* and Fix-it shops that sold windows. For new windows to be produced, old ones had to break. They were connected in time in that way; as a new window was born an old window died. The spirits made sure of it. They were angry that a mug had been produced across the country and the one in Dr. Garcia's office was still breathing.

Gina listened, empathetically, respectfully, calmly, as he dove down his rabbit hole, waiting for him to resurface. She decided a few things at that moment. For one, she would send a note to his psychiatrist and let her know that he had stopped taking his medication abruptly and was possibly experiencing an increase in his symptoms due to that, although, he had not yet started his mood stabilizer and that may be key in reducing his symptoms. Two, she may need to consult a colleague because she had not dealt with such a complex client before. And three, she could use a drink after the week she had just had.

CHAPTER 19

UNKNOWN

He thought that he might do well with a dog. Somedays his loneliness was so crushing that he thought it could kill him. Ironically however, killing others brought him to life. It lit a fire inside him that kept him warm when he was so cold, he could crack and break. Surely, a dog would help.

He considered going to a shelter, but the thought of interacting with a representative was awful. Especially the thought of being scrutinized so deeply over the state of his home and if he seemed *good enough* to adopt a dog. Perhaps he would look for a breeder on Craigslist, but he didn't have the patience to raise a puppy. This idea had now become so complicated in his head that he needed to take a walk.

He wandered through a neighborhood, occasionally seeing strangers walk their dogs. Large ones, small happy ones, old ones that could barely take a step. Nothing made him angrier than a dog in a stroller. It was so unnatural. He would become so angry upon seeing one that he often considered tossing it into the street when he saw a stroller-dog coming. He really had to fight the urge to do so in the middle of the afternoon on a crowded corner.

He loved a long walk. He would be a great dog owner and the dog would be great protection in addition to being a companion. The man turned down a suburban street. He heard a dog bark and saw it poke its nose through a hole in a fence. The man lowered himself so that he was eye level with the hole and the dog sniffed his face. The dog backed away and the man took the opportunity to look through the hole and see what kind of dog it was.

A black lab, probably only two or three years old, darted back and forth through a backyard comprised primarily of concrete. The dog deserved better. He could give him better. He looked across the street and saw another dog, sitting at a chain link fence on someone's property. The man walked over and the dog growled. It was a larger dog. A mastiff.

He continued to walk down the sidewalk and another dog ran the length of a fence to follow him.

Maybe I will come back and just take one of these. All of these dogs, waiting around for their owners and where are they? Maybe I will come steal one. It would be better off in my care.

The man walked a few blocks to a coffee shop and sat on the patio, drinking an iced tea and watching the neighborhood bustle. It was early evening. People would be coming home soon. If he were to take a dog it would have to be at night, and the dog may bark. The man considered this. A family from a nice suburban area might go looking for it too.

Getting caught was not a concern of his. He was bound to get caught eventually for something he had done, but to get caught for taking a dog, that was foolish. More than anything he would hate to have the dog taken back by the family. He would never survive it. He had a better idea anyway.

The man walked out of the suburbs and continued toward the lower end of downtown. He made his way along the river, through the trees, and through the tents. There were homeless camps along the river, under freeway overpasses, in certain alleyways... and many of them had dogs. A dog deserved more than a tent. The man would give it that.

The man walked past a large community of tents, and back into downtown, searching for the perfect target and the perfect dog and a more isolated victim. He found them both, deep on V street just as the sun had set. *Perfect.*

A woman sat with her back against an abandoned building and a dog sat with her. The man approached them with caution, he did not want to scare the dog. The woman eyed him suspiciously as he approached.

"Hello," he said, walking up.

"Hello..." she said warily.

"May I pet your dog?" He asked, crouching down to be level with the animal. The dog wagged its tail and approached him. He offered his hand and the dog licked it excitedly. The dog was a mutt, probably pit bull-terrier mix. He had dirty black hair and white paws covered in mud.

It's honestly too easy, he thought as the dog sat down beside him.

He looped a leash around the dog in a slip knot fashion and stood to leave. The woman, realizing what was happening stood and lunged at him, panicked.

"What are you doing? Give him back!" She shouted in a raspy voice.

She was older, and small, with matted gray hair stuffed under a beanie and filthy torn clothing. Her skin was dark and leathered by years of abuse by the sun.

The man walked to a stop sign and tied up the dog. He rolled his eyes as the woman shuffled after him begging him to stop. The streets were empty, not a car in sight aside from those parked down the block outside of an apartment or house. He took several long strides toward her and threw a hard punch, hitting her in the mouth and sending her toppling backward. She cried out, grabbing her mouth and burst into tears when she saw blood on her hand as she pulled it away.

"Stop!" She yelled.

And he hit her again because she was being loud. Then he hit her again because he liked it. His fire was lit, and he couldn't stop now. He hit her over and over until she lay in a broken heap on the curb. He turned back to the dog and saw it cowering against the stop sign pole. He approached it and the dog backed away, tail between his legs.

"It's okay boy, you're okay… it's okay." He stroked the dog's coat gently until it settled down. They sat together on the street corner, in front of the dog's owner and her battered body as she stained the street with her blood. When the dog seemed ready, the man stood and they left.

The dog resisted at first, wanting to stay with its original owner, but after a few sharp yanks of the leash he followed in step with his new master.

CHAPTER 20
CHARLOTTE

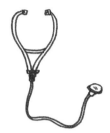

I t was late evening and Vera's sister Charlotte stood at Starbucks waiting for her coffee order at the pickup counter. There was a sign on the glass that divided the baristas from the customers that read:

> *The whole world is short staffed, please be kind.*

Charlotte rolled her eyes.

Truer words were never spoken, she thought.

Starbucks was beginning to close for the night. Charlotte collected her drink quickly after her name was called. With her vanilla latte in one hand and cell phone in the other, she checked her work emails and she headed out into the street to walk back to the hospital.

They were extremely short staffed. Because of this, Charlotte had recently found herself wearing several hats and being spread between other areas in need of employees. She was still relatively new to her job at Sutter, so she had no seniority and was occasionally covering shifts in the emergency room and other specialties for which she could fill a space with her level of expertise.

The night Charlotte had performed CPR on the customer at the Thai restaurant was not even the first time she had performed CPR that day. She later found out from a friend in the hospital that the man who had collapsed over dinner was epileptic and that the woman he was with was not his wife, but his *mistress*, and she was unaware of his seizure disorder.

Charlotte preferred to *stay in her lane* and only wear the hat of *Charlotte Kowalski, Urology PA* but understood that she was needed where she was needed and there was not much she could do about that. Especially if they had a slow day in Urology. Sometimes she would split her time between Urology and the ER. Today she had assisted in two vasectomies, changed a catheter, and consulted on a patient experiencing erectile dysfunction in his later years. After her urology tasks were complete she headed straight to the emergency room to assist where she was needed.

This evening Charlotte was working late. She took a break to stretch her legs and thought that some fresh air would help her clear her head and maintain her sanity. The walk to Starbucks was very short and she had just enough time to walk there and back before her break was up. She passed several other hospital staff members in scrubs with the same fresh air idea as she walked by *Sutter's Fort*, the historic park across from the hospital.

Charlotte entered the hospital through the automatic sliding doors and went to the staff break room to finish her coffee before heading out to the ER. It was just after 9:15p.m. when she returned to work.

She started off consulting on a few injuries in bays two and three, then she had to interpret labs for someone who had been there for over an hour waiting on their insurance to go through before they could get started on helping them with anything.

There was a patient who had dislocated their shoulder, which she examined and helped reduce, to get it back into the socket. Next she moved to drain an abscess, then provide stitches for a child who had fallen and split open their forehead, after that she had a patient come in with broken glass shards in his legs. Apparently he had dropped a plate on himself while cooking. He had been drinking quite a lot. It was a busy night. The ER bustled loudly, and Charlotte was grateful that she had her coffee.

Char and her husband had finally conceived a child after trying for roughly one month. She had taken three pregnancy tests over the past three days. All positive. She felt lucky. She knew friends who tried for years without conceiving. She had friends that were in their early thirties and going through fertility treatment as well.

Charlotte had limited her coffee intake significantly after learning of her pregnancy, making sure to keep it to less than two hundred milligrams of caffeine a day, if at all. She intentionally waited until late evening before having her coffee because she wanted to make her only cup for the day count and she knew that she would need the energy in the ER.

Charlotte was standing at a monitor, sending a prescription in for a patient, when a stretcher burst through the door loudly.

"Female patient, we are thinking about seventy years old, beaten badly. Looks like she has a fracture to her mandible, periorbital hematoma and lacerations around her eyes and mouth. Missing a few teeth. We found them in the street with her but there isn't really anything we can do about that." A young, handsome paramedic spoke clearly to an ER doctor as they wheeled the patient in. Two other paramedics followed in suit.

The doctor withdrew a flashlight from his pocket and lifted the woman's eyelid looking for a pupillary response.

"Okay, bring her this way please?" The doctor, Tyrese Jones, directed the paramedics with the stretcher to a bay and called Charlotte over after the patient had been placed into a bed.

The woman had no identification and in addition to her brutal beating, she was filthy. Charlotte guessed that it was probably an incident in the street with a homeless attack. It was not uncommon for homeless women to be injured in such a way. Rapes and assaults were high with this demographic of the less fortunate.

They assessed her quickly. Broken jaw, eye socket, wrist… She was missing a few teeth, one of them was cracked in her mouth, another was loose and hanging. Her nose was broken in an awful position, flattened to her face.

Dr. Jones spoke to her softly, assuring her that they would do everything they could to help her but that he was going to have to reduce some of her fractures, starting with her nose. He withdrew a syringe and vial of lidocaine with epinephrine and injected her in several spaces around her nose, eyes, and just below her nasal septum to deaden the nerves prior to setting her nose back into place.

The woman did not wince. She was alive, but not responsive to conversation. She laid in the hospital bed with her eyes shut as Dr. Jones prepared her for the procedure. He looked to Charlotte to continue with the lidocaine inside her nose as he went and changed his gloves.

Dr. Jones returned with a long silver blunt edged device to be inserted into the patient's nose that assisted him with pushing the broken bones back into place. The woman reacted to the pressure and movement of her fracture and groaned loudly in pain.

"I know, I know, I'm sorry," Dr. Jones mumbled to her softly as he reset the break and bandaged her up.

"What do you think happened to her?" Charlotte whispered to him.

"Looks like she got into a little fight…," Dr. Jones muttered gently.

Charlotte liked him. He was one of the nicest providers that she had worked with in the ER, and they were relatively close in age. She suspected that he was in his mid to late thirties. He bent his neck and rubbed his dark cheek against his shoulder to scratch an itch before continuing with the patient.

"Ma'am, can you hear me?" He asked the woman. "Can you tell me your name?"

She groaned again, murmuring something about a dog. A tear rolled down her cheek. Charlotte had not seen someone so badly beaten in a long time. The woman's eyes were red with burst blood vessels that stood out brilliantly against the dark purple bruises of her skin. Tears streamed down her face as she lay in a broken heap afraid to move.

Charlotte and Dr. Jones examined the rest of her body. She had a few broken ribs and dark bruises on her torso. They were concerned with internal bleeding and would get an ultrasound to look for further damage. Two of her fingers were crushed on her right hand. It looked as though they had been stomped on. Her gray hair was matted with blood. Dr. Jones looked thoughtfully at the woman and turned to Charlotte.

"Let's get her a CT, please, to rule out brain injuries." He turned to walk away and Charlotte stayed with the patient for a moment before leaving to work on his requests.

She continued to mutter about a dog in a raspy voice. Charlotte checked her again for bites, wondering if perhaps a dog had been involved in the attack, but did not see any. If she had to guess, she would say that the woman was attacked by a larger man, based on the severity of her injuries. It appeared that they were injuries made by hand, not by a weapon. She had taken a very bad beating but luckily was still alive. As Charlotte drew back the curtain to give the woman some privacy, she wondered where the attacker was now.

CHAPTER 21

GINA

Gina unlocked her front door and entered her home to the smell of garlic and the sound of pots and pans. She closed her eyes and inhaled what she felt love must smell like. She kicked off her heels and hung her purse on the banister by the stairs. Before heading into the kitchen Gina went to the bar cart and opened a bottle of Sangiovese. After she had filled her glass, she placed the bottle gently on the gold cart and looked down at its reflection displayed in the mirror shelf. Gina could see her face past the bottle in the mirror and she looked exhausted. She noted the dark circles under her eyes.

She carried her glass into the kitchen, taking a sip as she walked into the room. Her taste buds embraced the crisp and rich red wine as garlic filled her nose and warmed her body with the essence of a loving Italian home. Her boyfriend was at the stove stirring a sauce and drinking a short glass of whisky over ice.

Gina walked up behind him and put her arms around his waist, hugging herself to him.

"Hi," she said.

"Hey baby," he said stirring the sauce. He lifted the spoon and blew some of the steam off to cool it, turning to her.

"Try this."

Gina tasted the sauce he had been working on.

"Too much salt?" He asked.

"It's perfect. Is it almost ready? I've had a hell of a day and I could use some dinner with my wine," she said, rubbing her neck.

"Yeah, just a moment."

Gina sauntered to the round kitchen table and sat down, crossing her legs, and lifting one of her feet into her lap to rub the sole. Her boyfriend, Matteo, was plating their food.

He carried it to the table and set it down. Pasta primavera. It looked *divine*. If Matt could do anything, he sure as hell could cook. And kiss. And dance. And he was good with his hands, both in bed and around the house. He was basically the whole package.

"*Mangiare.*" He kissed her on the cheek.

Matteo Dellucci was Italian American. He told her that his family had moved to the United States several generations ago from Sicily, prior even to the birth of his own grandparents. He was born and raised in Sacramento, but deeply infatuated with his Italian heritage. He grew up dumbstruck by the fact that they did not speak Italian to each other and had vowed to Gina that when they had children, their home would be an Italian speaking household. It would be better for them to get into college that way anyway. He felt that being bilingual was a necessity, and a deep privilege.

Gina was already bilingual, raised speaking English and Spanish, but she didn't like to interrupt him when he was daydreaming. She thought it was sweet that he wanted to bring another language into their home, and especially sweet when he talked about kids. Their children would, *of course*, be trilingual.

Matteo minored in Italian in college and studied abroad in Italy. After he graduated, he spent a full year abroad, visiting distant Sicilian family members whom he was meeting for the first time, practicing his Italian, seeing the sights, sleeping with tourists, and pretending he was a local. He had met Gina in Italy while she was on a vacation with some girlfriends after she had finished her PhD. They were in love by the time her trip was over and he decided it was time to come home to the states.

"Thank you, baby," Gina said, taking a long drink of wine. "You wouldn't believe the day I have had."

Matteo pulled out a chair and set his plate down next to hers. "Bad day at work?" He asked.

"Crazy day. Like, certifiably insane. My clients were just going out of their minds today. You know, more than usual… They were both so angry. I have never seen either of them behave like this before. It was just a lot to absorb and I had a hard time shaking how upset I felt as I was leaving work today. I really need this drink." She said, draining her wineglass and standing to retrieve the bottle for a refill.

"I've got it babe," Matt said, walking out of the room to grab the bottle for her.

He returned and filled her glass. Gina watched the rich red wine as it poured from the bottle, it soothed her. She focused for a moment on her senses; her breathing, slow and easy… the smell of her drink -vanilla, figs, forest leaves, dried cherries- smoky and fruity… the look of the liquid, an intoxicatingly rich maroon, *like blood.*

She shook that last thought from her mind, unsure where it came from, and took a bite from her steaming pasta dish.

"I could use a new bouquet of flowers."

"Oh yeah?" Matt grinned at her. "What'd you do with the last one?"

"My client threw them at the wall. I need a new vase too."

Matt laughed.

"I'm sorry. That's not funny…" He took her hand and smiled at her. "Of course, I will buy you more flowers."

Gina slurped up a noodle. "Thank you."

They ate in silence until Matt stood and went into the other room to turn on their sound system. He liked to play music while they ate. Usually something without words, just to fill the silence. It was often jazz or piano. Tonight, he put on Santo & Johnny. *Sleepwalk*. This song always reminded Gina of Italian mob movies. She felt like it was a wedding song that was played in movies like *Casino*, *The Godfather*, pretty much anything with Robert De Niro and Joe Pesci.

Matt walked back into the room, swaying left to right and took Gina's hand, lifting her from her seat. She laughed and almost spilled her wine as she stood. *Sugar Song* came on next. Matt pulled her close and took her wine from her hand, setting it back onto the kitchen table. They swayed back and forth, and he guided her into a little spin then pulled her back to him. Gina leaned her face into his chest as they danced slowly in the kitchen. The song finished and played into *Sweet Lelani* after that. Gina pulled away and looked up at Matt.

"Our food is getting cold." She smiled.

"Yeah, you're right. But you looked like you needed that."

He was right of course. She did. She really needed that. It felt good to be held and spun around gently. She felt most intimate with him when they slow danced. Sometimes they would even dance together without any music.

They sat back down at the table and ate the rest of their dinner, music filling the background with warmth and passion. Once dinner was finished, Matt cleared the plates and started on the dishes. Gina sat on the counter next to the sink, drinking her Sangiovese and talking about an article she had recently read about psychedelic medicine being at the frontier of mental health treatment in some facilities.

Matt was an excellent listener. He smiled and nodded, and

always seemed genuinely interested in her stories, even though their lines of work were different from one another. Matt worked as a Nutritionist. Lucky for Gina, because not only did she not have time to cook, even if she had the time, she wouldn't know how. Matteo was phenomenal in the kitchen, and he was always making healthy dinners for them. When she had a hard day at work, she could always count on coming home to a hot meal.

They moved to the couch, and each poured themselves another drink. Matt rubbed Gina's feet and told her about his day while she finished her bottle of wine. By the time they had finished their glasses off, they were both a little bit drunk.

Matt pulled her into his lap and kissed her neck gently. They made out on the couch like teenagers before heading upstairs to their bedroom to continue their night. Matt was even better in bed than he was in the kitchen and after the day Gina had at work, it felt amazing to come home and be loved to the extent that she received. *Especially tonight.*

Tomorrow is another day. Gina thought to herself as she closed her eyes. The two of them laid naked on top of the covers together. Matt ran his fingers down her back, tracing small shapes into her skin and Gina felt her eyes get heavy with sleep until she gave into the weight of her eyelids.

Gina stood in the middle of a forest, barefoot. She felt damp bark against the bottoms of her feet and small grains of dirt creeping between her toes. It was dusk, but the forest floor was made significantly darker by the looming shadows cast down by the trees. It was cold.

Gina didn't recall how she got there. She looked around, scared and vulnerable. She was still naked.

Where am I?

She rubbed her bare shoulders with her hands, trying to warm herself. Her skin felt tight as it all shrank to keep in heat. Her breasts hurt from the cold so she cupped them in her hands as she walked forward, trying to be light on her feet because every few steps she would walk over a particularly sharp piece of bark.

The forest smelled of rich wet tree bark and pine needles. She looked to her right and saw the light of a fire flickering. She set in the direction of warmth, only mildly aware of her nakedness. More than anything, she was cold and thought that whoever was over there might be able to help her.

As she approached the fire, she felt fear creep up her spine.

What if this person hurts me? Who else would be alone in the forest like this?

She was suddenly too aware of her exposed body. Her soft skin illuminated by the moonlight through the branches of the trees. She reached down and picked up a rock from beneath the dirt. It was large enough to fit fully in her fist. It was very cold, and she felt her whole body shiver as she closed her fingers around it.

Gina crept up behind a bush and peaked through the leaves to see if anyone was sitting by the fire.

She gasped.

Her clients, Mark Langdon and Howard Young sat around the fire together on tree stumps that had been pulled forward to use as chairs. The flickering flames illuminated their faces, casting devilish shadows as the light played with their skin. They were each wearing a purple windbreaker.

Gina took a step back, hoping to abscond without being noticed by either of them. On her second step, she heard the sharp snap of a twig break beneath the ball of her foot.

Shit.

Gina looked up quickly to see if the men had noticed the sound. Howard was looking her in the eyes.

"Dr. Garcia," he said in a dull voice. It was posed as a question, but there was no surprise in his tone.

Mark stood and approached her. Gina turned to run but

Howard was at her other side as she spun around. Heat rushed to her face as she remembered her nudity and she tried to cover herself. Howard smiled gently.

"Here," he said, handing her a purple windbreaker. "We have extras."

Gina looked over her shoulder as she took the windbreaker in her hand and noticed that there were windbreakers littered everywhere. They were all around the clearing where they were sitting. Hanging from the trees like laundry out to dry, piled around the fire pit like bean bag chairs, folded in neat stacks next to the bushes.

Gina's breath hitched as she looked back at Mark and Howard, smiling at her.

———

Gina woke with a start, gasping and sitting up to look around the room. For a moment Matt scared her, until she realized it was him. She looked down at her naked chest and stood to put some clothes on.

It was just a dream...

She walked into her deep closet and flicked the light on, closing the door slightly behind her so that the light wouldn't disturb Matt and wake him.

Gina fished around her dresser for a pair of black panties and stepped into them, pulling them up onto herself. She felt immediately better, as if the fabric were hugging her, telling her she was safe. She reached for a white t-shirt and pulled it snugly over her head. Just for good measure she popped on a pair of socks before returning to bed.

Gina switched off the light and walked back to her side of the mattress. She looked up at the moon out the window as she pulled back the covers.

Gina gasped.

A figure stood across the street, facing her home.

Gina was frozen in place. One hand on the comforter, one hand on the windowsill, she stood there, staring back. After a moment, the figure turned and walked down the sidewalk, away from their house.

Gina looked over at Matt, wondering if she should wake him. She crawled into bed and stared at the ceiling, mind racing until darkness crept over her again and she fell back asleep.

CHAPTER 22

VERA

Vera drove to the gym with her windows down, letting the warm spring air fill her car and blow her hair around. She rolled her neck and turned up her music, allowing herself to become lost in her thoughts for a few minutes. She was procrastinating on studying for midterms. She just didn't feel like it today.

Vera felt as though her equilibrium had been off since her attack at Mosaic and her incident with Aaron, understandably so. She wanted to be alone and do something for herself today. She had it all planned out. She would go to the gym, work up a good sweat, and then grab lunch on the way home. At home she would shower off, change into her sweats, and watch Netflix in bed. No texting, no friends, no homework. She just wanted a Saturday to reset her brain.

She bobbed her head along with the beat of her music and found herself singing along to *Days* by The Drums. The soft, upbeat melody felt therapeutic combined with the breeze that poured in from her open window. She turned into the parking lot and scanned for a spot, finding one right in front. She smiled.

So far so good today.

Vera checked her blood sugar before going inside. *270 mg/ dl.* Pretty high. Vera had intentionally let it get high though. She struggled with what she often referred to as the *diabetic gym paradox*. She would come in to workout, be doing cardio, and her blood sugar would drop rapidly. She once had to stop and sit down because it tanked so fast, she thought she might fall off of her stationary bike. She always brought juice boxes and glucose with her but no matter what, when she got low she would have to sit down and wait until it came back up.

On top of that, she was at the gym trying to get in shape and drop a few pounds but was finding herself binging sugar because she couldn't get through a workout without getting low. It was infuriating. She tried drinking Gatorade at the gym instead of water because it contained so much sugar, but even that wouldn't raise it enough at the rate at which she was working out. All she wanted to do was ride the spin bike or do a few miles on the elliptical, maybe run on the treadmill. But every time she tried her blood sugar got low.

So she started eating prior to the gym. She would have breakfast and deliberately not take insulin, then she would work her blood sugar back down to a normal level. It had been working well for her, plus she got out of taking an injection, and it helped her to conserve insulin. *Win, win, win.* Kind of... It still did not feel great having high blood sugar, but if she timed it right it went up and came back down quickly, and was not high for very long. It was either that or her endocrinologist had suggested micro-dosing glucagon by injection, and this felt easier.

Inside she made her way to the elliptical and climbed aboard. She got herself into a groove of motion, placed in her earbuds, and turned up her gym playlist. It started out with a throwback, 50 Cent's *Disco Inferno*.

After a mile, she checked the app on her watch to see what her blood sugar was at. *260 and dropping. Good.* She glanced up at the TVs mounted in front of the equipment. There were several of them in rows in front of the ellipticals, spin bikes, and treadmills. There were a few on the walls over by the weights as well. Just something for the gym goers to watch lazily as their minds wandered during their workout.

The TV directly ahead of Vera had the news on. The one further to her left was playing the movie *Step Brothers* on it and she was regretting not having looked at the TVs before choosing her elliptical. Now she was stuck watching the news.

Once again Vera checked her progress. She was at a mile and a half and her blood sugar had dropped to 248.

Excellent. It's still going down.

She started to glance around the gym to people watch when a story on the news caught her attention. The news ticker at the bottom of the screen read:

Do we have a Midtown Murderer our Hands?

Vera continued pumping away on the elliptical, swinging her arms and legs in sync with her music as she read the subtitles on the screen. Once again the beautiful Asian American reporter that covered the 7-11 crime scene, Kristi Suzuki, introduced the setting.

"Police are appalled to see the appearance of a second dead body in the last ten days. This one turned up near H street and was found by a neighbor of the residence," the captions read, generating word by word.

"I was out walking my dog," The woman said. She looked

to be about thirty years old, maybe forty, with bright red hair thrown into a messy bun on top of her head. She paused to ash the cigarette that she was smoking into the street and looked down at her gray Shih-Tzu. The dog wagged its tail. The woman gestured to the dog as the captions continued to generate in sync with her lips.

"He got off his leash and ran into an alley behind some trash cans. I went after him and saw her all leaned up against the wall." Vera's eyes widened as she read the captions, trying to keep up.

Kristi Suzuki nodded to the woman and looked back to the camera.

"Police have not indicated that this murder is connected to the last one, however, it has been acknowledged that neither of the victims were shot. It appears that they were both beaten to death, and both had stab wounds."

The camera panned over to the police cars blocking the alleyway. They sat parked with their lights flashing red and blue. A pair of feet were visible from behind one of the trashcans and the camera man zoomed in on them. The woman was barefoot. Her shoes looked as though they had been kicked off. One black heel lay nearby, and the other was nowhere in sight.

Vera noticed that other gym goers had stopped their exercises and were staring up at the TV as well. A woman on an elliptical nearby was staring intently at the TV that she was sharing with Vera's elliptical.

Kristi turned to a tall African American police officer with his hair in a tight professional fade. He looked at Kristi and then at the camera as he spoke. The captions lagged for a moment before displaying everything he had said at once.

"We are asking that everyone carry out their days with additional caution until we know what we are dealing with. Go to work and go home. We are by no means implementing a curfew, but we ask that people living in the Midtown, Downtown, and East Sacramento area keep an eye out for each other. At this point we don't know if these two cases are connected. What we do know is that two people have been found dead. Be careful out there."

"Thank you, Officer Jackson," Kristi Suzuki said as she turned back to the camera. Jackson nodded and walked off screen.

Vera quickened her pace on the elliptical as the screen went to commercial. She felt herself beginning to sweat and checked her Apple Watch again to ensure that her blood sugar was still dropping. *200. Good.* Vera pushed herself that day at the gym, thinking that with two murders in her neighborhood it wouldn't hurt to be in better shape.

She allowed her mind to wander as she got deeper into her miles. Vera drifted into a dreamlike state, allowing her vision to split and blur while she stared forward into space. After half an hour she checked her progress on her watch and checked her blood sugar. It was continuing to decrease and she knew that she should stop before it got too low.

107 and dropping.

She slowed her pace and let herself down from the machine, taking a minute to find her footing, as if she were getting off a boat and needing to readjust to land.

Vera felt her phone buzz and checked the screen.

New Message- Alison

Vera slid her thumb across the screen and opened the text. Alison was asking if Vera wanted to meet up and go out of town tomorrow. She suggested Auburn but Vera felt like getting out of the area all together after seeing the news.

She typed back: *Let's road trip.*

She smiled to herself at the thought of spending the day outside in the sun. The weather was warming up quickly and Vera wanted to get up to Tahoe and hike around, but she wasn't sure if the snow had melted all the way yet.

As she headed out of the gym, she browsed Google for ideas

of where they could go. She imagined the sun on her skin and the breeze playing with her hair. She pictured Alison by her side and the sound of birds chirping in the trees. She needed a day like that. Alison responded.

Let's do it!

CHAPTER 23

VERA

Alison's white Jeep Wrangler sped down the highway headed toward the small town of Sonora. The past week had been remarkably hot and the girls decided to take advantage of the nice weather and go for a mild hike and a dip in some natural pools at the end of the trail. They were headed for *God's Bath*.

Vera had been once before with a group of friends but had no idea how to get there herself. Luckily, Alison frequently visited and knew the way well enough that she could have drawn Vera a map solely from her memory of the road. This was part of the reason that Alison drove. The other reason she drove was because her car was significantly more fun to take out for a road trip.

Small black and brown bugs speckled the white paint of Alison's jeep as they tore down the road squishing those who were unlucky enough to fly past as they approached. Alison switched on the windshield wipers as a particularly plump one hit the glass with an audible *splat*.

"*Eeeek!*" She shrieked, laughing, as the wipers dragged the remains across her field of vision in a gold and yellow rainbow of slime.

"Vera, did you see the size of that one?? My poor baby is getting a new coat of paint today. It's going to come home a totally different color."

Vera snickered and cranked up the radio. *Born to be Wild* by Steppenwolf poured out from Alison's ratty speakers. Alison looked at Vera, eyes wide with adventure, just as the course rang.

"BORN TO BE WIIIIIIIIIILD!" They both shouted as loud as they could. Vera drummed on the dashboard and Alison shook her hair around to the beat.

"Booooorn to be WIIIILD!"

Vera stood up in her seat as they turned off the highway. She let the wind blow through her long, dark hair and tussle her bangs about. Her t-shirt clung tightly to her skin as it was pulled backward by the force of the jeep as it raged ahead. Vera put her hands up and felt the air flow roughly through her extended fingers. She felt alive today. More than she had in months.

Alison had a way of bringing that out in people. She was a beacon of light. She looked up at Vera from her big heart shaped sunglasses and grinned.

"Sit the hell down! You're going to get us pulled over and I'm not paying a ticket because your dumb ass couldn't keep your butt in your seat! Put your seatbelt on!" She teased.

Vera obliged, shoving her playfully as she settled back into her seat.

"Pass me a *Coke*?" She asked when Vera was seated again. Vera reached into a little cooler that they had packed and pulled out a bottle for Alison. She insisted that the bottled *Coca-Cola* was vastly superior to canned and wanted the novelty of drinking out of glass on their road trip. It was not lost on her that they couldn't bring it with them to the pools for risking it breaking, so they bought a set of cans as well. Vera didn't mind because she only drank *Diet Coke* anyway and unfortunately, they did not have glass bottles of diet.

Vera cracked open her can with a satisfying hiss and passed Alison the opened bottle of her regular *Coke*. They drank in silence for a moment as Alison drove. Vera turned the music down as she tied her hair up in a messy bun to keep it from blowing in the wind.

"Did you hear that we have a murderer in midtown?"

Alison laughed. "Yeah, right." She rolled her eyes.

"Seriously, we do. They found two bodies within like a week from each other," Vera said casually, hanging her arm out the side of the jeep and playing with the air.

"No fucking way. Where?"

"One was by Sac State, by that 7-11. The other was somewhere on H."

"Good thing we are getting out of town."

They sat silently for another moment.

"Want to know something wild?" Vera asked, hesitantly.

"Hmm?"

"The first body that they found was the body of the guy who robbed Mosaic while I was working."

"Shut UP!" Alison took off her sunglasses to look at her. Either for dramatic effect or genuine disbelief. As if maybe if she looked her in the eyes, Vera wouldn't be able to lie to her.

"I am dead serious. They found him the morning after the robbery. I think he was killed later that night when he ran away."

Alison considered this for a moment. Vera had let Alison in on all of the intimate details of that night while they were drinking together at the kickball game. Something about Alison made Vera want to talk. That and the beer. And the fact that she was uncomfortable because she didn't know anyone at the game other than Aaron, and she was hoping to have a friend that she could confide in. Alison was a wonderful listener, and not the least bit judgmental. She always responded on cue, with the perfect little gasp or one-liner to make you feel like you were a fantastic storyteller. She always made Vera feel as if she were totally engaged and invested in the outcome of the story.

"How are you feeling about that?" She asked Vera.

"I'm not sure, kind of in disbelief, but also glad that I know where he is now, so I don't have to worry about him coming back to Mosaic."

"Yeah, but it isn't like he had hunted you though. No offense. What you went through was awful, I can't even imagine, but the odds of him coming back were crazy low, and now nonexistent since he is dead. At this point the scary thing is that there is someone out there killing people. Who was the second person?"

"I'm not sure." Vera said, and that was true. She had not even seen the woman, only her feet. "Some woman. I saw it on the news yesterday at the gym. A neighbor found her body behind a dumpster."

Alison shuddered and took a long pull from her *Coke* bottle. She slowed to park the car. Gravel shifted under her tires with a soft crunch as she turned her steering-wheel.

"Well, on that happy note… shall we hike?" She suggested. Vera smiled and collected her things. She grabbed her backpack, containing: insulin, glucose, a water bottle, and an apple. Before they set out, they each stuffed a few treats from the cooler into their bags as well.

It wasn't much of a hike. It was really more of a trail walk to the pools but there was some occasional uphill. Vera yanked a navy baseball cap onto her head and they set forward. Alison had her long blonde hair secured in a high ponytail as she walked in front of Vera, leading the way. Vera watched the sun bounce off of her silky strands, giving it a soft white-gold glow.

The air was crisp and warm. It was April, but Spring in

California had been unpredictable in recent years. It was subject to capricious weather for those transitioning months of spring and fall; ranging from forty degrees to ninety degrees, rain to hail, sunshine to fire storm, and winds that set fires out of control and burned down whole cities. Today however, the sun shone brightly in the cloudless blue sky and warmed Vera's shoulders and the back of her neck.

They walked in silence, admiring the trees and the rocks around them. The trail snaked along, thin and dusty, as they made their way along the Clavey River. Soon large rocks came into view as they approached the swimming hole.

God's Bath got a lot of foot traffic during the summer, but it was empty today as they made their way to the pools. The large granite rocks were flat and they walked up the incline as if it were a ramp. The girls choose a spot to set their stuff down that was shaded by a lacy shadow of leaves from the trees above.

The granite rocks sat above the water, making jumping points for hikers who came out to swim. Some people would go so far as to climb the larger boulders so that they could take a larger fifteen to twenty-foot jump down into the water. From where Vera and Alison had chosen to sit the drop was no more than five or six feet.

Vera sat down and fished into her bag for a *Sierra Nevada Pale Ale*. She passed a green can to Alison as well as she set out her small blue and white towel. Alison cracked open her beer and laid down, propping herself up on her elbows. She took a sip and tilted her head back, letting the shadows of the leaves dance across her face.

Vera glanced around at the vast emptiness of the area. She had never been here without other people. A yellow butterfly fluttered past and landed delicately on the rim of her beer.

"Don't… move…" Alison whispered as she pulled out her cell to take a picture. Vera flashed a smile and stretched out her arm so that the butterfly was closer to Alison.

"It's so cute!" She said extending the phone to Vera so she

could take a look. Vera examined herself, setting her beer down on the granite. To her surprise, the butterfly did not fly away. It protested the movement mildly by batting its wings and readjusting its position on the can.

Vera looked at the photo of herself. The can was closely outstretched and the butterfly brilliantly in focus with its golden-yellow wings and black patterns within them. The sun bounced off the can with a soft white shine, and Vera smiled widely in the background. The bill of her navy cap shaded her eyes and her dark hair lay in her sloppy low bun on her shoulder. It was one of the better photos she had ever seen of herself.

She caught sight of Alison unlacing her shoes to take them off, in her peripherals. She was sure that every photo of Alison was stunning. She was someone who came off as naturally very photogenic. She handed the phone back and Alison shot her a wicked smile.

"We should go skinny dipping." She glanced around, implying a 'why not?' Seeing that there was nobody else there.

Vera laughed. "Fuck it, sure."

Alison squealed and jumped up, stripping off her shirt and the green bikini top she had worn. Vera kicked off her shoes and peeled away her layers of clothing, hurrying to catch up with Alison who had taken off running buck naked, beer in hand, headed toward the mouth of the pool.

The second Alison's toes met the edge, she leapt off and pulled herself into a ball, sailing a few feet down and into the turquoise water, beer and all. She resurfaced laughing and drank from her beer, which was undoubtedly fifty-fifty pale ale and river water.

"Come on!" She shouted up at Vera.

Vera felt a little shy, standing there naked and bruised, looking down at Alison. It had been a week since her attack, and her bruises were starting to turn yellow and fade. Her cuts were mostly healed and had scabbed over as well. Vera hoped that she would be healed back to baseline by next week.

Alison swam in little circles waiting for Vera. If she were to skinny dip with anyone it would be Alison. Alison was fearless, and Vera admired her confidence. Her sister Charlotte was similar in that way. It was the kind of confidence that was contagious and Vera allowed herself to dismiss the thought of her naked imperfections before diving in. She took a long pull from her beer and removed her Apple watch, tossing it into her pile of clothing, then ran to the edge of the round opening and jumped clumsily in after Alison.

The cold water knocked the breath out of her and she opened her eyes under the clear green water to have a look around. Bubbles scattered around her, quickly rising to the surface after she had displaced the water with her splash. She came back up with a gasp and shouted at Alison, laughing.

"You didn't tell me it was freezing!" Vera's voice echoed in the tube they were in. They were surrounded by tall walls, and it would be impossible to climb back out. Vera felt uneasy and regretted diving in.

"It's not that bad, once your body goes numb." Alison giggled. "Come on." She dove under with a splash, leaving a ring of white ripples. Through the clearness of the water, Vera could see Alison's distorted shape swimming through an opening in the wall of the tunnel that led to the larger pool.

Oh, thank God.

Vera took a breath and pulled herself back under, following the way Alison had gone. She opened her eyes and swam toward the opening with wide strokes. It looked like a small opening, but as she got closer, she saw that it was much larger than she had expected. It was probably four or five feet across.

Vera emerged through the other side and took a sharp breath of air as she burst up through the surface of the water. She brought her hands to her head and slicked back her wet hair, treading water with her legs. Alison was still holding her beer, treading water too. She looked like a mermaid. She had taken her hair out of the ponytail and it floated around her like a blonde cloak, drifting softly through the water. Vera noticed that Alison's skin was covered in goosebumps.

"You're freezing too, liar!" She splashed at her and Alison darted away, putting some distance between them.

"Stop, it's cold!" She laughed.

The two of them glided through the water in large circles trying to warm up but eventually decided to get out, shivering. They swam through the large pool to where it became shallow again and the granite welcomed them back with its gentle incline. They trekked back up to their towels dripping and shaking with laughter and cold.

Vera dragged her red towel out from the shade and into the sun so she could lay out and dry off. Alison did the same and retrieved two fresh beers for them as well. In the sun they warmed quickly. It beat down on them un-eclipsed by clouds or trees and Vera felt her prickly goosebumps shrink back into her skin. After a few minutes, it felt nice, laying naked on the warm granite. She felt a soft breeze roll over her skin.

She and Alison were laying side by side on their stomachs, tanning their backs, both hesitant to flip over and be totally exposed in their nudity now that they were out of the water. Alison reached out a tanned arm and touched Vera's CGM that had been placed on the back go her arm.

"What's this?"

"It's called a continuous glucose monitor."

"What does it do?" She asked lazily, eyeing it with her head sideways in her arms.

"There is a little wire under my skin that reads the level of sugar in my blood, and the monitor part reads that number and will transmit the score to the app on my phone through Bluetooth. I can see it on my smart watch too."

Vera reached forward and grabbed her watch from out of her pile of discarded clothing. She strapped it onto her wrist and showed Alison the score with a graph. *135*. She was grateful that her blood sugar was within range when she showed her. She often found herself showing people the app and having her blood sugar be completely out of a healthy range, feeling embarrassed by the roller coaster she was riding.

"That's so cool," Alison said, closing her eyes. "Medicine has come a long way."

"It really has," Vera agreed.

"Does it ever get caught on stuff since it sticks out from your skin?"

"Oh, all the time…" Vera groaned, memories flooding back to her. "I catch it on doors a lot. Like when I try to shimmy out of a tight parking spot, I will catch the edge of it on a car door and it will pull it hard, sometimes it pulls it clean off. Especially if it is placed on my leg or torso. Or like when I pull my pants down to use the restroom, I have accidentally caught it in my jeans and nearly pulled it off."

"Ouch."

"I have had guys accidentally pull it off in bed before too, because they forget that it is there. They'll run their hands down my side or up my arm and rip it off if they're being kind of rough. Even if they aren't being rough though, just catching it and pulling it hurts because it is under my skin."

"I can't even imagine having something attached to you all the time."

"Yeah…," Vera trailed off. She had always had something attached to her as long as she could remember though. For many years she used an insulin pump as well and would catch the long tubing on doorknobs, desk drawers, even her own thumbs as she changed her clothes, and it would yank off the pump site that was attached to her skin. She shuddered at the memory.

"One time I was on the bus and I had the CGM on the back of my arm and someone came up behind me and literally tore it off. They said I was too young to need a nicotine patch or something. Something totally unrelated."

"Are you serious?" Alison asked.

"Yeah, and either way, even if it was a nicotine patch, what the hell gives you the right?? That's assault."

"You should have hit him."

"Believe me, I wanted to. He looked like the kind of person who might hit back though."

That thought hung between them for a moment until they settled into a new subject. They sat in the sun, drinking beer and snacking on chips that they had brought.

Vera told her about what had happened with Aaron and how he had not called since then. They agreed that it didn't seem like a very good fit either way. They talked about school and about Mosaic. Alison told her about how she and Philip were probably going to move in together soon. They daydreamed about other road trips that they would take together and other adventures that they would have as the sky began to turn orange in the late day.

The girls got dressed and packed up, getting ready to leave and drive back to Sacramento to get some sleep before class the next day. Before they left they paused to take photos of the swimming hole at sunset, admiring the way the sun hit the water and made it sparkle.

"Ugh, the bugs are starting to come out," Alison said after a few minutes of silence.

"Let's get the hell out of here."

Vera heard one zooming around her ears and swatted at her head, pulling her baseball cap back into place on her sun-dried hair. She felt a mosquito land on her arm and slapped it just as it had started to drink from her. The mosquito erupted into a red stain on her skin.

"Ew," Vera said under her breath, wrinkling her nose at the sight. The blood from the burst mosquito dripped down her arm and she couldn't help but wonder if it was more than just her own, and whose blood had stained her skin.

She had spent all day totally removed from Sacramento,

physically and mentally. But in that moment, she found the news of the murders creeping in from the corners of her mind. Vera felt a shiver run through her as the weather began to turn cold with the setting sun. She wiped the blood on her shorts and followed Alison in the direction of the Jeep, looking back over her shoulder with the sudden eerie sensation that they were not actually alone out there.

CHAPTER 24

UNKNOWN

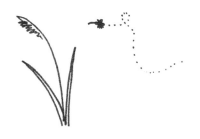

Today felt like a good day to take the dog to the river. He decided that he would call the dog Duke. It felt like a strong name, and he would have to be a strong dog if he were going to belong to the man. He knew that.

It was a warm, sunny day in Sacramento. He and Duke made their way through town to the trail along the river. They walked along the bike path at the top of the levy for some time before peeling off and into a smaller, windy trail that weaved through the trees and bushes on the river's edge. The soft, dusty dirt gradually became sand as they approached *Paradise Beach*, a popular access point in East Sacramento.

The beach was busy for an April day, but it was Sunday and the weather had warmed so much that locals were out taking advantage of the sunshine. College girls in their small bikinis were sprinkled across the beach, lying on towels and working on their tans while drinking *White Claws*. College boys, trying to show off, were seen throwing a football around loudly and crushing cans of light beer.

The man pulled the dog close on its leash and continued down the trail to an area with less traffic. They found a beach's edge where the sand became soft, fine dirt again, completely devoid of college kids. However, this beach still had some occupants.

Older men and women sat around, smoking cigarettes and drinking beer, admiring the weather. A young woman with bright red lipstick and greasy hair sat on the beach in her bra and underwear, clothes piled beside her. She passed a joint to a guy standing next to her. He was shirtless but wore red basketball shorts and had set his shoes beside her pile of stuff. A pit bull ran by, fetching a stick and then swimming it back to a Filipino man with a Raiders hat.

The man continued down the trail with Duke, still searching for a quieter beach. The dirt became rocks and they passed a man standing alone, fishing in silence. A few minutes further down the trail and they were finally alone.

The man picked up a stick from the ground and threw it out into the river to see if Duke would fetch after it like the other dog had been doing. To his surprise, he did. Duke went bounding into the river after the stick and swam right back, bringing it to the man. He smiled. He had chosen a good dog. He threw the stick mindlessly for Duke and began to lose himself to his thoughts. He remembered his first dog growing up. *Daisy.*

Daisy had been the family dog. He was nine when they got her. She used to sleep at the foot of his bed and protect him from the monsters in his dreams. He would toss and turn and cry out, and Daisy would come and lick his face to wake him up. He would open his eyes and see her there, licking his tears away.

When his father started hitting him and his sister, Daisy was there to lick those tears away too. When his sister got sick and needed treatment, Daisy was there. When they couldn't afford treatment anymore and she just laid in the bed dying, Daisy would sit with him while he hid in his bedroom so that he didn't have to listen to his sister in pain.

When his father got drunk and cracked a bottle of rum over the boy's head, Daisy was there to lick up the floor and lick the blood on his face.

That day he saw his father stumble into his sister's bedroom after the incident and the boy followed, dripping down the hall-way. The boy saw his father try to smother his sister with a pillow. Thankfully Daisy was there to bark.

When he pushed his father away to stop him and his father struck him so hard that he broke the boy's collarbone, Daisy was there to bite the man in the child's defense.

But when Daisy bit the boy's father and his father threw her into the wall, Daisy wasn't there anymore.

The next time his father tried to smother his sister with a pillow Daisy wasn't there, and he succeeded. His father said that he was putting her out of her misery, but the boy knew better. His father felt that a sick child was a burden and an expense.

The next time the boy had nightmares and awoke to the sounds of his own screams, Daisy wasn't there.

The boy had no Daisy. He had no sister. He had no mother. He had no father- just a monster who lived in his house and dressed in his father's clothes.

Now, as a man, he had Duke.

CHAPTER 25

VERA

One of the best decisions that Vera had ever made was not to take a Monday class. Especially since she got roped into a Friday class. If it is within reasonable power, give yourself a three-day weekend as a college student- a rule Vera lived by.

Vera slept in on Monday morning and went to the gym once again. She used her usual method of breakfast without insulin, to make her blood sugar high enough to exercise it back down into range. Today it shot straight up and instead of coming down it continued to increase. Vera ended up stopping her workout to take an injection and decided to go home after that because she didn't feel well. It was an imperfect method, but it worked more often than not.

After her failed workout attempt, Vera showered and changed

into light wash jeans and a red t-shirt. Since she had the time she gave her hair a quick once over with her curling iron, making big barrel waves and brushing her bangs out just right. She went with contacts today and consulted the mirror by the front door on her way out.

Oh girl, you're making tips today!

She gave herself a smile, pleased with her appearance, and walked down the street to where she had left her car before heading for her shift at Mosaic.

⸻

Vera pulled into the Mosaic parking lot with a familiar crunch of the gravel under her tires as she turned in. She parked her car and sat in the driver's seat for a moment before getting out. She looked at the entrance.

Her memory flashed the flutter of loose bills trailing behind the man who had robbed her as he ran from the scene.

A flash of the register smacking the wall and coming down onto her head entered her mind.

A flash of his body, dead in the street, surrounded by a pool of his blood as the police lights flickered red and blue on the dark red stained cement.

Vera swallowed the lump in her throat and released her seatbelt.

She walked into the pub, timidly, as if it could bite her. She saw that their glass fishbowl had been replaced with a tin bucket that had a little tipping blurb taped to the outside.

"Feeling Tip-sy?"

Her mind flashed with the memory of smashing the glass bowl over the head of her attacker, bills bursting out of it and flying around the room like frightened bats as the robber fell to the floor with a yelp and a thud.

Vera walked behind the counter and set her purse down where she usually put it. She stared at it and picked it back up, wanting to place it somewhere else.

"Hey Vera."

She glanced up nervously and saw Sam smiling at her from behind the bar.

"What?" She asked.

"I said, Hi." Sam's expression softened.

"Oh." Vera looked back at the empty space on the counter waiting for her purse. She set it back down reluctantly and cleared her throat.

"Hi," She said, walking to the register to clock in. She looked down and noticed that they had a new register box. This one was white.

"You see the window?" Sam asked as he hung up freshly clean steins on hooks.

Vera looked over at the window that had been shattered, half expecting to still see a snowfield of broken tempered glass. Instead, she saw a beautiful new window to the brew house. It was like it had never happened.

"It looks good." She forced a smile and looked at the steins he was hanging. "Are these new? A lot of them were broken that night."

"Oh yeah," he said, extending one to her. Vera took it and turned it in her hands, examining it before handing the stein back to Sam.

They still had a bunch of old steins that had survived the attack, and the new steins were slightly different, giving it a mismatched eclectic aesthetic. It went very well with the chic interior that Mosaic was beginning to cultivate.

A man walked up to the bar just then and ordered one of the new hazy beers on tap from Sam.

"Could you grab that, Vera?" He asked.

Vera lifted a stein from the hook and fumbled with it clumsily as she filled it with some nervous effort. She felt jumpy and on edge. She turned to carry the stein over to the customer as a song in the background ended and played into *Crazy Train*. Ozzy's laugh flooded out of the speakers and Vera dropped the stein in surprise.

Her mind flashed back to the sound of his laughter as she crept out of the bathroom, terrified, realizing she would be unable to scream for help because the music was so loud.

The stein shattered on the floor and the sound made Vera jump. She looked at the mess she had made and then up at Sam, embarrassed. The customer looked at her as if she had just dropped his child.

"I-I'm so sorry, let me pour another, I-I don't know what happened…," Vera stammered.

"It's okay Ver, I've got it," Sam said, stepping over the mess to pour a new beer and smooth things over with the customer.

Vera slipped into the back to grab a broom. She stood in the brew house, broom in hand, and looked around completely lost in thought. One of the tanks had about a dozen little dents in it from where the man had beat on it with the wrench. Vera's mouth was like cotton. She took the broom to the front and went to grab herself a glass of water before cleaning up her mess.

Sam approached her while she was squatted down sweeping up the shards of stein.

"Sorry about that." She said without looking up.

"Are you alright?" Sam asked her gently. "Is it too hard for you to be here?"

Yes.

"No…," Vera sighed. "I don't know. I'm just remembering a lot from that night. I haven't been back here since it happened."

Why did I agree to come back here at all?

"It's not very busy. Do you want to sit down for a second and take a little break to collect yourself? I can handle the shift myself honestly if you want to go home, but I know it's a job and you're working for the money, so if you want your hours I get it." Sam dragged a trashcan toward her so she could dispose of the glass.

Vera grabbed a towel and blotted at the floor to soak up the beer, thinking that she probably should have grabbed a mop while she was getting the broom.

"Yeah, I think that is a good idea. I'll just sit for a bit."

Vera went over to the bar and sat down with her water. She looked around the pub and allowed herself to relive her experience just to get it out of the way.

Her thoughts were interrupted as a man walked up behind her to order. She heard him coming before she saw him. There was the soft *tap tap tap* of a pair of crutches that made her turn around out of nosiness and curiosity.

The man was about five-foot-three and three hundred pounds, he was very round. He leaned into the bar and ordered a couple lagers from Sam, pointing at the menu. As he extended his hand to point out the beer that he wanted, Vera noticed that he only had three fingers. He was missing his pinky and ring finger on his right hand.

Vera looked at him curiously, trying not to stare. She peeked down, wondering if he was in a cast since he was on crutches. The man had a prosthetic leg opposite to the hand that was missing fingers. He looked over at Vera and gave her a crooked smile. He was missing several teeth.

"Hello," he said.

Vera noticed that his breath smelled sweet.

"Hello," Vera returned politely.

Sam set down the two beers for him and was called by someone else quickly at the other end of the bar.

The man struggled to collect his beer and use his crutches. He seemed to have enough trouble holding the one stein with only three fingers. Vera looked at him thoughtfully.

"Would you like a hand to your seat?" She offered, hoping that he would see the offer as sincere and not take offense.

"Oh, you're so sweet. Thank you, yes."

Vera climbed down from her stool and grabbed both glasses for him. He slowly led them outside on his crutches.

Tap. Tap. Tap.

He was seated at a small round table next to the ivy wall with a woman. Vera set the glasses down.

"I noticed you were alone; would you like to join us?" The man asked as he pulled out his seat.

Vera smiled. "Actually, I work here. I am taking a little break. But I could sit down for a minute." She took a seat at their table with them.

As the man clumsily lowered himself on to his stool Vera noticed that he had a CGM on his arm.

"Are you diabetic? I see you have a continuous glucose monitor," She asked gently.

What the fuck Vera? You are going to offend him. Where is your filter?

He smiled at her sadly. "I am."

"I only ask because I am as well." She said, trying to explain herself so that her question came off as mildly less invasive. She showed him her arm.

"You?" He asked, shaking his head. "You're too young."

Vera smiled at him. "I've actually been diabetic for about fifteen years. I was diagnosed young."

"Bah." He waved her off.

His female companion spoke up. "Are you *type one* then?"

"I am," Vera said.

"Marty here is *type two*. He has had a tough time getting the hang of it, but he's had it for about forty years now."

Marty scowled at her and then looked at Vera.

"Take care of yourself." He instructed. "You see this?" He lifted his hand to her, wiggling his three fingers around. "This should scare you."

Vera cleared her throat politely.

"And this?" He gestured to his prosthetic leg. "This is new. I'm still on crutches, but eventually I would like to be able to walk with just a cane. I lost it a month and a half ago."

His female companion shook her head.

What the hell did I get myself into?

"Complications." He scolded Vera with a little slur. Vera wondered at that moment how long he had been here and how many steins he had gone through already. She also wondered why he was ordering at the bar instead of his lady friend with ten fingers and two perfectly good, flesh and blood legs.

Vera gave him a soft smile and stood to return to work.

She exhaled roughly as she returned to the bar with Sam. He smiled at her.

"Marty sucked you into a story?" He asked.

"Is he a regular?" Vera inquired, grabbing a glass to dry with him.

"Sort of. He just started coming around, but he has been here a few times in the last week or so."

"Hmm." Vera hung up the stein she had dried.

The rest of their shift was quick and mechanical. They spoke very little, rushing around, clearing tables, pouring drinks. The tip bucket got more and more full. By the end of the evening, they each had a nice stack of bills to leave with.

"Hey Vera?" Sam asked as he finished counting the drawer to the cash register.

"Hmm?" She asked as she wiped down a counter.

"Do you want to get a drink at The Emerald Lounge tonight? I still kind of feel like I owe you one." He smiled shyly.

Vera considered it. She looked around. They had pretty much finished closing already. The chairs were stacked and the tips were distributed. She had already mopped.

"Is that the name of the bar from the other night where we ran into each other?"

"Yeah," he said brightly.

"I sort of just stumbled into there." Vera laughed.

"Well? Would you like to grab an old fashioned?"

Fuck it, why not?

"Fuck it." Vera smiled. "Why not?"

CHAPTER 26

VERA

The Emerald Lounge was nearly empty as they descended the stairs into the speakeasy-style bar. It was, after all, a Monday evening. Vera looked around and felt as if she were seeing it for the first time again. The emerald green wallpaper with swirly damask patterns emanated elegance. The bar with its dark wood and gold trim had a more antique feel that didn't quite match the wallpaper, but was a close fit and made the bar feel cozy.

The bar stools stood on gold legs with dark green upholstered seats that looked like they might be velvet. The booths were, of course, that same gaudy gold that Vera remembered from her first visit. A large mirror on the wall extended the room into another dimension, dragging out the deep green wallpaper.

Sam and Vera approached the bar and each climbed onto a

stool. Vera looked up at the rows of exotic looking liquor bottles in different shapes and colors. She let her eyes fall to the bar counter in front of her and took in all of the garnishes and fresh ingredients: Orange slices, lemons, limes, mint, rosemary, basil, cranberries, cinnamon sticks...

A female bartender with thick natural red hair thrown up into a stylish bun and green eyes that matched the intensity of the walls approached them to take their order. Sam ordered them each an old fashioned and she turned to make them.

Vera watched the bartender's hands. They moved with such speed, confidence, and elegance as she crafted their cocktails. It was an art. She set the drinks onto the counter and smiled at them before turning to leave.

"Enjoy," she said softly, as though she didn't want to break the silence of the bar. It was very quiet in the emptiness. Soft indie music played in the background. Vera thought she heard *The Lumineers.*

"Cheers," Sam said, raising his glass.

Vera clinked hers against his and took a sip.

"Sorry again about what you went through at Mosaic. Was it really weird being at work today?"

"Yeah, a little bit. But now that I have gotten that first shift back out of the way, I think it will be easier. We made good tips tonight too."

"Yeah. Plus, we have implemented a new buddy system so that nobody closes alone. I think it was overdue. Unfortunately you were the one to pay for that."

Vera shrugged. "I get why it took a while though, it's just more ways to split tips. If you can close alone, it is more money for you. I would prefer not to close alone anymore though. That or I will just take an opening shift."

Sam smiled at her sadly. "I think that is more than reasonable."

Vera poked at the curly orange peel in her drink and stirred it around with her pinky.

"How was your date on that Saturday? I hope it was good at least." Vera cleared her throat and tried to be playful, realizing that it sounded cold and accusatory as the sentence left her mouth.

"Ahh, I was hoping you wouldn't ask about that," he said chuckling lightly shaking his head.

"Oh no, was it bad?"

"It was awful."

"So you're telling me you asked me to cover a shift for you, at which I was attacked, and you didn't even have a good time on your date?"

"That's why I am buying you a drink! I feel *terrible!*"

Vera rolled her eyes. Truly, she wasn't angry. Nobody could have predicted the situation, and it wasn't Sam's fault. *Shit happens.* Maybe she was becoming a bigger, more mature person. Or maybe the whisky was softening her mood.

Vera sipped at her old fashioned, thinking that she might like another and contemplated if it was a good idea since she had class in the morning. She noticed Sam humming along to the song that was playing softly in the background.

"What song is this?" She asked him.

"This is...," Sam raised his eyes to the ceiling as if the answer was up there. He paused, searching his mind for the name of the song. "...I Saw You Close Your Eyes, by *Local Natives.*"

"Hmm." Vera listened for a moment. "I like it."

"Yeah, it's a fun one."

"I thought that I heard the Lumineers playing when we walked in."

"Oh, for sure, they definitely were. They play a lot of this style of music here. Do you like the Lumineers?"

"I do. I've always wanted to see them live."

"Oh, they are great live," Sam said, tipping his glass to his lips to take another drink.

"What was the last concert you went to?" He asked, repositioning his seat to face her.

Vera played with the orange in her drink. "The last show I went to was *Glass Animals*. They were fantastic."

"I *love* Glass Animals. They are great. I would love to see them live," Sam said enthusiastically.

"What about you?" Vera said, turning her seat to face him as well.

"The last concert I went to was J. Cole. I have absolutely no memory of it," Sam laughed, "Which is a shame because I hear he is great live."

"Well, it sounds like you had fun though," Vera snickered.

"Yeah, I mean, I hope so. The last concert I remember going to was The Red Hot Chili Peppers. They are awesome."

Vera drained her glass as they continued to talk about music. They listed songs that they liked, songs that they didn't, bands that were underrated, bucket list concerts they wanted to attend, and bands that you couldn't pay them to see.

Sam flagged over the bartender and ordered another round for them. Vera accepted, completely forgetting that she had to be in class tomorrow. It was a 9:30 a.m. class anyway, nothing she couldn't handle.

"Would you rather see *Palace* or *Alt-J*?" He asked.

"*Palace*. Would you rather see *Guns N' Roses* or *Metallica*?"

"Probably *Guns N' Roses*. *The Rolling Stones* or *Queen*?"

"What kind of question is that?"

"You have to just pick," He insisted.

"Uh, I don't know, maybe *The Rolling Stones*?"

"Aww Vera, you're sick for that," Sam said, shaking his head laughing, "I don't think we can be friends anymore."

Vera shoved him.

"Careful! You'll make me spill my drink and then you'll owe me another. You don't want to burn through your hard-earned tips too quickly," He teased.

Vera rolled her eyes.

"Do you know who *The O'My's* are?" Sam asked her, taking another sip.

"I do! I love them!" Vera said animatedly.

"Did you know that they'll be at the *Ace of Spades* this month?"

"Shut up, when?"

Sam pulled out his phone to check the date. "I dunno, let's see." The *Ace of Spades* was a small concert venue downtown on R street. That side of town had a fun and lively night life. There were a handful of bars around there and the street was usually closed off so that foot traffic could take over the road. Typically, only smaller name bands played at the Ace because it was such a tight setting, but once in a while you could find a gem. Vera saw *Portugal. The Man* play there when they were just becoming popular. The next place she had seen them play after that was at *Coachella*.

Vera leaned toward him to get a peek at the screen of his phone.

"Looks like Friday night. We almost missed them." He laughed. "I'm glad we checked. I would have been so upset. I don't know why I thought they were a week later."

Vera looked at him, her eyes wide with mischief.

"Should we go?" She whispered, as if it were a secret from the bartender.

"Absolutely. I'm buying tickets now."

They both looked up at their empty glasses.

"One more." Sam smiled, holding up a finger.

The red headed bartender mixed them each another cocktail and Vera ordered a side of fries after finding out that they had a tiny mystery kitchen when the bartender asked if they wanted anything before it closed.

It was a good call, it would keep her blood sugar from getting low from the alcohol. Cocktails were a beast. Vera's blood sugar always cooperated well with beer but the sugar in the cocktails would increase her glucose levels, and then they would crash once the alcohol was being metabolized. French fries would be a saving grace.

Sam held up his fresh glass to cheers Vera again.

"To *The O'My's*," He announced.

"To *The O'My's*," She echoed.

What just happened? Oh, my... Vera thought grinning to herself.

CHAPTER 27

GINA

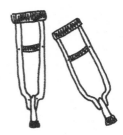

Tuesday rolled around. Gina had slept like shit all weekend. Monday included. Nightmares every night, weird ones too. She kept dreaming about her client's problems and their lives, things that she couldn't talk to her boyfriend about due to patient privacy, but that she felt like she had to talk to someone about. She considered getting a therapist of her own as she poured herself a cup of coffee in the break room.

She tipped some sugar into her mug, mixing it thoughtfully with the wooden coffee stirrer. Her mind wandered back to the vivid dreams she had. She pictured Howard holding the purple windbreaker out to her and wondered what about the windbreaker was so familiar.

She headed back to her office and pulled out her laptop to set up for the day. She decided to review her notes from Friday to see if there were any particular topics that she might want to avoid today so that she didn't set Howard or Mark off. She pulled open Howard's chart. There it was... the windbreaker.

> *Client exhibits paranoia. He complained of a man that had been following him. He described the man's clothing but not his face. He reiterated that the man wore a purple windbreaker and black baseball cap. Client has not mentioned this encounter in past appointments and it is unclear if this was a delusion of his paranoia or if he were lucid at the time of the incident. Will follow up.*

Gina leaned back in her chair and held her coffee mug to her lips, resting it there, and taking in the warm and rich scent before taking a sip.

I'll have to remember to ask him about this man today.

Gina checked the time on her delicate Anne Klein wristwatch. It was just about 8:30 a.m., time for her first appointment. She stood and smoothed her burgundy blouse before walking into the waiting area. Her heels made a soft thunk with each step on their office carpet as she made her way toward the reception desk. When she arrived where the clients were sitting, she had to stop herself from audibly gasping.

Howard and Mark were seated side by side on the soft blue couch in their waiting room. Mark flipped through a gardening magazine and Howard was scribbling something into a composition notebook. Her mind flashed to the image of the two of them seated around the campfire together as flickering light cast shadows dancing across their faces.

She backtracked her steps and approached the reception desk.

"Hey, Kierra," she said in a hushed tone to the young woman seated at the desk in front of her monitor.

"Hey Gina."

"Do Mr. Langdon and Mr. Young know that they are early?"

"Mr. Langdon does, yes. His appointment is at 10:00 a.m. Mr. Young, I am not sure."

Gina looked over at them, both absorbed in what they were doing.

"Okay, would you let him know that his appointment is not until after lunch, please?"

"Of course."

"Thanks," Gina whispered as she turned back to the lobby.

As she approached her clients, the front door opened and Matteo walked in with a bouquet of white roses. Startled, Gina smiled at him and shuffled him back toward the reception desk.

"What are you doing here?" She grinned.

"Bringing you new flowers," Matt said, leaning in to kiss her on the cheek. He looked around at the guests in the waiting area and they stared back silently. Gina shifted him so that has back was to the group.

"Babe, you can't bring me flowers to work unless I am on lunch. I don't want my clients to see people associated with my personal life," Gina said, taking the flowers. She tried to be serious, but in that moment she was so happy to see him.

"My apologies, love," he said with a whine. "See you tonight," he whispered.

"Goodbye," she sang, tossing a pen at him on his way out.

Gina took a moment to collect herself and set the bouquet on the counter in the front office area where the clients could not see it.

She walked back into the seating area and turned to a third person sitting near Howard and Mark.

"Good morning, Mr. Alvarez." Gina said brightly.

Martin Alvarez looked around the waiting area before standing. His eyes landed on Howard, scribbling frantically in his journal and grazed over Mark.

Gina cleared her throat politely.

He stood, struggling with his crutches, and hobbled forward to follow her to her office with a *tap... tap... tap.*

Once they were settled snugly into her office, Gina smiled at him from across the room.

"So, Mr. Alvarez…"

"Martin."

"Martin."

"Actually, call me Marty. Martin was my father."

"Alright, Marty. Tell me what brings you in today?"

Martin Alvarez, seventy-one-years-old, was a type two diabetic who had recently been struggling with his mental health. Well, that wasn't true. He had been struggling with his mental health for nearly his entire life, he only recently began seeking treatment for it.

He grew up in the Bay Area. Martinez, CA. He worked as a mechanic for many years. He had always struggled with his weight, significantly more so than his friends and peers. Diabetes ran in his family. His father was type two diabetic as well. Martin experienced relentless bullying for his weight throughout his youth. When he was diagnosed with diabetes at thirty-one. People said it was his own fault, that he deserved it.

He tried all of the online tricks and tips for managing care. He tried the keto diet, it worked for a while, but he always felt hungry. He tried exercising, however he worked long hours and had a difficult time maintaining a regiment. He cut out sugary drinks and snacks, but he missed them deeply; they reminded him of a simpler time during his youth. He struggled to change such a substantial amount of his routine and diet so late in life.

On holidays, his family scolded him for trying to have pie or wine with everyone else. Slowly, he began to feel more isolated and more depressed by the way his life had changed. He still tried to eat well but he was too tired to get up and cook. He thought about going for a walk but walking didn't interest him, nothing interested him. He felt himself fall deeper into an anhedonic despair.

Soon, his physical health spiraled out of his control and high blood sugars ran consistently high for days, on to weeks, and then years. He began to experience some serious complications. He developed severe neuropathy, sleep apnea, and began to have difficulty with his eyesight. For the first time in fifty-five years, he needed glasses.

Once, he decided that he would try cooking for himself again. Unfortunately he nicked his hand cutting up vegetables during the process. The cut became so infected due to his lack of control of his blood sugar levels that he lost two of his fingers. He lost a third finger later on from a cat scratch that became infected for the same reason. His body didn't heal like other people's. His body was broken.

When he turned seventy, his wife, the love of his life, planned a trip for the two of them to travel to Guatemala. He felt as though he finally had something to look forward to. During their trip, he stepped on a sharp piece of glass at the bottom of the swimming pool in their hotel. Someone had broken a beer bottle.

The cut never healed properly and became infected, as his hand had. He was terrified to go to the doctor for fear of another amputation. He let it fester out of control. The infection spread up his leg, and by the time he finally went in, there was nothing that they could do. A normal course of antibiotics or a surgical cleaning of the wound may have saved his leg if he had gone in earlier.

He lost his leg earlier this year. It was removed by an orthopedic surgeon at Sutter named Dr. Kowalski.

Marty looked up at Dr. Garcia, wiping his eyes after his long story about his life. She listened quietly the whole time. He blew his nose roughly.

Textbook Major Depressive Disorder.

At the end of their session, Gina thanked him for sharing and they set up their next appointment. She liked Marty and looked forward to working with him more. She wanted to see him improve so badly that it hurt her.

He denied experiencing suicidal ideations. One thing she admired about his story was that at the end of it he said that he was coming to therapy now because he wanted to salvage the life that he had left. He wanted nothing more than to live out his last years at peace with himself and what his life had become.

Marty's appointment took the full hour and a half that Dr. Garcia had allotted for him. She typed up his treatment note quickly and then headed back to the lobby to retrieve Mr. Langdon.

Mark Langdon's mental health was deteriorating right before Dr. Garcia's eyes in his appearance alone. He sat in front of her today wearing the same gray sweats as last week. They had collected a compilation of stains varying from what looked like mustard, to coffee, to red wine, and to toothpaste. He had stopped shaving. He wore glasses today and until this point, Gina had not realized that he normally wore contacts.

"How are things today, Mr. Langdon?" Dr. Garcia asked warmly.

"Same as last week."

"You seem less angry than last week."

"Yeah, sorry about the flowers."

"All is forgiven. However, I can't allow you to lash out like that in the office again."

"Yeah, I know." Mark looked down at his hands.

Gina gave him a moment to gather his thoughts before prodding him with questions.

"Did your mother reach out to you again?" She asked gently.

He looked up at her, irritated that she had asked.

"Yes."

"Would you like to talk about that a little?"

"I guess," he groaned.

They sat in awkward silence for a moment as Gina waited for him to begin and he waited for her to ask him a question.

"What did she say when she reached out to you?"

"She said…," he hesitated. "She said that she wanted to finally divorce my father so that she could get remarried."

Gina waited to see if he would give her any more of a reaction than he had. His movements were slow today. His depression had him in a vice grip.

"She said that she couldn't get a hold of him or find him and wanted me to help her."

Gina nodded, understanding what the weight of that request brought down onto Mark's shoulders. He wanted nothing to do with his abusive father.

"I told her that I don't know where he is. She doesn't believe me."

"Is that true?"

"Of course it is," he spat. "Why would I lie?"

"It's just a question, Mr. Langdon." Gina shifted in her chair. "How did your mother respond?"

"She yelled at me. Said I was worthless. Said I owed this to her. Said I should help her." He paused. "She'll never find him."

"What makes you say that?"

"I just know." He looked out the window. "If she does, she'll never get a signature out of him."

Gina took his curtness as a sign that he was done discussing this with her for the time being. They talked briefly about his garden that he had been working on. The plants were all starting to die. He was taking it very hard. He told her about the magazine he had bought to see if he could salvage them, and when their time was up he said he would see her at his next appointment.

At least he didn't throw anything today.

<hr />

Finally, after lunch, Dr. Garcia had Howard. She had spoken with her colleague Elijah about his intensity and his diagnosis. Or, about a client with such an intensity and diagnosis, not by name of course. Elijah recommended that she reach out to his psychiatrist and keep in close contact with her. They also discussed some techniques to help keep him calm when he had an episode. Today she would focus on what was triggering his symptoms, what treatments would likely be effective for him, and what goals they could set together for a healthy routine that might help hold him together.

Howard sat on Dr. Garcia's soft gray couch and tapped his foot up and down. She noticed immediately that something was off with him.

His eyes darted around the room. He set down his notebook and Dr. Garcia could see that he had scribbled dozens of drawings that layered over each other compiling into a mess of ink. He had ink smeared on the edges of his hands from writing and drawing on top of a paper that was already covered by his work.

"How are you today, Mr. Young?"

Howard took a breath and expelled everything in his brain. He told her about his morning, the dreams he had last night, how his dreams connected to his reality, how his reality was ever changing, how he felt the need to write it all out so that he could keep track of his changing reality and document the variations.

He talked about his ride over here on the bus and his theories about broken glass once more. He continued on and on. Dr. Garcia waited for a break in his stories to interject, but there didn't seem to be one. He stood and began to pace the room, talking excitedly.

He picked up his notebook and brought it over to her desk to show her. Dr. Garcia took it from him and asked him to please have a seat back on the couch as she looked through it.

He sat down but continued to talk, telling her about each page one by one. He told her that he hadn't slept, he had been up for hours and hours, drawing. He couldn't stop. He had not slept since Saturday night.

Dr. Garcia flipped through his note book. The pages were chaotic with frenzied scribbles and swirls, drawings of what looked like maps of Sacramento on some pages, with detailed notes in the margins that ran sideways up the page and then back onto themselves. Another page alternated in red and blue ink, giving it a 3-D appearance on the page. He drew the schematics of what she assumed was his home. He drew pictures of animals, dogs in particular. He wrote full pages about his theory on the connection of breaking glass across the nation and the conspiracy about the glass producing companies needing them to break in real time.

She looked up at Howard.

Shit. He's totally manic.

Gina had read that individuals with schizotypal personality disorder were at a higher risk for having other associated personality disorders such as bipolar. Although, she thought that it generally went the other way, where a patient might have bipolar first and later be diagnosed with schizotypal.

Gina looked back at her notes about his medications. As far as she was aware, he had not yet started taking *Lithium*, a medication that was commonly used for bipolar personality disorder, but it looked as though his psychiatrist had in fact given him the bipolar diagnosis. She jotted a quick note and decided that it was in her best interest to maintain a better flow of communication with his psychiatrist.

He said that he would be seeing his psychiatrist later this week, so that was a good sign. Before Howard left the office today, he looked back at Dr. Garcia. She expected that he would comment on her *non-yellow shirt* and remind her that he liked the yellow one better. To her surprise, he said that he liked the burgundy on her.

"I have been enjoying the color red more and more lately. I even have been using red a pen in my journal. That dark red though, I like that one a lot. It speaks to me," he said, and then he shot Dr. Garcia a wicked smile, one she had never seen him wear before. One she was sure was driven by his mania, but nonetheless, it left her with a chill creeping down her spine as she watched him walk away.

She looked down at her blouse, wondering what about it he found attractive. He said the color spoke to him. It was a brighter burgundy, almost a blood red. She shook the thought from her head, trying to maintain an objective, non-biased perspective and relate his behavior to his mania.

Blood red.

She squeezed at her temples.

Blood red.

CHAPTER 28

UNKNOWN

It had been a few days since his last attack when he rescued Duke from the dirty woman downtown. He was beginning to feel restless and pent up. He needed to release some of his rage.

Duke had been nervous when he first brought him home, unaware of how to act in his new environment. He soiled the floor several times. The man was so angry, he thought about snapping the dog's neck. But he loved the dog, so he resisted his urges.

He was having a lot of nightmares again. Nightmares about the abuse he endured for years from his father. Nightmares about the last moments he spent with his sister before her cancer progressed. Nightmares about the night his father smothered her, "*to put her out of her misery.*" The man would never know for sure what the truth behind that was, but he had his suspicions of a motive. His sister was too expensive to keep alive. His father was a toxic drunk. And his mother was gone.

The man grabbed his coat off of the hook by the door and set out into the night. He considered bringing Duke but knew the dog might bark, and that was the last thing he needed. The fire in his chest burned hot. He walked through the streets for some time until arriving at the top of midtown, near the *Motel 6*.

Perfect.

The place crawled with what the man considered to be *undesirables*. People who were utterly expendable. People who would not be missed. His blood lust growled like an animal deep within him. He walked around the back of the motel, where there was an alleyway littered with trash and belongings. It looked as though someone had set up to live there. He continued back around the bend to the front. There were *undesirables* hanging around the pool and across the street at a neighboring diner.

It's too public. The man thought reluctantly.

However one man in particular caught his eye. He dug through the trash, *eating* the food scraps that he could access.

You desperate thing, you.

The man decided to get a room at the motel and offered the homeless man a place to stay. With some hesitance for his safety, the homeless man revealed that his name was Raul and agreed to accept the man's *kindness*.

They ascended the stairs together and the man unlocked the door to Raul's room for the night. They stepped inside together. Raul looked at him awkwardly and mumbled a thank you, extending his hand for the key. The man checked the time, 9:00 p.m. It was too early. He would come back later. He handed the key to Raul and shut the door behind him as he walked out.

The man walked across the street to the diner and decided to have some dinner as he waited out the night. He ordered pancakes. A short stack with eggs and bacon. He used the strawberry syrup and watched as it flowed out of the spout and on to his pancakes with a steady, deep red flow. He ate and looked out the window, watching as the streets became less crowded, even the homeless seemed to dissipate. He cut his pancakes with jagged, unsteady motions, becoming restless and anxious about getting back to the motel room. Red syrup dripped down his chin.

He sawed at the pancakes as they soaked up the deep red liquid. With a stab of his fork, the syrup seeped out of the pancakes again when he cut into them, pouring across the plate, staining it red as well. *Beautiful.*

When he was finished, he went to the restroom to wash his sticky hands. He looked up at his reflection as he washed and noticed the red stains on his face. He licked the corner of his mouth. *Strawberry.* He wet a paper towel and wiped his face clean. He smiled at his reflection.

Showtime.

The man slipped the knife from his meal into his sleeve as he left and walked across the street. He walked toward the motel, excited, and took a breath to compose himself before going to the office.

"Excuse me, I seem to have lost my key. I was in room six," he said to the woman at the service counter. He gave her his name, his fake name of course, and she set him up with a new key.

"You're lucky," she said, "I was just about to close up for the night."

"Thank you," He gushed.

Very lucky.

The man climbed the stairs to the room, feeling as though wasps were buzzing around his head and stomach. He felt himself smile. He couldn't help it. He took a breath to steady himself and unlocked the door with the card. It made a small *click* and he was in.

Raul was fast asleep in one of the two queen beds in the room. He had laid out his own sleeping bag on top of the covers and was sleeping inside of it.

Oh, too easy.

The man approached him carefully, grabbing a pillow from

the bed next to him. In a swift motion, he pushed the pillow down over Raul's face, *smothering him* and keeping him silent.

Raul thrashed beneath his weight, but the man was much larger than him. Raul kicked his sleeping bag open, revealing his vulnerable body. The man withdrew the knife from the diner and stabbed at him sloppily and frantically.

The knife was dull, but with enough force it did the job. It was quiet in the room as the man muffled his victim's screams with the pillow. The bed squeaked as Raul fought against the man but once he stopped, *true* silence permeated the room as if someone had put the scene on mute. Raul's sleeping bag filled with his blood.

The man smiled.

Before bringing Raul up, he had taken part of the shower curtain off of the rod, just the plastic interior lining so that the bathroom would still appear untouched as the white fabric curtain remained hanging in place. The man slipped the plastic lining under the sheets in the bed to protect the mattress from his victim's blood. Once he was prepared, he set out to walk Raul to his sleeping arrangement. He did not expect Raul to set out his own sleeping bag, and that gave him an extra precautionary guard.

The man stuffed Raul back into the sleeping bag and zipped the bag up around his wounded body. He rolled him onto the floor with a light thud. The man tore the sheets off of the bed and balled them up with the curtain lining to be disposed of.

The man checked outside of the door before leaving with Raul. The city was quiet.

He dumped Raul's body in the alley behind the Motel, leaving the knife in the eclectic pile of belongings of the homeless person who had set up back there.

The man went back up to the motel room to wash his hands and wipe things down. Once the motel looked as it had before, he shimmied himself into the second queen bed and fell fast asleep within minutes. He would check out in the morning and thank the receptionist for being so kind and printing him a new key. Maybe he would even have another stack of pancakes.

The man dreamed in red that night. He dreamed of stabbing Raul and watching his blood pour out as strawberry syrup, making a sticky mess of his hands.

In reality, Raul continued to bleed into his sleeping bag as his body laid in the alley behind the motel.

CHAPTER 29
VERA

Vera tapped her pen against her desk as her calculus professor, Dr. Muir, handed back their exams. She slipped a paper onto Vera's desk, upside-down. Vera flipped it over to see a ninety percent written in red sharpie.

Happy hump-day, Hallelujah.

She smiled to herself and glanced out the window. A gray squirrel scattered up a tree next to her building. The sun was shining brightly through the leaves and she longed to be outside.

Vera sat through her lecture, took notes, and worked through several problem sets before collecting her things to leave with the bustle of the class as they were dismissed. She took out her phone to text Alison and see if she was on campus yet. Her phone vibrated to let her know that Alison had responded moments later.

At Round Table Pizza!

Vera hiked up her backpack and headed through campus, admiring the changing leaves on the trees and the blooming flowers. Her eyes watered and she sneezed hard.

Sacramento was the *"City of Trees"* and Vera had never experienced allergies so bad in her life. She had been told by other people she knew who were not Sacramento natives that they had bad allergies as well. She had also been told that even if you lived in Sacramento you would develop allergies at some point in your life. It was inevitable. Everyone would suffer and sneeze together.

Vera wiped her eyes on her sleeve and walked into the common area on campus that housed a handful little restaurants and fast food joints. It also contained several conference rooms, study areas, and a student store where you could buy snacks and testing materials during exams. It was referred to as *The Union*. The larger Hornet Bookstore with all the Sac State merchandise was across the way in a separate building.

Vera made her way through the busy automatic doors and into the building, headed toward *Round Table*. One nice thing about the *Round Table* was that it was the only place on campus you could get a beer.

Vera checked the time on her phone. It was approaching 1:30p.m. and she had not eaten lunch yet. She got in line and ordered herself a small personal pizza and a fountain drink. A beer sounded good but she had one more class and didn't want to feel lethargic after drinking.

She took her order number and headed outside. She scanned the outdoor patio until she saw a hand shoot up from a table and wave her over. Vera approached timidly, not expecting Alison to be with a group. She was sitting with her boyfriend Philip and two of his friends.

"Hey Vera!" Alison grinned.

"Hey." She smiled shyly at the group. "Hey Phil."

"Hey Vera, good to see you again." He gestured toward the other two guys at the table. "This is George," he said referring to the guy in a navy *Delta Chi* fraternity sweatshirt. "And this is Alex." He gestured to the other guy sitting with them. He was wearing a backward Sac State hat and a *Bar Stool Sports* t-shirt.

"Hey." They said in unison.

Vera pulled out a chair and took a seat next to Alison at the edge of the table.

"When's your next class?" Alison asked.

"Three o'clock," Vera sighed. "I'm tired already."

"Been partying Vera?" George teased her.

"No," Vera smiled, happy that the new people were friendly. "I had an early class. I have a long day on Wednesdays."

"At least you're getting your classes out of the way though." Alex offered.

"I wish," Vera groaned. "I still have a late Friday class."

"Yeah, Vera is a book worm and she is in class until the sun goes down." Alison nudged Vera playfully.

"Are you coming to the kickball game tomorrow night?" Phil asked as he took a sip from his beer.

Vera opened her mouth, unsure of what she sould say, when a *Round Table* employee walked up with her mini pizza. Vera recognized the employee as a girl in her finance class and gave her a small smile.

"That looks *so* good! I should have ordered some. Babe, want to split a pizza?" Alison said, flashing a smile at Phil.

"I have my Justice and Public Safety class in like…," Phil checked the time on his phone, "…like 25 minutes. I don't have time for pizza."

"Are you a criminal justice major?" Vera asked.

"Yeah, almost done too. I have five more classes and I am out of here." Phil grinned. "*Georgie* here is a Criminal Justice major as well."

George nodded.

"Hey Phil, did you hear that the cops found another body with the same M.O. as the last two?" George asked, leaning into the table and keeping his voice low.

"No way. Where'd you hear that?" Phil retorted.

"My older brother works for *Sac-PD*. He said that they found a homeless guy over by the *Motel 6* on N street. He was stabbed a bunch of times just like the others. They're trying to keep it low key so that they don't panic people, right now it just looks like it was an attack by another homeless person in that alley. They found the knife by a tent. A fucking *IHOP* knife too. The cops are looking at this from a larger scale though since the attacks have not been stopping."

"Who the hell cares?" Alex joked sarcastically. "They're just homeless people. The less of them on the street the better."

Vera shifted uncomfortably. The conversation had taken an unexpected turn. She looked over at Alison. Alison rolled her eyes and shook her head.

"You're such a dick Alex."

"What? Am I wrong though?"

"Yes."

"Whatever. All I'm saying is, if he starts killing college students, that's when we're going to have a problem." Alex finished his beer and set his glass back down. "I'm late for Fluid Mechanics with Dr. Brown. I'll see you guys later."

He stood with his red backpack slung over his shoulder and walked back inside.

"He's such an ass," Alison said to Vera, picking up a slice of her pizza.

Vera chewed thoughtfully, absorbing everything that had just been discussed.

Another body?

George and Phil stood after another few minutes.

"We're out of here too. I'll text you." Phil leaned down and gave Alison a kiss, then gave Vera a little wave as he walked out.

"Nice to meet you," George said as he followed after Phil. Once they were gone Vera checked how much time she had before her next class. It was nearly 2:40 p.m. She picked up another slice.

"When's your next class?" She asked Alison.

"I have Abnormal Psych at three o'clock. I'll walk out with you."

Vera swallowed her pizza and took a sip of her *Diet Coke*. She used her tongue to clear food from her teeth before continuing their conversation.

"What do you think about this '*Midtown Murderer*' thing?"

Alison shrugged. "I'm not sure. Not that much has been publicized about it yet. I'm not sure how scared we need to be."

"Do you think we should, *like*, not go out at night?"

"I mean probably not alone, but regardless of there being a murderer on the loose, do you go out alone at night anyway?"

Good point.

"No." Vera drained the last of her soda, making a slurping sound with her straw to get the bottom of the cup.

"Are you going to come to kickball tomorrow?" Alison asked with a yawn.

"I don't think so. I don't really want to see Aaron."

"What about George?" Alison teased. "He's cute right? He's got a killer body. I see him at the gym sometimes."

Vera laughed. "You're something, you know that?"

"Well obviously Alex is off the table. He's a pig."

"Yeah, I mean George was cute, I guess."

And he absolutely was. Cute was an understatement. He had a very dark complexion, he looked like he was some sort of Puerto Rican or Black, or both. He was devastatingly handsome.

In the distance, outside of the patio, Vera saw Sam walking by on his way to class. He saw her and waved. She waved back and smiled.

"Who was that?" Alison grinned, chewing on the crust of her pizza slice.

"My friend Sam. He works at Mosaic."

"Mhm." Alison smiled.

"What?"

"Nothing," she teased. "Let's get to class."

They both stood and collected their things. Vera refilled her soda and chewed on the straw as they left the patio and headed toward their respective halls.

One more class to go for the day.

As Vera walked through the trees toward Tahoe Hall, she caught herself searching the crowd for Sam. She shook the thought away as well as she could and headed into the building when she approached it.

God Vera, what the fuck has gotten into you with this Sam thing recently??

As she opened the door to her classroom, she cast one last glance over her shoulder.

Oh well.

CHAPTER 30
GINA

G ina stared at her computer screen, hugging her cup of coffee between her hands. The mug read *Mental Health Matters*, a gift from her mentor when she had finished her PhD program.

She was tired and had been up late, re-reading documents from when she was in school and researching personality disorders and violent outcomes. Something felt off about Howard recently.

She was concerned for his wellbeing regarding his mania, but more than anything she was beginning to feel concerned that in a manic episode he could be reckless or dangerous. If she were being honest with herself, he kind of just gave her *the creeps* recently.

In addition to Howard, something felt off with Mark Langdon as well. She had a gnawing curiosity about his father and felt that he did in fact know where he was, based on how he responded to her questions during their last session. He was hiding something. Maybe… or maybe it was in Gina's head.

Gina sighed loudly. She was exhausted.

Despite her nights of late studying and feeling run down by her case load, her passion for mental health and psychology was unwavering. Her friends teased her for "taking her work home" when she read from *Psychology Today* at coffee shops, *Psychiatry Today* in bed, and when she chose psychological thrillers on movie night. She was hooked. She had never experienced a passion for learning like this in any regard other than mental health.

Gina had considered going to medical school for Psychiatry, and sometimes she wished that she had, but the financial debt for her education was much lower with her PhD, and she was still seeing patients in the manner that she wanted. Perhaps more so. Her appointments were more than just medication management as they might have been in Psychiatry. They were problem oriented and together she and her client unpacked an issue and worked toward a solution.

Gina sipped her coffee and smiled softly to herself. The warmth ran through her chest and sent a shiver of goosebumps flooding across her skin. She was reminded of stepping into a hot tub and wondered why the body would sometimes produce goosebumps from heat as well as cold.

Ugh, a hot tub… I don't remember the last time I was in a hot tub… I could use a vacation…

Gina imagined herself in a red bikini, stepping into a hot tub in the Caribbean with a drink in her hand. Matteo would be there and smile at her as she climbed into his lap. *Bliss.*

She thought back on when they had met in Italy. He was so young and handsome. A little scrappy. His Italian was very good and Gina had thought that he was a local. To her surprise, he was not, he had just been there long enough to pick it up with ease and perfection.

She remembered going to dinner together in various bistros

and *vinotecas*. She remembered his soft smile when he poured wine for them in his apartment. He had a roommate who was a little bit younger. Gina remembered liking him.

What was his name?

She pulled her attention back to her present and squeezed the bridge of her nose with a little pinch, trying to keep herself awake and focused.

Gina looked past her computer at the stack of papers on her bookshelf, fighting the urge to go over and continue reading through them. She had not been home last night. Matt was always supportive when she worked late, and she didn't do it often, but once in a while when she had a particularly difficult client she would study late and sleep on her gray couch with a blanket. In the morning she would run home, shower, and change early before work.

She preferred not to put herself in that position, but she was an early riser anyway and did not like to drive late at night. Especially with the recent news about the murders.

It was late afternoon and Gina decided that she was probably done for the day. She caught up on her chart notes and had a few errands to run before going home. She just had to get through an afternoon staff meeting and then she would be free.

She yawned.

Almost done Gina. Home awaits.

Gina rolled her neck and sipped again from her mug, thinking about how she couldn't wait to go home and lay in Matteo's arms.

CHAPTER 31
HOWARD YOUNG

H oward walked through the park, admiring the trees, the birds, the rose garden, but not the people. The people made him anxious. On his way over, he saw a broken beer bottle in the street that made him shudder. Today, another bottle was born. He understood the connection in space and time but found that it still unsettled him. Nobody else seemed to understand it and frequently people tried to convince him that he was wrong, or they would often use the verbiage "crazy," which he didn't like.

Howard knew he was sick, or some kind of sick. He understood that his brain worked differently than the brains of other people. Dr. Garcia never said *normal people*; she would say a "non-depressed person" or a person who is not living with bi-polar, etc. Her phrasing made him feel better about himself but sometimes he would wonder what it would be like to have a *normal* brain and be a *normal* person and live a *normal* life that was unplagued by the universal connections exposed to him by broken glass and paranormal activity.

He walked quickly along the flowers scanning the area. It was early evening and the sun was setting softly. He could probably get a few more laps in before the sun set, but he should head home soon. He took a walk through the grass at the park and headed over to a bench where he took a seat. He took a deep breath and released it shakily, trying to control his breathing. He felt unbelievably restless. His knee bounced as he sat.

He looked down at some of the names and pictures that had been etched into the bench. He saw the name John and thought of his father. The thought disturbed him so much that he reflexively slapped the seat of the bench, hard, and stood to leave the park all together.

He tried to remember the breathing exercises that Dr. Garcia had taught him. He took a deep breath in, picturing his father's face of disapproval. He released a breath, picturing his father telling him he was more trouble than he was worth. He took a deep breath in and heard his father tell him to man up, and that men don't cry. He released a shaky breath and pictured his father telling him that he was crazy and that his decisions were an embarrassment. He took a deep breath in and remembered the day his father stopped picking him up from his high school campus.

Howard was beginning to feel overwhelmed. He opened his booklet and flipped through the pages of drawings and notes. His mania had begun to crash and he was feeling increasing amounts of anxiety and paranoia again. He ran his hand over the pages, bumpy with layers of pen scribbled about. It helped to settle his nerves. He looked down at the map he had drawn of Sacramento. He had done it by memory, and he was proud. He knew the area well.

He glanced up and saw a figure in a purple windbreaker and

black cap staring at him from across a street. Howard stood, startled to see the man again. He started to cross the street but had to stop to allow a truck to pass first. Once the truck had cleared, the man had vanished. Howard looked around, searching for him and saw him walking fast up a street away from him.

Howard turned and took quick strides in the direction of the bus stop. He looked back and did not see the man anymore.

Where did he go now? Howard thought.

He began to feel angry.

The bus arrived shortly after he approached the stop. Howard climbed on and took a seat in the back. He peered out the window, looking for the man. He heard a glass break and snapped his attention to the interior of the bus. Howard stood and looked around.

"Sir, you must be seated. We are going to go now," the driver said.

Howard lowered himself into his seat. In his peripheral, he saw a flash of purple. He swung his vision to the origin, expecting to see the man, but it was a teenager with a purple backpack. Howard released a breath and dug a small pocket knife out of his bag. He opened the blade and closed it in his fist. The quick sting startled him at first, but when he released his grip and looked down at the scarlet blood flowing slowly into his palm, he felt more at ease.

What a beautiful color.

He used to cut himself when he was isolated. It helped to distract him from his paranoia and allowed him to feel something that he knew was real. Dr. Garcia had insisted that they work on that behavior together and try to put a stop to it. Howard agreed, but today, he didn't feel like he could help himself.

He looked back out the window and watched the houses pass as they drove. He focused his attention on anything purple that he could see. Purple bags, purple shirts, purple signs; they passed a purple house and a purple car. After some time on the road, he saw a woman in a purple dress as the bus waited at a stoplight.

Dr. Garcia.

She crossed the street and walked into a convenience store. Howard turned his neck to try to keep watch of her as the bus started to move again. At the next stop, Howard got off.

He arrived at the corner store just as Dr. Garcia was leaving with her bags full of items. She walked across the street and to her car. It was a black Mazda. Howard thought it suited her. He had never seen her car before. The license plate had an unusual amount of zeros in it and it caught his attention. As she backed out of her spot, her tires ran over an empty travel-size shot of vodka; it cracked and broke. Howard clenched his teeth, hearing the glass break.

Dr. Garcia exited the parking lot and drove down the street. Howard followed out of the lot on foot and stood at the end of the block. He watched her turn into a neighborhood. He walked in the direction that he saw her turn, wondering if he would be able to find her. He did not have a car of his own, but he knew what hers looked like and figured he would be able to find it on foot. Howard walked quickly, wasting as little time as possible.

The sun set slowly, but the sky began to turn dark with time. Howard stumbled around the neighborhood. He had been walking for nearly forty-five minutes. Just as he was about to give up, he heard a garage door open and turned to see which house was making the noise.

A light brown, two story house with a freshly manicured lawn and white mailbox owned the sound. As the door rolled back, Howard could see that a black Mazda sat parked inside. Dr. Garcia walked out of the garage in a pair of sweatpants and a white tank top with a black bag of garbage. She took her bag to the street and lifted the lid of one of the cans on the curb, placing the trash inside.

Howard stood outside, watching, unsure why he was there, but he felt very strongly drawn to Dr. Garcia's presence after seeing her.

CHAPTER 32

VERA

Alison hooked Vera through her arm from behind, taking her by surprise as she walked to the parking lot after class on Thursday afternoon.

"Hey!" Alison chirped.

"You scared the *shit* out of me." Vera laughed, catching her breath.

"Guess what?" Alison grinned.

She was always so bright and full of energy. Vera felt her allergies weighing down on her and wanted to get home and grab a *Zyrtec*.

"What?" She smiled back, trying to match Alison's energy as they walked out to the parking structure by the school gym.

"I said *guess*, Vera!"

"You got an A on your Abnormal Psych exam?"

"Uh, no, I wish."

"You were reached out to by a modeling agency?"

Alison shoved her. "Shut up Vera. I'm serious."

"You're dropping out of school and becoming a stripper because the pay will be better than anything you'll get with your degree?" Vera laughed.

"Oh my god, I'm going to kill you. No!"

"I give up. Let's hear it."

"The kickball game was canceled! The entire other team got food poisoning. I think they all went out to lunch together today as a team building exercise and now nobody can play against the *blue team*. Isn't that hilarious?"

"Um, I guess so, in kind of a sick way. Why the big production over this?"

"Well, that's not the exciting part." Alison skipped in front of Vera and walked backwards ahead of her so that they were face to face.

"There's a Kings game downtown tonight. Do you want to go? George and Alex and Phil and I are all going. You should come. I'll buy your ticket. They're dirt cheap anyways. Nobody ever wants to see the Kings play."

"Hey, I like the Kings."

"I do too! That's why you should come!"

Vera smiled. She didn't have any other plans, and Thursdays were a good day for her to go out because she didn't have classes until late in the day Friday.

"Fuck it, why not." She grinned at Alison as her whole face lit up with excitement.

"Yay! This will be so fun. I'll text Phil now. The game is at seven o'clock. Do you want to come by Phil's house before it starts? He lives with George downtown on S and eighteenth street."

"Sure. That sounds fun. I'll text you."

"Okay, see ya then!" Alison hurried off toward her car and

Vera walked to the elevator and pressed the button to call it down.

The doors slid open and she stepped in. Just as they were starting to close, she heard someone call for her to hold it and a brown hand shot between the doors just in time. They reopened and George stood in front of her with his backpack, panting from rushing to catch the elevator.

"Oh, hey." He said, striding in.

"Hey." Vera smiled. She felt a little shy suddenly. Alison had gotten in her head yesterday when she talked about him being cute.

The doors slid shut and Vera's mind flashed back to the couple pressed up against the wall in the elevator the night that her car got swiped last week.

Damn, I would love to be pushed into one of these walls.

Vera cleared her throat. "Alison told me about the Kings game tonight."

"Oh yeah? Are you going to come?"

"Yeah, I'm looking forward to it. She said that we are meeting at your house before the game?"

"Yeah, that's the plan so far."

"What time?"

"Whenever you want." He smiled. "I'll be home."

College boys…

"I'll text Alison and probably come around the same time she does," Vera said politely.

"Sounds good."

The elevator doors slid open on the fourth floor of the structure and George stepped out.

"I'll see you later, Vera." His voice was smooth, and she saw him give her a little wave as he walked toward his car while the doors were closing. She felt her stomach flip once she was alone.

Vera smiled, really beginning to look forward to the basketball game. She hadn't been to a single game this year. She used to go a lot with her sister and Char's husband, but Charlotte had been so busy recently, and Vera admittedly had not thought about going to a game until now.

The doors to the elevator slid open at the top of the parking structure and Vera stepped out, walking toward her car.

"Oh, are you fucking kidding me?!"

A red paint ding decorated her driver door. She looked around. No red car in sight.

"I'm about to wring someone's neck." She mumbled under her breath.

She pulled out her keys to unlock her car frustratedly and drove to Mosaic- the only appropriate remedy for when your car gets fucked with at school.

The gravel in the Mosaic parking lot made the usual crunch as Vera turned in. She locked her car and walked inside. She could see through the window that her coworker Michelle was working today.

"Hey Michelle," Vera said as she stepped in. She saw Marty sitting at the bar with his crutches leaned against the stool next to him.

"Hey Vera," Michelle replied as she fiddled with the music, trying to pick a station. *Adele* poured out from the speakers and Michelle turned to face her.

"What's up?"

"Nothing. I was just thinking that I would get some beer to go. I am going to a Kings game tonight."

"Oooh fun," Michelle said brightly. "What'll it be?"

Michelle put her hands on her hips. She had curled her long brown hair and pulled it back into a ponytail. Her blonde highlights peaked out from within the curls. Today she wore high-waisted jeans and a mustard yellow cropped top.

Her tanned arms were covered in colorful tattoos. Roses, leaves, and other flowers. Butterflies and bumble bees filled the spaces between her botanical garden of ink. She had a leafy vine that wrapped around her wrist and onto her hand. From below her small yellow top, the body of a snake was visible against her ribs.

Her red lipstick gave her the appearance of a classic pin up doll, especially as she passed steins to the customers seated at the bar. Michelle was a hot commodity at Mosaic and brought in a lot of tips.

Her shiny Doc Martens squeaked softly as she walked to the register to help a customer while Vera looked over the menu to pick a beer to go.

"What are you thinking?" Michelle asked again as she approached Vera after closing out her customer.

"I think I'll get a four-pack of the session and a four-pack of the West Coast IPA."

"Sure," Michelle beamed. She grabbed the packs from the cooler and carried them over to Vera.

"Anything for here?"

"No, I'm okay," Vera said. "Thanks though."

"No prob," she responded, tapping Vera's debit card on the counter before she turned away with it to ring her up.

Vera collected her beer and gave a small wave to Marty as she walked out. He smiled back, confused.

He probably doesn't remember me… That's awkward.

Vera climbed back into her car and drove home to change and have dinner before heading to Phil and George's place.

Vera pulled up to the house and parallel parked her car on S street. She looked up the steps to the porch and checked her cell phone for a text. Nothing.

Alison had better be here.

Alison had told her 6:00 p.m. It was 6:08 p.m. Not really fashionably late or anything, but they were going to walk to the game and Vera wanted to have a beer with everyone first.

She was feeling anxious about entering the house without her friend, not knowing the boys very well. She deliberated momentarily.

Screw it.

She grabbed her small black purse from the passenger seat and exited her car, crossing the street toward the house.

George and Philip had a nice little set up. It was an older yellow house wedged between two white houses on either side. The steps that led up to it were painted a soft eggshell color and a wrap-around porch was set up with a red table and chairs set for when they wanted to sit outside. Vera knocked and heard laughter inside. A moment later the door swung open and Phil stood there with a goofy grin on his face.

"Welcome!" He swooped his arm wide as if to present a game show prize to her, inviting her into his home.

"Thank you," Vera chuckled nervously. "Is Alison here yet?"

"Not yet but she should be in a few minutes."

Philip turned and walked into the living room. He was wearing a purple *De'Aaron Fox* jersey and dark jeans.

"I brought beer," Vera said, forcing some confidence into her voice and holding up the cans.

"Wow, perfect timing. I just finished mine." Philip smiled, shaking his empty can.

Vera followed him into the living room and set the packs of beer down on their coffee table.

George was sitting on their brown couch in front of the TV wearing a white *Domantas Sabonis* jersey.

"Hey Vera," he said warmly as she sat down across from him on a worn, small black ottoman.

"Hi George," she said. Her stomach flipped as she said his name.

Get a hold of yourself Vera, would you?

"HEY BITCHES! Are we ready for the game???" The front door burst open and Alex walked in wearing a black Sacramento Kings hoodie and joggers.

This guy… where the hell is Alison?

Vera rolled her eyes and cracked an IPA. George noticed her reaction and snickered to himself. Vera blushed.

"Oh nice, beer!" Alex reached over Vera and helped himself to one of the sessions.

"May as well get into it," Philip said, smiling and reaching for one himself.

"Pass me one Vera?" George asked.

"Sure." Vera smiled shyly and passed him one of the West Coast IPAs. He cracked the can and took a long drink.

Alex plopped down on the couch next to George and looked around.

"Where's Allie?" He asked Philip.

"She should be here any minute," Phil responded, checking his texts to verify.

"Okay, because we should try to leave around six-thirty if we want to talk."

"I'll give her a call." Phil stepped outside to ring Alison. Vera was left alone with Alex and George.

Vera picked at the tab of her beer for a moment, trying to figure out what to say to the two of them. To her relief, started a conversation together about the kickball team and the recent gossip between their friends shortly after Phil left. Vera was spared the *getting to know you* conversation that she was dreading.

After a few minutes of listening to their conversation, Vera began to wonder if Alison was going to bail on the game tonight since they were having a hard time tracking her down. After another moment the door creaked open and Phil stepped inside.

"Look who I found!" He sang as Alison followed in behind him.

"Hey guys!" Alison beamed to the room. Her long blonde hair was braided back and she wore a purple *Fox* jersey to match her boyfriend's. She wore her jersey over a gray hoodie and looked remarkably balanced in her cozy-sporty set. She strode over to Vera in her black leggings and slip-on *Vans* and took a seat beside her.

"Did you bring these?" She asked Vera brightly.

Vera nodded.

"Aw Ver! You are so sweet." She gave her a big kiss on the cheek. Vera laughed.

"*Girl*, you're too much. Stop." Vera wiped her cheek, embarrassed.

Alison cracked an IPA and took several big gulps.

"I have some catching up to do." She laughed.

"Yeah, finish up guys. It's six-thirty. We can each take another for the walk over," Alex commanded.

"Bottoms up," George chirped.

They all tipped their beers back to finish as much as they could, grabbed their things, and headed out the door to walk to the *Golden 1 Center*.

They walked in a pack. Alex, George, and Philip in the front with Vera and Alison following in the back. Vera and Alison passed the last can of Mosaic IPA between the two of them. It was a nice night, not too cold.

Vera was glad she had decided to wear her sneakers since they were walking. She followed in step with Alison quickly.

Vera wore a black Sac State crew neck that just said *Sacramento* across the chest in white. It was the best she could come up with for the game. Maybe she would buy something there. She did have a purple Kings baseball cap that she tossed onto her head last minute just to splash in a shade of color.

They arrived at the Golden 1 Center arena by 6:50 p.m. and got in line to have their tickets and bags checked. Vera's bag was slightly too big and one of the security women was giving her a hard time about it. After explaining that she had medical supplies in it, she was ushered over to a separate line with a backpack X-ray scanner. Vera looked back over as her group swiftly entering the arena. She scowled as she was left behind.

I'll never find them in there. I hope they wait for me…

A man waved her down and looked at her bag.

"They said I have to come over here if I have medical supplies in here."

"What is it?"

"I'm diabetic. I have insulin and stuff in here."

He grunted. "Sure are a lot of *'diabetics'* coming through here with big bags," he said, with an attitude like he didn't believe her.

Vera was stunned. "Yeah. There are a lot of us, it's more common than you'd think."

"*Sure.*" He said, looking into her purse. "Where's the medicine? I don't see anything."

Vera pulled out a rose-colored zipper pouch that Charlotte had given her as a gift. It was stylish and not obviously filled with medical supplies, which was why Vera liked it.

She zipped it open and exposed its contents. A few syringes and a bottle of insulin lay inside with a tube of glucose and her blood test meter.

"Okay," the man grunted.

Vera zipped her things up and walked through the metal detector. As she did, she had a distinct childhood memory flash through her mind of being at the airport and having her hands wiped down for explosives as they checked through her medical belongings and equipment. She had been on an insulin pump for many years when she was younger too. Airport security was very wary when the insulin pumps started becoming more popular in medical care- especially post 9/11. Vera had hers in 2005.

One time when she was running late for a flight, she was stopped by security to be searched. They dumped out and checked each individual needle that she had in her bag. She nearly missed her plane. Vera shook the thought from her mind and trailed inside with the crowd.

Once she was in, she searched for Alison and the boys. She finally found them at one of the concession stands ordering beer and popcorn.

"Hey! What took you so long?" Philip asked as she approached.

Vera knew he didn't *actually* care and was only asking to be polite, so she just shrugged. The group had their hands full, and it was apparent that they were on the move. Vera looked over at the line, wondering if she should just meet them at the seats so she could grab a drink too.

"I'm going to grab a beer really quick. Where are we sitting?" She asked.

"I got you one already." George smiled.

"Oh!" Vera said, surprised. "Thanks George."

"No problem." He gave her a silky smile.

She took the tall can of *Bud Light* from him and took a sip, trying to hide her childlike smile with the can so he couldn't see her blush. He saw anyway and smiled into his beer before turning to follow everyone to their seats.

They filed into seats in section 110 and walked down halfway. The seats were pretty good. They were seated Alex, George, Phil, Alison, and then Vera as they settled in. The game began almost immediately as they sat.

The Kings scored the first three pointer of the game and the crowd responded with light cheers and applause as people were still arriving and finding their seats. They were playing the Denver *Nuggets* tonight.

Alison looked at Vera mischievously and proposed a drinking game like the one they had played at kickball. The rules were: Drink when the Kings score on a three pointer, drink when the mascot- *Slamson the Lion*- comes out, drink if you end up on the big screen when the camera goes around the audience, and finish your drink if the Kings win- no matter how full your beer is.

Vera liked how competitive Alison was. She was fun and seemed to bring out a buzzing energy in the group.

Slamson, the Kings mascot, was running the length of the court waving at fans and poking fun at people. He ran up and down the aisles and the camera man followed him, displaying him on the big screen for everyone and alerting the audience if he was near their seats.

Vera took a sip from her can. He was coming near them.

"He's coming! He's coming!" Alex shouted, pointing to the Lion.

"Get ready!" Alison said, holding her can to her lips and watching the big screen above the court to drink if they appeared on camera.

At the last second, *Slamson* turned and ran back down the stairs.

"Aww, so close!" Philip shouted.

The Kings were playing well, and it was a high scoring game. By halftime, the scoreboard read 69-59 with a Kings lead. The halftime buzzer rang, and the crowd stood, shuffling back to the concession stands for refills and merchandise as the *916 Kings Dance Team* ran on to the court to do their halftime performance.

The five of them stood and let the crowd carry them back to the food court. They snaked through a sea of people and headed to a set of escalators toward the tall glass walls of the arena. On the second floor they made their way to the Biergarten.

Sierra Nevada was always on tap and they each got a pour in a proper cup, instead of their previous cans. They stood at the railing that overlooked the court and gazed down at the halftime show from above.

Vera smiled. She was having a great time. Much better than kickball would have been. George appeared at her side.

"What did you get?" He said loudly over the noise.

"Just their classic Pale Ale. You?"

"I got a hazy something or other." He laughed. "Want to try it?"

"Sure," Vera said, taking a sip. She didn't prefer hazy beers, but it was hard to say no to the conversation starter with George. They stood together at the railing, making small talk over the noise and mostly going off of nonverbal conversation since it was loud.

Vera would point at someone in the audience doing a silly dance and he would laugh. George would point out a couple that was drastically over dressed, the girl in eight-inch heels and her date in a full suit and they would chuckle. After a moment, Alex nudged them to indicate that it was time to head back for the third quarter.

When they arrived back to their seats, they filed in- Alex, George, Vera, Alison, and Philip. They continued their drinking game with their fresh beers for the duration of the second half. By the end of the third quarter, their beers were empty again.

"Can I grab you another, Vera?" George asked loudly.

"Of course, I'd never turn down a beer." Vera giggled.

George smiled and took her empty cup from her, leaving with the other two boys to grab more for the group. Alison looked at Vera with her mouth open in playful shock.

"*What* is happening over here?" She teased.

"I don't know." Vera laughed. "We're just hanging out."

"Okay." Alison smiled.

"He's pretty nice though. You were right."

"I didn't say he was nice; I said he was *hot*, but I'm glad you think he is nice too." Alison shouted over the crowd.

Vera shoved her, laughing, and Alison took one last sip of her beer. Suddenly, she inhaled sharply, her eyes wide and pointed forward, toward the court. Vera followed her finger and saw that she and Alison had made it on the big screen. They cheered and stood to do a little dance for the audience before it flashed over to a different section of the crowd.

"No way!" Vera shouted happily.

"Damn, we're out of beer!" Alison yelled, smiling.

The boys returned with their drinks a few minutes into the fourth quarter and Alison told Phil what had happened in giddy, drunken excitement.

The Kings and the Nuggets were tied 119-119 in the last minute of the game. All five of them sat on the edges of their seats hoping to see a Kings win. The crowd hollered and the arena buzzed with suspense. Twenty seconds left and number 40, *Harrison Barnes*, had the ball. He sailed down the court, the clock was running out, he shot for a three, *and missed*.

"NO!" Alex cried out.

The Nuggets got hold of the ball, number 15, *Nikola Jokic* made his way down the court and took a soft push shot under the net, scoring as the buzzer rang. The final score read Kings 119, Denver Nuggets 121.

Fuck.

The five of them deflated in their chairs.

"Well, bottoms up anyway," Alison said, raising her can.

"I guess," Alex scowled.

They all held their cans to their mouths and finished what was left as they gathered their things and exited with the disappointed crowd.

"Should we drown our sorrows?" Philip suggested as they funneled out into the cool night air.

"Why not?" George sighed. "Where to?" He looked at Vera. "What do you think Vera?"

Vera liked that he was giving her so much attention and putting her in a spotlight.

Does this dude like me? She wondered enthusiastically.

"Uh, what about *Streets* again?" Vera suggested. They had gone to *Streets Pub and Grub* last week after kickball.

"Sure, always down for *Streets*," he said to her with a smile. "To *Streets*!" He instructed the group.

They all shuffled out of the downtown commons near the Golden 1 Center and up K street. They walked quickly, excited to make their way over to their new destination. As they approached a dead end on K, they turned down an alley to cut to their left, headed the parallel street, J. The pub would be on J street a few blocks up.

Alison and Phil jabbered away about what they were going to order at the bar, and Alex was shouting on the phone with a friend about what the Kings players should have done differently if they wanted to win that game.

Vera walked step-in-step with George, and they made small talk about school. Vera looked ahead and saw Alison skipping forward until she stopped abruptly and nearly fell.

Vera strained her eyes to see what she was doing and picked up her pace out of curiosity when Alison released an ear curdling scream.

Phil raced to her side and pulled her back by her waist after seeing what she was looking at. Vera and George ran ahead to see what had scared them so badly.

They looked down at a battered body, fresh blood pouring into the street around them. The victim gurgled softly, still alive. Alison began to cry, hard. She was having a panic attack. She stepped back and Phil went to settle her down. George pulled his phone from his pocket and called 911 to report it.

Vera looked at the victim, wanting to help, but there was nothing she could do. There was nothing any of them could do, and the ambulance would never get there in time. She looked down at the poor mangled man in front of them, full of holes, as he was visibly stabbed dozens of times, mutilating him. She watched him carefully, and saw the man draw one last shaky breath before going still.

Vera looked to George, fear in her eyes, and he nodded, understanding the question. With his eyes, he said that he was thinking the same thing.

Yes, it was the Midtown Murderer.

CHAPTER 33

VERA

Vera sat at her desk, furiously taking notes on Professor Wong's lecture. She would not get another D. She would get an A on the next exam for sure. If she got another D, she would scream.

"Well, that about wraps things up for tonight. Any questions?" Dr. Wong posed to the class.

"No?" He said, glancing around. "Okay, don't forget that your portfolio assignments should be nearly done by this point in the semester. They are worth a significant amount of your overall grade so don't wait until the last minute."

Vera swore that he looked right at her as he said that last part. She packed up her school bag and headed out toward the courtyard.

The sun was still shining brightly that Friday evening. The

days were becoming longer and it was now staying light much later.

Vera checked her phone and saw that she had a text from Sam.

Looking forward to tonight! :) Meet at the Snug?

Sure, see you then! Vera typed back as she walked toward the parking structure to retrieve her car.

The Snug was a cute little bar near the concert venue. It was cozy and dimly lit with nice music. The drinks consisted of fancy cocktails with lots of garnishes. It was right up their alley since they had been spending time in *The Emerald Lounge* together.

She felt a little bit guilty that she was seeing Sam tonight after she had just been to the game with George the night before. However, it was not a date with George. They were in a group. And she wasn't sure if this was a date with Sam either... but it felt like it might be.

In addition to the guilt Vera was feeling about being close to both of the boys, she was a bit of survivor's guilt. If you could call it that... With the recent murders in the area, she wondered if she should be out enjoying her time like this or if she should stay in out of respect for the lives lost.

The news was documenting very little on what was *actually* happening with the Midtown Murderer, so Vera was having a difficult time understanding her feelings about the situation and navigating how scared she *should* be feeling.

After stumbling upon the body last night, she definitely was feeling aware that this was more than a couple stories on the news. It was real. It was real and someone really died at her feet last night.

After the incident, Phil took Alison home and George wanted to give them some space at the apartment so he continued to the bar. Vera stayed out with him and Alex as they walked to *Streets of London*.

They sat outside under the string lights and talked about what had happened. George was so composed. Vera suspected that he was familiar and comfortable with the idea of crimes like this, as he was studying criminal justice. She had not asked what he planned to do with his degree yet and was unsure if he wanted to go into law enforcement like his older brother or pursue a career on something more related to the court systems. There were many directions he could take his education, but Vera mostly associated criminal justice degrees with police officers.

Alex had rambled on and on about how he couldn't believe it. He was pale. Vera was surprised to see Alex personality shift so much from his usual annoying and rowdy self to almost that of a scared child. The incident seemed to humble him immediately and he was visibly trying to cope.

George bought the round of beer and tried to talk Alex down as well as he could. After a while, they changed the subject and avoided the topic all together. Vera thought that she might either be in denial or shock about the situation. She felt nothing. She felt excited for her concert, and a bit of guilt for feeling excited and not allowing herself to have an emotional response to their discovery of a body. Although, the reality of the death was hitting her a little more today than it had in that moment. She did her best to push the thoughts aside for now.

Vera waited for her usual elevator car, checking the time on her phone and trying to plan out her evening. The elevator doors opened and *Acqua di Gio* poured out. The same couple as from the last Friday stepped out together, caught red handed in embrace. Vera rolled her eyes and stepped in.

Jeez, typical Friday for you two?

As the doors of the elevator opened on the top floor, Vera braced herself for more damage to her car. She walked over and inspected it carefully, seeing nothing out of the ordinary. She smiled to herself and unlocked the door.

So far so good for this Friday!

Vera put her keys in the ignition and went to start her engine. Her car wouldn't start.

Oh no.

She tried again, and again, and again.

"What the fuck is wrong with you?!" She shouted at her car, banging her fists on the steering wheel. She leaned her head back into her seat and groaned.

A tapping at the window startled her and she jumped.

"Hey Vera," George smiled from behind the glass. "Car troubles?"

"Yes," she sighed.

"Want some help?"

"Yes," she sighed again.

George smiled and gestured for her to hop out of the driver's seat. She stepped out into the parking structure and he slid past her and into the car. He fiddled with the ignition for a moment and then gestured to a light on her dashboard.

"Your battery is dead. No big deal," he said politely. "Let me bring my car over here and I'll give you a jump."

"Thanks George."

"My pleasure," he said softly. Vera felt her stomach flip at his silky voice.

He got out of the driver's seat and walked a few rows down to where he had parked his car. Vera looked at her hands, embarrassed.

He pulled up in his white Toyota 4-Runner and hopped out, situating his jumper cables on Vera's battery and then his own. Vera went to start her car. The sound of it coming to life made her smile and George smiled in return.

"See, no big deal," he said.

"Thanks for your help."

"What are you getting into tonight?" George asked, leaning against his truck and crossing his arms casually.

"I am going to a show at the Ace of Spades."

"No kidding? Who is playing?"

"*The O'My's.*"

"Hmm, I've never heard of them. Are they good?"

"Yeah, I like them."

"I'll have to check them out on my drive home today," George said as he removed the jumper cables.

"You holding up okay after last night?" He asked, his expression softening.

"Yeah, I think so. I think I am in shock."

"Understandable. Everyone processes these things differently. Be careful tonight though. I hope you aren't going alone." He said.

"Oh, uh, I'm not...," Vera said feeling a little embarrassed, "And thank you. I'll be careful."

"Cool," he said. "And hey, if you ever need a jump again, shoot me a text, I'm on campus late on Fridays too."

"I don't have your number, Vera replied.

"That's an easy fix," George said, plucking Vera's phone from her hands and entering in his cellphone number.

"Now you do." He smiled. "I'll see you later. Have fun at the concert."

George climbed back into his car and drove out of the structure. Vera listened to her engine run and sat back down in her driver's seat.

She would think about whatever was happening with George later. One man at a time. Tonight, she had the concert with Sam, and she was really looking forward to that. Vera smiled to herself as she backed out of her spot and put on the *O'My's.*

CHAPTER 34
GINA

Gina pulled into the driveway of her house utterly exhausted. She had promised Matteo that she would take care of dinner tonight since he had made dinner every day prior, and because he had made earth shattering love to her earlier in the week. She just blurted it out in her post-coital bliss. *"Let me make you dinner tonight."* It felt like a sweet gesture at the time, but then she didn't end up coming home. She figured she would do it tonight, but *God*, she was tired and didn't feel like cooking.

She also had forgotten that if she were to make him dinner, she had to go to the store and pick something up because they were in need of a grocery run. She was more than halfway home before she remembered that unfortunate detail and had already passed the closest grocery store. Frustrated, Gina had pulled off to the first corner store that she could find to see if she could find anything edible.

Gina pulled the car into her garage and gathered her things to carry it all into the house. Inside, she set her grocery bag on the counter and removed the contents of the plastic bag. Egg noodles, tuna, a can of peas, *Lays* potato chips, and some cream of mushroom soup.

Tuna casserole it is.

After changing out of her work clothes, Gina whipped dinner together quickly and preheated the oven. She mushed her concoction into a casserole dish and started to clean up her mess. She was happy that Matt was not home yet because she knew he would be put off by the looks of what she had made; however, she had made this dish dozens of times and knew that it tasted much better than it sounded. She was looking forward to a nice comfort-food dinner.

She disposed of her tuna cans in the kitchen trash and then thought twice about it and tied up the bag, hoisting it out of the bin. She didn't want the kitchen to smell of tuna all night and the garbage was getting full anyway. Gina carried the bag out to the front of the house, keeping it at arm's length, and threw it in the trashcan at the curb. She looked up at the sky. It was a pale navy blue as the evening settled in, a full moon glowed brightly overhead.

Gina stretched her neck and turned to head back into the house. As she entered the garage, she glanced back over her shoulder with the strange feeling that she was being watched. She did her best to shake the thought from her mind.

Wine will help.

Gina returned to the living room and retrieved her bottle of Sangiovese from the gold bar cart. She uncorked it gently and poured herself a glass.

With some momentum, Gina slid in her socks into the larger living room and reached for the remote to the stereo, turning on some music. The house felt so quiet. Classical piano poured out of the speakers and Gina laughed, changing the music to something that was more suited to tuna casserole and sweatpants. Time of the Season by *The Zombies* began to play and Gina bobbed her head in satisfaction to the intro.

Dundundun- ahhh- dundundun- ahhh- dundundun- ahhh

"What's your name? Who's your Daddy? Is he rich like me?" Gina sang out loud as she pranced into the kitchen to wash the dishes she had used. She hummed along to the words that she didn't know and picked up the pace when it got back to the ones that she was familiar with.

"Tell it to me slowly. Tell you what? I really wanna know..."

Gina slid into the living room to collect her wine glass that she had left behind after choosing the song.

"It's the time of the season for... LOV-ING...."

Gina bobbed her head and danced around in a circle, trying not to spill her wine glass as she moved. She felt tired, and silly, as the wine warmed her and helped her to relax after her long day.

She slid into another spin.

BANG!

A loud clatter outside startled Gina, causing her to drop her wine glass. It shattered on the floor and shards went everywhere.

"Fuck!" Gina exclaimed, jumping back.

Before addressing the mess she had made, she went to the front door to turn on the porch light. She opened the door and looked around. Her garbage can had been knocked over and trash poured out into the street.

"Goddamnit...," Gina grumbled under her breath.

She looked back at the spilled wine and then at the trashcan, rolling her eyes and deciding which to address first. She pulled on her nearest pair of sneakers and went to retrieve a broom from the cabinet in the hall.

Gina swept up as much of the broken glass as she could and used nearly a dozen paper towels trying to mop up the red wine.

What a waste of wine..., she thought, shaking her head as she cleaned.

Gina took the dustpan out to the front yard, leaving the door unlocked behind, and addressed the trash can after tipping the contents of the dustpan into the bin.

Once she had tipped it back upright and collected most of the garbage, she put her hands on her hips and looked down the street, wondering what had knocked it down. The sun had set further since she had arrived home and she hurried back inside, feeling uneasy in the dark.

As she walked in, the preheat timer went off on the oven and Gina rushed into the kitchen to put her casserole in so that it would have time to cook.

She poured herself a new glass of wine and turned down the music. The neighbor's dog began barking loudly and she started to feel nervous about the noises she was hearing outside. She wondered if an animal was loose in the neighborhood, like a stray dog or a coyote. She briefly allowed her mind to wonder if it was a person, but quickly shook that thought away.

There is no reason to get yourself worked up.

She thought about the man that she had seen on the sidewalk last Friday when she had woken up from her nightmare. A chill ran down Gina's spine and she chased it with red wine.

The house was too quiet, that was it. She hated it when Matteo worked late. She went to the living room, shut off the music and turned on the TV, hoping that the sound of people would make her house feel less empty.

Gina plopped onto the couch, kicking her shoes off, and curling up with a blanket. The news rang out from the TV and another story about the Midtown Murderer was on.

Oh, not this again…, Gina thought.

She had been trying her best to stay vigilant and be aware that the murders were happening without scaring herself into a stupor.

Suddenly, Gina heard a loud pop and darkness followed. The power had gone out. *Or been cut.*

Gina was in total darkness. She heard movement outside and found herself suddenly terrified. She lived outside of Midtown and the murders were happening there. It wouldn't be the killer... He wouldn't come out this far...

From what the news reports, but what if there have been more killings outside of Midtown?

Gina stood, desperate to call Matt. But where had she put her phone? She must have left it upstairs when she changed. She made soft, quiet steps toward the stairs, unluckily stepped hard on a shard of wine glass that had escaped from the dustpan as she was cleaning.

She jumped, startled by the pain. As she leapt up, she inevitably had to come back down, and landed on the wounded foot, pushing the glass in further. Gina cried out as pain shot up her leg, nearly knocking her off balance. She limped to the stairs, guiding herself with the wall, hands outstretched to find the banister.

She found the stairs and took anxious steps up each one, trying not to trip. She babied her foot, putting as much weight as she could on the other. Her foot felt wet, and she knew that she was leaving bloody footprints after each step.

She heard a *BANG* outside that sounded like her trash can had been knocked over once again. Whoever was out there was right outside of her house. She limped into the bedroom and felt along the wall for her dresser where she had put her purse. It wasn't there.

I left it in the fucking car...

Gina heard movement downstairs in her home. She glanced nervously round the corner, seeing the glow of a flashlight searching her living room. Her eyes widened with fear.

Fuck, fuck, fuck.

She saw the light grow brighter, indicating that whoever was in her home was headed for the staircase. Gina turned back to her room and felt along the wall, past her dresser, and toward her closet. She fumbled for the doorknob, missing several times. On her third try she found the brass bulb and closed her hand around it, taking a breath to steady herself before opening it quietly.

She stepped inside and lowered herself to the floor on her hands and knees. Gina crawled forward with one hand extended to keep her from hitting a wall. She wanted to find a corner to tuck herself in.

Gina backed herself to the wall, pulling her knees to her chest, tears streaming down her face as she tried to keep her breathing quiet. She heard footsteps ascend the staircase with a *thump, thump, thump...*

Gina squeezed her eyes shut. Her mind raced with the images of mutilated bodies and the headlines that she had seen on TV about the Midtown Murderer. She opened her eyes and listened carefully, hoping to hear her invader *thumping* their way back down the stairs.

She saw the beam of a flashlight illuminating from the crack under her closet door.

He's in the bedroom...

Gina clamped her hands over her nose and mouth, trying to silence her breathing.

He can't know I am in here, the room is empty, he'll leave when he doesn't see anyone... she thought, but then, she remembered the trail of bloody footprints that would have led him up the stairs, and right to the closet.

Her heart sank.

I'm going to die.

She reached for the delicate gold cross that hung from her neck and prayed that it would be quick.

The door burst open and Gina cried out, blinded by the white beam of the flashlight.

"Baby? Are you okay?"

Gina opened her eyes.

Matteo.

"Matt?" She cried out breathlessly.

"Babe, what happened? I saw blood. Are you okay?"

In the light of the flashlight, she saw his face and crawled toward him, sobbing. He held her on the closet floor and brushed her hair behind her ears. He took her face in his hands.

"Gina, baby, what happened? Why are you bleeding?" She struggled to find her words.

"I'll be right back, I am going to go see what happened with the power. Stay right here," he said.

Gina's lip trembled as he left her in the dark closet. She took a breath to steady herself. A few moments later, the power came back on. With her fingers still on her cross, she exhaled a sigh of relief.

Matteo returned with their first aid kit and carried her to the bed. She gazed out the window as he tended to her foot and worked to pull the glass shard out. Gina winced at the pain.

Out the window, she saw their trash can laying sideways in the street, trash littered into the road. She swore, for a moment, that she saw the figure of a man standing beside it.

CHAPTER 35

VERA

The Snug was crowded as Vera squeezed herself inside after
having the bouncer check her ID at the door. She headed
straight for the bathroom to take a look at herself before
locating Sam. She got ready in such a hurry after the time delay
with her car battery, that she forgot to look in a mirror at the final
outcome before getting into her Uber.

She gave herself an up and down glance in the mirror.

Not bad Vera. She smiled and applied some lip gloss.

Vera had decided to wear black jeans and black heeled ankle
boots. She wore a loose-fitting gray tank top that she had tied in a
knot to give it some shape to her body. You could see the black lace
of her bra peek out from the sides slightly and it gave her a sexy-
flirty concert goer look. She wrapped it all up with her favorite

dark denim jacket and some silver earrings. She tossed her dark wavy hair up in a clip and was ready to hit the Ace of Spades.

When Vera exited the restroom, she saw Sam sitting at the bar by himself looking at his phone. Just then she received a text.

Saved you a seat at the bar.

She walked up and took the stool beside him.

"Hi," she said.

"Hey!" He grinned.

That smile.

Charlotte would be so excited to see this. She had been pushing Vera to go out with Sam for ages. Sam wore a dark olive-green corduroy jacket with a black t-shirt underneath and a pair of black jeans. He looked casually sharp, the kind of effortlessly attractive that made other people's heads turn. The jacket brought out the green in his hazel eyes.

The bartender approached them as she sat down.

"Can I get something goin' for you guys?" He asked distractedly, glancing around at the other bar patrons and doing the math in his head to make sure he could handle everyone.

"Vera?" Sam looked at her to order first.

"What was it that your friend said was amazing here? Remember? Sanjay and Vince were arguing about it at *The Emerald Lounge?*"

The bartender tapped his finger impatiently.

Sam laughed. "That was a Moscow Mule and I think they were talking about the bar down the street from here actually. This place makes a good Moscow though."

Vera shrugged. "Alright, I'll take a Moscow, please," she said, directing her attention to the bartender who gave her a curt nod and looked at Sam.

"And you?"

"I'll take one as well, thanks."

Sam turned to Vera and gave her an up and down glance. "You look nice," He smiled. "Are you excited about the show?" "Yeah, really excited, I have always wanted to see them live." Vera grinned.

The bartender set two Moscow Mules down for them and Sam passed him a card to open a tab.

"Cheers," Sam said, lifting his cup to her.

"To *The O'My's*," Vera beamed, clinking her copper mug against his and taking a sip from her tiny cocktail straw.

They drank and talked about everything from school, to work, to life. It was loud at the bar so they sat huddled together to hear. Sam smelled like cologne, but Vera didn't recognize the scent. That alone made her happy, no *Acqua di Gio*, and whatever he was wearing smelled amazing and made her want to be closer.

As they finished their first cocktails, Sam waved the bartender back over.

"Another?" He asked.

"Definitely."

"Should we try something else?"

Vera considered her options, thinking that she should probably stick with vodka to lessen the severity of any hangover she may develop.

"I think I want a lemon drop. But no sugar on the rim."

That was the last thing Vera needed. She checked her blood sugar level on her watch briefly- *still looking good.*

Sam ordered a lemon drop for Vera and a whisky sour for himself, fearlessly braving the impending hangover. The bartender returned after a moment with their drinks.

Vera took hers and crossed her legs with her drink in her lap, looking around the room and observing the people nearby.

"Do you think everyone here is going to the concert?" She asked Sam.

"Probably at least a few of them, but it's hard to tell. It is a Friday night."

Vera looked over and saw that Sam had his phone out.

"Hold still," he said, snapping a picture of her.

Vera laughed and he snapped another.

"You just look so elegant with your lemon drop," he teased.

Vera rolled her eyes, reaching for his phone to take a look. The lighting was awful, but if she flipped the filter to black and white, it did look kind of elegant with her slim and delicate martini glass. It possessed a soigné aesthetic.

They finished up their drinks and settled the bill, ready to head into the Ace of Spades for the show.

The line for the concert was not too long and they managed to get in quickly. The inside of the venue was hot and stuffy. The Ace of Spades was dark and small. They headed to the bar to order another drink as they waited for the show to start. They each got a beer, something easy to hold in the crowd that wouldn't spill everywhere.

All at once, the lights dimmed and the opening artist walked on to the stage, greeting the crowd and playing into their first song. It was an artist named *Topaz Jones*.

The crowd started to sway and bob their heads. After two cocktails, Vera was starting to feel loose and ready to dance. As she rocked back and forth next to Sam, he watched her fondly and she looked up at him and blushed, realizing that she was being observed.

Even in her heels Sam was a whole head taller than her. Seeing that Vera was embarrassed, he started to bob and sway as well so that she would not stop dancing. Vera grinned and kept at it. After a few songs, the stage went dark again, and the crowd began to cheer for *The O'My's*.

There was a moment of silent buzzing energy when the band arrived on stage and the lights were turning on to illuminate the set. The stage glowed red as the band started to play.

Vera and Sam squeezed their way into the packed crowd and *The O'My's* opened with the song *My House*. Sam and Vera swayed and raised their arms up, bringing them down only to take a drink from their beers and put them back up.

The crowd seemed to flow with each other like waves on a beach. They swayed in motion with one another so as not to collide in such a small space. Vera closed her eyes and bobbed her head along with the music. As the song ended, and the audience erupted in whooping applause as the band played into their next song- *April 29th*. The slow start made Vera smile. She loved this song.

The song reminded her of easier times. She first heard the song in high school, and she listened to it nearly every day for the entire summer. It reminded her of swimming with her friends and staying up late and looking at stars. She pictured herself sitting on the roof of her house with Charlotte as they passed a cigarette back and forth between them, thinking that they were cool.

She thought about sneaking out to watch the sunrise with her high school boyfriend and what her first real kiss was like. He tasted like watermelon *Jolly Ranchers.*

Outside of her mind, one song played into the next, and Vera swayed along with Sam, losing herself in her thoughts and the music.

She continued to think about her adolescent years. She thought about the night that she woke up to her mother's screams that same summer. She heard her wailing, and she crept into the hallway to see what had happened.

Vera peered into her mother's bedroom to see her tossing around the bed, convulsing and crying out. She ran to Charlotte's room and pulled her out of bed, unsure what to do.

Charlotte rushed to her mother's side and tested her blood sugar. Their mom was a type one diabetic as well. Her meter read *21 mg/dL.* Vera had never seen a number so low displayed from a glucose test. She didn't understand. Her mother was going into shock.

"Vera!" Charlotte cried out in tears, "Call an ambulance!"

Her voice seemed so far away. It echoed in Vera's empty head. "Vera! Snap out of it!"

Charlotte jumped up and grabbed her by her shoulders as their mother fell off of the bed and onto the floor, shaking.

"Vera, call an ambulance and stay with mom. I need to find the glucagon shot to help her." Vera used the first phone she could find and sat on the floor with her mom, weeping, and dialed 911.

Charlotte rushed back into the room with a syringe and jammed it into their mother's thigh. She immediately stopped moving and Charlotte sobbed. For a moment, they were sure she was dead.

After seconds that felt like an eternity, she began to stir and mumble. She was disoriented, but alive, and her blood sugar levels ran tremendously high for the rest of the day. The spike of glucagon she had been injected with stimulated her body to break it all down into a large influx of glucose. The lesser of two evils, *of course*, because at least she was alive.

When the ambulance arrived, they thought Charlotte was the one who needed medical assistance because she was crying so hard. Vera sat off in the corner, in shock, and terrified for her own life as she reflected on the severity of a diabetic emergency.

What if I don't feel a low? What if I don't wake up?

In reality, their mother had been drinking. Her blood sugar took a dive related to a combination of all the alcohol in her system and the insulin that she had on board. She also had drunk quite a bit.

Vera wiped a tear from her eye, tuning back into reality. She checked her own blood sugar on her watch, *140*. She was maintaining spectacular control this evening. She was always careful, especially when she drank. Vera was so traumatized by that experience that she took every precaution necessary to keep herself safe while still living what she felt was a normal college life. It was a tricky balance. She exhaled and looked at the beer in her hand uncomfortably. Vera squeezed herself out of the crowd to find a restroom.

She took a couple breaths in the restroom and tried to shake the mood she had just lost herself in. That memory was too big for her date with Sam, and she didn't have room for it tonight. She dusted herself off, applied some more lip gloss, and headed back out to the concert. Sam was waiting for her by the door.

"You all good?" Sam asked over the music.

"Yeah, I'm okay," Vera said, making herself smile.

"It's the kind of music that makes you think, huh? I love their songs, but the tempo can kind of get you into your head." He smiled. "That and the beer," He said, shaking his can. Vera smiled softly.

"Want to get back out there?" He asked.

Vera nodded, tossing what was left of her beer into the trash as she followed Sam back into the crowd.

The band played into *The Wonder Years* and to the audience's surprise, *Chance the Rapper* came out to sing his parts. The Ace of Spades erupted with euphoric energy. Vera looked at Sam with wide, excited eyes and he had the same look on his face. They danced side by side, and then together. The crowd opened slightly, and Sam gave Vera a small spin as the next song played out of the speakers. She lost herself in the music again and felt her mood elevate back to where it had been at the start of the evening.

When the crowd closed back in around them, they were packed together face to face. Dim lights danced across the faces of the concert goers. Vera laughed, looking around at everyone singing along to *Girl It's Been Fun.*

She looked back at Sam as the spotlight drifted across his face, blinding him momentarily. He laughed and looked down at Vera. For a moment, everything stopped, and he bent his neck down and kissed her. He tasted like beer and peppermint gum.

Vera pulled herself up on her toes and wrapped her arms around his neck, kissing him in the moving sea of people as they swayed back and forth with the music. She pulled her body to his and they rocked with the flow of the audience. Sam tangled his fingers in her hair and undid her hair clip as his hands got caught. Her hair fell down her back and he slipped his hand up her neck. The concert was dark and intimate, and the music created an electricity between them.

When they pulled apart, Vera smiled and turned back around to dance to their last few songs.

Eventually, the concert came to an end and the lights at the venue turned on. With a drunken groan everyone flooded out like vampires avoiding the bright bulbs.

They poured into the street after the show, giddy and sweaty from being confined in such a small space. It was late by the time the concert ended. They left the venue around midnight.

The cool air felt good against Vera's skin. Sam smiled at her and took her hand.

"Burgers?" He asked.

Vera laughed, "Yeah, I could eat."

And she *should* eat after drinking so much if she didn't want her blood sugar to drop and end up getting low while she was sleeping. Her mind flashed back to the memory of her mother. She had not had nearly enough to drink tonight to reach a point like that but eating before bed was the most appropriate way to handle any night that involved alcohol for her.

They walked next door to the venue and each ordered a burger at the little restaurant, *Burgers and Brew*. Sometimes after a show, the artists would go there to eat, and fans could get autographs. Sam kept his eyes peeled for the band.

"There is no way they are coming here tonight," Vera teased, chewing a French fry.

"Hey, you never know." Sam winked, stealing a fry from Vera and dipping it in his root beer float.

"You're wild for that," Vera said, nodding her head toward his beverage of choice.

"Want to try?" Sam challenged.

"Pass. I don't like root beer."

Vera never drank root beer. She was a *Diet Coke* or nothing kind of girl. The diabetes didn't many soda options and she developed a mild aversion to other, non-diet sodas because they were so much sweeter than she was accustomed to.

"Suit yourself…," Sam sighed dramatically, taking a long sip from his straw with an exaggerated exhale to detail how *refreshing* it was.

Vera snickered.

They ate their fries and exchanged bites of burgers to taste the different specials. They talked about music and how much fun they had, and by the time the burger joint was ready to close, Vera was ready for bed.

"I'll walk you home," Sam said, noticing her release a yawn.

It was a long walk, but it was a refreshing night, and Vera enjoyed the crisp air. Plus, she was happy for the opportunity to walk off some of the food she ate, she was *stuffed*.

Sam was a perfect gentleman that evening. He walked her all the way to her door, kissed her goodnight, and excused himself. Vera had considered inviting him in, even sleeping with him that night, but the fact that they worked together held her back.

She wanted to take some time to think things over. And she was exhausted. She dragged herself upstairs, one foot in front of the other, and collapsed onto her bed, still dressed in her concert clothes.

CHAPTER 36

UNKNOWN

His father had gone too far this time. The boy had not slept in days. Since his sister's death, he could not sleep, for fear of being smothered by his father as well.

He wasn't sick like his sister, but he knew his father didn't care to raise children alone. He knew he was a burden. A punching bag at best. Since the death of Daisy, he couldn't breathe. He became prone to anxiety attacks, hyperventilating until he learned to self soothe. This was no way to live.

Most days, he was home alone while his father was at work. He liked to be alone. Nobody hurt him when he was alone. When he was alone, he was powerful. He hit his toys, beating them into submission. He broke things around the house. He was angry and he was tense. He felt as though the only way his muscles would relax was if he heard the sound of something smashing.

He buried Daisy alone. It was much harder to dig a hole than he had expected. He did it in the dead of night so his father wouldn't see. He didn't know how his father would react to a burial for the dog. That night, the boy tossed and turned, hearing the sound of scratching at his door. He would stand and open the door to let Daisy into his room, but the hallway would be empty.

One evening, the boy's father brought a woman home. She was lazy and slouched. She wore small, ratty clothing, and they smoked cigarettes in the living room together. She had curly blonde hair like corkscrew pasta. That was the only thing that the boy remembered about her that he liked. His father poured them whisky, and they drank it on the couch. The boy watched through the banister of the stairs.

When they started to kiss, the boy watched, confused by the type of affection he was seeing. They moved to his sister's room, the one she and Daisy had died in, and the boy saw red. Anger flooded through him like magma, searing what was left of his heart. He was a husk. He was a vessel for rage and nothing more.

He stomped up the stairs crying and slammed the door to his room, trying to focus on his breathing, trying to slow it down.

He heard the woman cry out and he stood, enraged. He went to his father's room and smashed the mirror, threw things around, making a mess of what he could. He shoved the bed, pushing it slightly on the floor with a heavy scraping of posts on the wooden boards. The butt of his father's shotgun stuck out from under the bed.

The boy lifted it with some effort, thinking very little about what he was doing. It was heavy in his hands. He dragged it across the floor with a scrape and down the stairs with a *thud, thud, thud...*

He carried it into the room where his sister and Daisy had died. He had decided what he would do now. The only life that belonged in this room were the lives that had been taken.

His father didn't notice him enter as he hovered over the woman on the bed. The boy fumbled with the gun, trying to navigate the trigger, it was already loaded.

Too easy.

The boy lifted the heavy gun, pointing the barrel at his father and pulled the trigger. The shot went through his father and into the woman. His father collapsed, bloody, and the woman screamed in pain.

The boy was knocked off his feet by the force of the gun, pain radiating through his arm and chest. He looked at his shoulder, scared that the kickback from the gun had blown his arm clean off.

His arm hung limp, his shoulder dislocated from the socket. The boy cried out in pain and fear and the woman wailed loudly. Not knowing what to do, he threw his shoulder against the door frame, attempting to get the arm back into its socket. On his second try, it worked. The pain of resetting it hurt as bad as when it was knocked out.

The boy went to the kitchen and grabbed a knife from the block, his wounded arm hung at his side, aching.

He walked back into the room slowly. The woman was losing color in her face, she begged him for help. The boy was so angry at her for lying where his sister had laid. For breathing the air in her room, in her bed, where she deserved to be breathing and wasn't.

He brought down the knife, *hard*, and finished what he had intended to do.

By the end of it all, covered in sticky blood, the boy showered himself clean, packed up his satchel, and ran out into the street. He would never go back there.

He held out his thumb to hitch a ride, like in the movies. He inhaled the summer air and closed his eyes. Finally, he could breathe.

CHAPTER 37

VERA

"Tell. Me. Everything." Charlotte said, as Vera reached for a bouquet of yellow daisies.

"It was fun. We went out for drinks first, then to the *Ace of Spades* and saw *The O'My's*, then we had burgers, and then he walked me home."

Vera turned the bouquet around in her hands and set it back down, lifting another one with a variety of colorful flowers in different shapes and styles.

"More, Vera. I need details." Charlotte clapped her hands in emphasis.

"I ordered a Moscow mule and then a lemon drop. I wore black pants and black underwear and black socks..." Vera rolled her eyes.

"Come on! You know I have been waiting forever for you to go out with Sam. Did you kiss him? Did you sleep with him? How is he in bed? What did he wear? How big is his-"

"Charlotte!" Vera laughed. "Enough!"

"Give me something, girl. I'm married and all I do is work! You know I love to gossip."

Vera lifted a bouquet of white flowers and eucalyptus to her nose. "We may have made out a little at the concert."

"Ver! Hell yes, girl! That's what I'm talking about. And?"

"And nothing. It was nice. He's a good kisser. He pulled my hair a little and I liked it, and that was it. We got burgers when the show ended and then he walked me home and called an Uber, I think. I was too tired to have sex with him and I'm not really sure if I want to."

Vera fished around in her purse for a few dollar bills to pay for her flowers. She and Charlotte had met up in the morning to walk to the Midtown farmer's market.

Vera woke up in her concert clothes with a full face of makeup still on, around 5:00 a.m. She showered and changed into sweats, then crawled back into bed to sleep for another few hours.

It was a beautiful Saturday morning. The farmer's market was the busiest around 11:00 a.m. The girls had gotten there at 9:30 a.m. hoping to be a part of the Saturday morning energy before it got too crowded.

Vera paid for her flowers and carried them as they continued to stroll down the sidewalk at a leisurely pace, looking at the selection of local fresh produce.

"Why not?" Charlotte pushed. "He's so cute, and you said he was a good kisser. He seems like such a good guy."

"Char, stop trying to play matchmaker for me." Vera gave her a playful shove. "I haven't decided how I feel about the fact that we work together. Something I feel like maybe you have forgotten?"

"Oh, I see," Charlotte said, frowning. "Quit your job?" She teased.

Vera shook her head, grinning. "I hate you."

"You *love* me," Charlotte said, walking toward the section of the farmer's market that housed the crafts and handmade trinkets.

"Oh! Look at this! How sweet," Char said, lifting a white baby onesie. Across the chest in typewriter font it said,

Made in Sacramento.

Charlotte slipped some cash to the man tending the booth and bought it with a grin.

"Conner is going to love it!" She beamed.

"Wait what?" Vera said, eyes wide.

"Oh, *shit*." Charlotte slapped her hand to her face.

"Char, are you pregnant?"

Charlotte rolled her eyes. "Yes. I meant to wait until the end of the first trimester to tell you, but I forgot. Conner is going to kill me. I won't let him tell anyone."

Vera smiled widely.

"Don't say a fucking word," Charlotte hissed.

"I won't! I'm so happy for you." Vera grinned.

"Thanks, Ver," Charlotte said, her expression softening. Vera could see in her sister's eyes how excited she was by this news.

They walked up and down the rows of booths and art tables, smelling candles and looking at jewelry. They stopped by the food section and Vera bought a bag of kettle corn before deciding to exit the strip town where the market was held.

"I could use some coffee," Vera said as they headed through midtown.

"I think there's a shop up here," Charlotte suggested.

They turned up K street and made their way to the coffee shop, *Temple*.

It was busy with people. Vera and Charlotte got in line with their haul from the farmer's market and waited. Vera looked around; this seemed to be a popular spot to visit after attending the market. People sat with fresh produce and their own bouquets of flowers at tables, sipping from their mugs and conversing.

Vera had only been to this shop one other time. It was open

late and she was with a group that wanted to study. In the evening, every table had a laptop on it as the customers typed furiously away at their keypads, caffeinated and determined to finish their work.

Vera looked down at the copper floor. It was made entirely out of pennies, and she wondered to herself how many pennies were used to craft it. She looked up and saw that the line had moved forward. She took a step to fill the space and placed her order.

"A vanilla latte, please?" Vera requested politely.

"I'll just have a decaf hot tea please. Peach if you have it." Charlotte said to the barista.

Vera paid for their drinks and they relocated to a table outside in the sun.

"How is work going?" Vera asked, cradling her latte carefully. It had been accented with a perfect foam leaf. It almost pained Vera to drink it because she didn't want to ruin the design.

"Ugh, it's awful," Char said with a frown. "There have been so many attacks. I don't know if I told you, but I've been splitting my time between Urology and the ER and I've been seeing victims of the murder spree."

"Are there a lot of survivors?"

"Not really. We had one woman come in who survived an attack. Another guy was brought in but died inside."

"Fuck. That's terrible. Did I tell you I found one of the victims?"

"What?? Vera!"

"Yeah, it was after the Kings game I went to. We were headed to a bar and found someone laying in the street. It was so scary."

"You probably shouldn't be out at night anymore," Charlotte lectured.

"I heard that the killer is only going after homeless people," Vera suggested.

"I mean, yeah, right now that's what it looks like. But you never know. Just be careful."

Vera sipped her coffee, considering.

She was all excited about me being out at night on this date with Sam. I shouldn't have told her about the attack victim.

Charlotte's phone rang loudly and made Vera jump. Several tables looked over at the blaring alarm, annoyed.

"Jeez Char, what are you going deaf? Put it on vibrate like the rest of the population."

"Sorry," Charlotte laughed. "I'm on call today; I wanted to be able to hear it. *Shit*, and this is work too. I'll be right back." Charlotte stood to take her call and walked a few feet away.

Vera sipped her latte and watched people walk by. She saw George and Phil walk into a shop across the street. Out of her peripheral vision she saw Charlotte walking back toward their table.

"Sorry Ver. I have to go. Someone called out today at the hospital and they need an extra set of hands. Let's get Thai again soon though."

"Why? You wanna show off with your CPR skills again?" Vera teased.

"I saved that man's life," Charlotte snapped playfully. "Do you want a ride home? I need to start walking toward my car."

"No, I think I'll just walk home. Thanks though." Vera smiled.

"Alright, love you Ver. See you later. Stay safe!" Charlotte said as she hurried away.

Vera finished her coffee quickly and stood, wanting to catch George and Phil as they came out of the shop they had gone into. They exited just as she crossed the street.

"Hey guys," Vera called out to them.

Philip spun around quickly trying to find the source of the greeting. His face lit up when he saw Vera.

"Hey! What are you doing here?" He said brightly. George kept walking, not realizing Philip had stopped. He turned abruptly after realizing and headed back toward them. He approached with a soft smile.

"Hey Vera," He said.

Vera smiled. "I was hanging out with my sister, but she had to leave for work."

"Bummer," Phil said.

He gestured to her bouquet and kettle corn. "Quite a haul. Farmer's market?"

Vera nodded.

"Well, what are you doing now?" Philip asked.

"Nothing, I guess. I don't have plans for the rest of the day."

"Do you want to hang out? George and I were going to grab a six pack from the corner store over there and hang out at our place today. It's a lazy Saturday."

"Sure. Let me just walk home and drop off my flowers and stuff and I'll drive over," Vera said.

"Sounds good Ver. See you in a bit." George smiled.

Vera pulled up to George and Philip's place feeling a little bit anxious to be hanging out with them without Alison. She was wrestling her emotions regarding the situation Sam last night, and her possible feelings for George.

She would keep it light and keep an open mind. Either way, it would be fine, and she didn't have other Saturday plans.

Vera approached the door and knocked gently, hearing a muffled yell from inside the that the door was open. Vera twisted the knob and let herself in, kicking her sandals of at the door and strolling into the living room.

Phil was smoking from a bong and George was in the kitchen, pouring his beer from the can into a pint glass.

"Hey guys," Vera said, smiling shyly.

"Hey Vera." George grinned. "Beer?" He asked, turning his back to her to grab another glass from the cabinet.

"Uh, sure," Vera said, lowering her purse to the floor and walking into the kitchen. "Just something light if you have it."

George pulled a Mosaic pilsner from their refrigerator and cracked it open.

"Hey! You have Mosaic." Vera smiled.

"Yeah. I've been a few times since you brought those beers over for the Kings game. They're pretty good."

He handed her the beer. There was an awkward pause.

"Would you like a tour? I don't think you had one when you were here last."

"Sure."

George walked out of the kitchen gesturing for her to follow. He ambled down the hall and turned into a doorway. Vera followed.

"This is Phil's room, but I like to say it's Alison's room because she's here as much as he is and it's full of her stuff." He laughed.

Philip had a black and white Sacramento Kings poster of *De'Aaron Fox* above his bed and a painting of the Tower Bridge on the opposite wall. Alison had signed the corner indicating that she painted it.

His bed had a light gray comforter and white pillows. The room was relatively tidy for a boy's room. There was a hanging plant that looked like English ivy in a macrame potholder that descended from a hook in the ceiling and Vera assumed it was Alison's doing as well.

Phil had his coats hung by the door on black hooks and a snowboard leaned against the wall in the corner.

"A lot of Sacramento pride," Vera commented with a smile.

"Oh yeah. He's going for a theme though," George said, turning back to the hallway. He gestured across the hall to a small blue restroom.

"That's the bathroom."

Vera peaked in as they passed and noticed that it had been tiled with navy and white Spanish flooring. It was lovely. The boys lucked out with this rental.

George continued forward and into a room at the end of the hallway.

"And, this is my room." He beamed.

Vera stepped inside timidly, feeling like she was entering his private space. The walls were an off-white color, and he had a fluffy dark blue duvet over the comforter on his bed with minimal matching pillows.

He had a dark wooden bed frame that gave his room a distinguished feel, like an office. In addition to the bed, there was a desk that matched in color against the wall. It was covered in schoolbooks and his backpack was hung on the complimenting wooden chair.

The window in his room looked out onto a small balcony, which surprised Vera. The house had more features than she had expected. George had put out a bistro table and chairs set, similar to the one outside the front of the house but smaller and more intimate- almost European. An ash tray sat on the tabletop.

Vera directed her attention back to the interior. George had a bookshelf covered in knickknacks. Vera thought it was sweet, more of his personality was present in the clutter on the shelves. She noticed a rubber band ball, a Harry Potter book collection, a framed photo of him with George and Alex at the beach, and a pint glass full of loose bottle caps. Vera smiled.

She took one last look around and decided that his room was likely the master because he had a second attached bathroom with the same blue Spanish tile.

He smiled proudly. His room was slightly messier than Philip's but since it was larger it was not overwhelmingly cluttered.

"It's very nice." Vera laughed, taking in his grin. "Can we sit on the balcony?"

"Of course," George said.

They made their way to his sliding door and stepped onto the small balcony. Vera pulled out a chair and sat down at the table with her drink.

"So, I listened to *The O'My's*," George said, pulling out his chair and taking a seat at the table with her.

"Oh yeah? What did you think?" Vera inquired.

"They're cool. They have a very mellow sound, kind of sexy, I like their vibe."

Vera laughed. "I don't disagree."

"How was the concert?" He asked, leaning back in his chair and putting his hands behind his head.

Vera's mind flashed to Sam's fingers tangled in her hair as they kissed in the crowd and she suddenly felt embarrassed. She hoped that she was not visibly blushing, her face felt warm.

"It was good. They're good live." She smiled awkwardly.

"Well, next time they're in town let me know. I'd love to go. I haven't been to a concert in years."

"Why is that?" Vera asked, sensing something in his voice.

George smiled softly and let out a breath. There was a pause.

"Did you know I was a twin?" He asked.

"No."

"Yeah, I had a twin brother; we were identical. I mean, in looks, not really personality. He was brilliant, one of the smartest people I have ever known. He was so fascinated by the universe. He wanted to work for NASA."

George took a tip from his beer and set it back town, continuing.

"We used to go to shows together. Since we were in middle school, I think. We loved to go to the *City of Trees* festival together. When larger music festivals became really popular, we fell in with it. We went to a big concert in Southern California, and he took a lot of *ecstasy*, more than he could handle.

Press pills were really popular, I mean they still are, but with that scene especially. Anyway… I think he was dehydrated too. I'm not exactly sure what it was, but he lost consciousness in the crowd and never woke up. We went to the hospital and everything. He was in a coma for a few weeks and eventually passed away. It was really hard on my family. Really hard on me."

He said the last part slowly.

Vera looked at him, stunned.

"Wow, George, I had no idea."

"Oh, of course you didn't. I didn't mean to share so much. It was just kind of along the lines of the conversation. It was a few years ago and I have coped with it. Kind of. I don't think grief has a clear timeline. But I went to grief therapy and everything. It was really like losing half of myself though. They say that twins have that telepathy thing. It was weird. I can't explain it. Anyway, that was the last concert I had been to."

"What was your brother's name?"

"Alan."

Vera smiled softly, empathetic to his story. She wasn't sure were to take the conversation after that. She felt the need to acknowledge the fact that he had shared so much but didn't want to pry. She barely knew him after all.

"Who was your favorite artist at that show?"

George smirked and it grew into a grin. "We saw *Snoop Dogg* and I swear it was one of the best moments of my life until that point."

Vera shifted a little in her seat, unsure where to redirect the conversation.

"I was really into *Snoop Dogg* in middle school. Do you remember his song *Sensual Seduction*? When I discovered it I was all about it." Vera laughed. "And *Drop it like it's Hot*. My dad wouldn't let me get explicit songs on my iPod and he would check my iTunes account, so I had to get the clean version and I ended up learning all of the words wrong. My friends would sing it and know the words and I looked like such a loser."

George laughed, *hard*. Vera was pleased that she had shifted the conversation softly but effectively.

"What else did you have on that clean playlist?"

"I learned some *Eminem* songs wrong, I learned a *Fergie* song wrong, mostly hip hop and pop."

"I was angsty in middle school. I listened to *My Chemical Romance, Slipknot, A day To Remember*... all that."

Vera smiled at him and took a sip of beer. "I don't see that of you."

George smirked. "What do you see me as?"

"I don't know. Maybe a *Maroon5* kind of guy?"

"I don't even know how to respond to that. I don't know what that looks like." George laughed again.

"*Jesse McCartney? Fall out Boy?*" Vera teased.

"Stop Vera. I'll go get my iPod right now."

"Bullshit. You don't have an iPod here."

"Ah, you caught me. I don't. That would be somewhere at my parents' house." He grinned.

"Where is that? Let's go find it." Vera challenged playfully.

"They live in Santa Rosa. You're driving."

"Oh pass, that's too far."

"That's what I thought," he said.

They were quiet for a moment.

"Why did you move to Sacramento?" Vera asked.

"The million dollar question." George took a sip from his drink.

"I don't know. Just to try a new place on for size. I got into Sac State and I thought, why not? It's a nice area." He set his beer back on the table. "Truthfully, when I visited, the trees got me. They're beautiful. I enjoyed being on campus."

"They are nice. The allergies are murder though."

"Oh, one hundred percent." He chuckled.

"Do you ever go down to the river and hangout?"

"Of course. I've been here for a few years now. There isn't a ton else to do." George teased.

"I haven't been there yet this year. It's starting to warm up though. I'll have to head over there one of these days."

"If you're free tomorrow we can go. I'd say today, but I'm kind of feeling a movie day. If we go tomorrow though, I'll teach you how to skip rocks."

"Wow, what makes you think I don't know how to skip a rock?" Vera said playfully offended.

"I'm just teasing." He smiled. "Do you know how to skip a rock?"

Vera blushed. "No! But that's not the point."

He winked and took another drink from his beer. "Don't worry I'll teach you how to skip a rock."

She rolled her eyes. "Sure. I'll teach you how to drive stick."

"I would love that. I don't know how."

Vera smiled at how candid he was. George was charming and she was enjoying her conversation with him.

"So, movie day?" She asked.

"Yes." George said, standing. "I was thinking horror. How do you feel about that?"

Vera stood as well. "I love a good scary movie."

"Good," he said, walking back into the house.

They turned into the living room and saw that Philip had disappeared. They heard Alison's giggle from behind his bedroom door.

"Looks like Phil is out for the movie. Sounds like Alison is here." Vera grinned.

"More couch space for us," George pointed out, patting the couch cushion next to him and he sat down.

"How about *The Shining*? I like how they display Jack's descent into madness," he said, choosing a title from the list.

Vera nodded. "It's a classic."

They drew the curtains, made some popcorn, and settled in for a movie. It was nice. Vera felt that after all the chaos they had been through recently, a movie day was an excellent way to spend a Saturday afternoon.

CHAPTER 38
UNKNOWN

Duke pooped in the house during the day while the man was out. He was so angry that he thought about tossing the dog into the wall, but then he thought of Daisy. Instead he decided that he would take Duke out more frequently.

The man sat on a green park bench watching Duke run around in the grass, tearing after a squirrel that he had seen. It was a quiet evening. Birds chirped softly in the trees as the sun set on the horizon.

The man lit a cigarette and crossed his legs, leaning back into the bench. Duke barked loudly as he ran. The man looked over his shoulder and saw a woman unloading groceries from a car with her child. He scowled. The woman's daughter looked like his sister had. She wore a pink sweatshirt from *Gap*. His sister had one just like it. She wore it until it became ratty and torn. She was wearing it the day she died.

He flicked the cigarette and stood, thinking about going over there to talk to the girl. But he didn't know what he would say. And he didn't want to call unwanted attention to himself. The mother wouldn't like it if he walked over. He just felt drawn to her, as if a ghost from his past were reaching out to him.

The young girl looked up and he realized that his feet had carried him forward and he had nearly approached them completely. The mother was still busy unloading the car, too busy to notice.

Typical. Mothers never notice.

The girl smiled at him. No, it was at Duke was smiling at. The dog had arrived at his side. The man gave her a small wave and the girl waved back shyly.

A squirrel ran past in a flash of brown fur and Duke chased after it. The man stayed put, watching the ghost of his sister. She turned to follow her mother into the house and waved a timid goodbye over her shoulder.

The man walked back to his bench, flicking the ash off of his cigarette. He watched Duke chase the squirrel up a tree, where he proceeded to stand on his hind legs with his paws against the trunk, barking.

The man wondered what Duke would do if he caught the squirrel. Would he kill it? Would he play with it? He didn't think the dog would know what to do if he got to that point.

The man began to wonder what he, himself, would do if he got to that point. What would happen if he caught someone and kept them alive, what would *he* do? Would he take the time to nettle his victim? Harass them, play with their psychology a little? Or go straight for the kill?

Maybe, it was time to find out.

CHAPTER 39

GINA

Gina stood in the break room with her coffee mug cradled between her hands. She stared at her reflection in the black coffee before adding some cream and watching it swirl in. She had not been sleeping well.

Gina's nights were disturbed by nightmares about the Midtown Murderer breaking into her home and dragging her out of the closet, stabbing her over and over while she lay on her bedroom floor.

The sound of a door closing made her jump as someone entered the kitchen.

"Hey Gina."

She glanced up. It was the colleague she had gone to for help with her client Howard.

"Hi Elijah."

He poured himself a cup of coffee and turned to face her.

"Oh my, honey, you don't look so good," he said, bringing his hand to his mouth.

"Oh, great. Then I must look about as good as I feel."

They headed to the kitchen table and Elijah pulled out a chair for her, she slumped into it. He sat down with her after adding cream and sugar to his coffee.

"What's going on? Are you okay?" He asked.

"I think all of this news about the Midtown Murderer is going to my head. I swear I thought someone followed me home yesterday, and my power went out and I went into a full panic. I hid myself in my closet, thinking that someone had cut my power intentionally, and then I heard someone in my house. It ended up just being Matteo. He was just getting home from work." She exhaled.

"Oh gosh. That's a lot."

"Yeah, he fixed the power and we had dinner and I went straight to bed. I just felt awful."

"I don't blame you. The news is really scary right now. I know my husband hasn't been sleeping well either. He is pretty worked up about it. He volunteers at a homeless shelter sometimes, so he has been really affected by this whole thing. I've been telling him not to go to the shelter because I am afraid something might happen to him there."

"Wow, he is really close to this all."

"Yeah. So, I can empathize with the fact that you're having nightmares. I think we all are." He smiled softly. "I keep worrying something will happen to my Daniel. I don't know how I would cope." He ran his hand through his scruffy salt and pepper beard.

Gina shook her head and lifted her mug to her lips.

"How bad do I really look? I have to see my clients today."

Elijah took a minute to assess her.

"You look exhausted. Try splashing some water on your face. The coffee should help. And maybe some lipstick if you have it? I'm sorry but you just look washed out."

Gina chuckled. "I can always count on you for your brutal honesty."

"You asked." He rolled his eyes playfully. "I have to go. I have a client in a few minutes. Hang in there," he said, standing.

Gina stood as well to excuse herself to the ladies room. She walked down the hall and went straight to the mirror in the restroom. Her reflection was haggard. Her eyes looked sunken behind dark circles.

"Fuck," she mumbled.

She splashed some water on her face, careful to avoid making her mascara run, and applied some of her burgundy lipstick. She pinched her cheeks for some color and ran her fingers through her short hair. It was beginning to grow out again and Gina thought that she might like it long.

She adjusted her blouse. It was a cream color with some pale red accents. It went nicely with her lipstick today and it helped bring some life to her appearance. She exhaled roughly and headed back to her office.

Her first appointment of the day was Martin Alvarez, her type 2 diabetic with Major Depressive Disorder. He was seated in the waiting area, fiddling with a button on his coat when she approached to bring him back.

"Good morning, Mr. Alvarez."

He looked up and gave a soft grunt, collecting himself, and standing with his crutches. He followed her to her office with a soft *tap, tap, tap*.

He settled in on the couch and Gina pulled up her chart notes.

"How are you today, Dr. Garcia?" He asked.

"I'm well, and yourself?"

"I'm here."

"You are. That's a good start."

He grunted.

"How have things been since I last saw you?"

He hung his head. "Okay," he said into his lap.

Dr. Garcia gave him a moment to collect his thoughts.

"I saw my endocrinologist on Friday. I always feel terrible when I leave there. I feel like I am doing everything I can, and nothing is good enough. I have been trying to get my blood sugar levels under control and I'll have some good days, but a lot of bad days."

Dr. Garcia regretted the fact that she knew so little about his disorder. She knew only a basic amount about diabetes care, but she listened empathetically and tried to understand. She made a mental note to do some research on her own to help her be a better advocate for this demographic of patients.

She also had a colleague who was a Certified Diabetes Educator and had been practicing with her CDE for some time now. Gina thought to herself that she should have referred Marty over to her colleague instead of taking on this case, but it would widen her own scope of knowledge, and in the end make her a more well-rounded therapist.

Something to add to the resume, her mother would say.

Marty continued to talk about his health as his major stressor. He felt extreme guilt about the state of his life and his physical condition.

"How long has it been since the loss of your leg?" Dr. Garcia asked gently.

Marty sniffed and reached for a *Kleenex*. "A few months now," he said.

"How are you coping with that?"

"Well, I've been drinking a lot," he said, looking at his hands, ashamed. "Mostly beer."

He looked up defiantly. "But I found a place that I really like, and they accept me and are kind to me. I'm a regular there and everyone knows me. Feels like a home away from home."

Dr. Garcia smiled softly. "That's wonderful. I am in no way telling you how to cope. I am only asking what has been working for you. It sounds like maybe getting out of the house and being in that environment is helping with your mood. Do you ever go there and have soda? Or something else? And just hang out?"

"No, but I haven't ever really thought about doing that."

"Okay. Well, if you get to a point where you feel like you want to cut back the beer, you could always go and have something else to drink."

"Yeah, that's true," he said considering it.

After a moment he shifted and rubbed his prosthetic leg.

"There is something else I wanted to talk about," he said.

"What's that?" Dr. Garcia asked.

"My leg. The one that's gone. I get these pains. They're awful, unbearable sometimes. Sometimes it's like a calf cramp, it hurts so badly. But… but my leg's gone. I know that sounds crazy," he said, embarrassed.

"Oh, Marty, that doesn't sound crazy at all. That must be awful for you."

And in fact, it was not crazy in the slightest. Gina had heard many stories and read many articles about this scenario. It was common in veterans, and a characteristic that many amputees experienced.

Phantom limb.

It was a horrible condition that patients who had been through the loss of a limb sometimes experienced. These individuals would feel pain in their missing body part and be unable to tend to it because there was nothing there to massage or hold.

Gina had read that people who experienced this would sometimes use a mirror to trick the brain into seeing a second arm or leg, and that would help the brain cope to alleviate the pain.

Gina spoke to him softly, telling him everything she knew about this condition that he was experiencing. There were many documented cases of it, but it is still only mildly understood. The brain is a very tricky organ. Psychology is one of the great mysteries of life.

"Wait here," Gina said, standing to leave her office for a moment. She cracked her door, walked quickly to the break room around the corner, and lifted the floor length mirror off the wall, carrying it back to her office with her.

She opened the door softly and entered with the mirror. Marty looked confused.

"So," she said, "what we can try is placing this in between your legs, with the mirror side facing your right leg, the non-prosthetic one, and it will mirror the image of having two flesh-and-blood legs."

Gina pulled over a chair so that Marty could put up his *legs*, allowing full extension. He let her help place the mirror in his lap and position it for him. He looked down at the reflection, providing the illusion of two long legs. Marty bowed his head and cried.

Gina had not expected that, although she should have been ready for it. Maybe this was too much too soon after the amputation. He cried so hard that she had to take the mirror away and give him a minute to collect himself, for fear that it might knock over and break. He blew his nose hard and blotted at his eyes, chuckling.

"Oh, I'm sorry Dr. Garcia. I'm a damn mess," he said.

She smiled softly. "Whenever you are ready, we can try again."

He cleared his throat. "Okay, let's go again."

Dr. Garcia helped him to readjust the mirror between his legs. He looked down and wiggled his right foot, seeing the reflected image move with it. It gave him the appearance of a child wagging their feet.

"Oh." He choked up again and muffled his sob with a laugh. "Look at that. It's like it's still there."

He rubbed his right leg. His hand reflected in the mirror, projecting the image to his mind that he was rubbing a hand along *his left*.

Dr. Garcia smiled at him. She crouched down so that they were eye level.

"So, the trick," she said, "is when you are experiencing pain and cramping in your *phantom limb* you can use a mirror like this to rub out your other leg. Then while you massage your right leg and look in the mirror, it will trick your brain into thinking that you are massaging out the left leg. Theoretically, it should help with the pain."

He looked up at her with wide eyes. "Thank you."

"Of course, Marty," she said softly. "You should tell your physical therapist and your orthopedic doctor about this pain that you are experiencing, just to keep everyone in the loop." Gina returned to her desk.

"I am happy to help from a psychological level, but they probably have more tricks for this than I do seeing as it is their specialty. Hopefully, this will give you some sort of relief for the time being though."

He was still looking at his leg in the mirror. He looked up at her and smiled sincerely.

"Of course. And thank you. This means more to me than assisting with the pain. This is something I can do when I am missing my leg."

"Yes. It won't bring it back though. I don't want you to get too absorbed in the idea of the mirror. You need to work on coping with the loss still, but I understand that it is a humongous adjustment that will take time."

"Of course. Of course."

Gina smiled. When their appointment was over, he left the office standing a little bit taller. Gina was very pleased with herself and felt an amount of pride in her profession that she had not felt in weeks.

On to the next.

CHAPTER 40

VERA

It was a beautiful evening; Vera had a feeling it would be busy as hell at Mosaic as she pulled on her jeans for work. She wiggled her legs in and jumped a few times to pull the tight denim over her butt before zipping them up. She grabbed a *Rolling Stones* graphic tee off of the hanger and tossed her hair into a ponytail before heading downstairs to leave.

"I'm headed to work. Don't wait up," Vera called to her roommates.

"Are you closing tonight, Vera?" Shanice asked, eyes wide with concern.

"No, I have the mid-day shift. I will be off around eight-thirty. I think Sam is closing," she said.

Shanice released an audible sigh of relief.

"Be careful," she said.

"I will be. I'll see you guys later. Either way, you don't have to wait around for me, go on with your evenings. I'll probably just turn in early and watch some TV in bed," Vera assured her.

She grabbed her keys from the hook by the door and headed down the block to where she had street parked her car.

Vera drove to work with the windows down, letting the warm spring breeze tussle her bangs and run through her hair. She allowed her mind to wander to her conversation with George and played some *Snoop Dogg* on her drive over, smiling. She sang along loudly until she heard the gravel crunch under her tires as she turned into the parking lot at the pub.

It was busy as ever. Pubs and breweries in Sacramento have a unique window of the year where they bustle with customers. There is roughly a six-week time period between late March and early May when the weather clears up and hovers at a polite temperature, drawing people out of their homes in droves to go eat and drink outside on patios. By the end of May, the weather is so hot that the business slows, and in the dead of summer, nobody wants to be outside.

Vera walked in and saw her coworker Michelle was already there pouring. She was beautiful as ever, hair pulled back in a messy bun, usual shade of red lipstick, tattered blue overalls and a brown tank top. Her colorfully decorated skin added so much to every look. She smiled when she saw Vera walk in.

"Hey girl!"

"Hey Michelle," Vera beamed.

"It's been a minute. I'm excited to work with you!"

"Me too." Vera smiled. She clocked in and grabbed a bus-bin to clear the empty glasses from tables.

Business moved steadily and they had fun talking together, catching up on the latest school and work gossip. Michelle talked about the regulars and what everyone was up to so that Vera would be able to keep up with the conversations when they came in.

It was always key to stay up to date with what was happening in the lives of the regulars if you wanted to make good tips. It made them feel recognized and cared for, like family of the pub, and Vera prided herself on that kind of customer service.

At 5:00 pm. Michelle gave Vera a kiss on the cheek and said her goodbye. Vera laughed and wiped the lipstick mark off her face.

"See you Ver! Let's hangout soon!" She called.

"Bye Marty," she said to their regular with the crutches. She gave his shoulder a little squeeze as she walked out. He smiled.

"That Michelle is so kind," he said to Vera as Michelle exited.

"Yeah, she is. One of many reasons we like her." Vera smiled. "She also pours a good beer."

"That she does." Marty said, raising his glass.

Shortly after Michelle left, Sam arrived. Vera had not seen him since their date on Friday and was feeling a little shy.

"Hey Vera," he said brightly as he walked behind the bar.

"Hey." She tried to match his energy. All she could think about was his tongue in her mouth. She shook the thought from her mind.

"Has it been busy?" He asked.

"Not too bad. It's been busy but it is manageable."

"Tips look good," he said, appraising the tip bucket.

Vera nodded and turned to help someone who had approached the register.

Sam looked over at the bar and noticed his regular.

"Hey Marty," he said.

"Afternoon Sam."

"You been staying out of trouble?" He teased.

"As far as my wife knows," Marty chuckled.

The day continued at a steady pace. Vera poured beer after beer and went through several bottles of wine. Sam even made a few cocktails despite it being afternoon.

The dart board that the owner had put up was getting some use and everyone seemed to be having a good time.

It was odd for Vera to think about what had happened when she closed a while back. Everything seemed so *normal* now. It was strange. She had experienced such a traumatic event here. Looking around now, she watched the customers laugh and drink with each other, blissfully unaware of the violent robbery that had occurred only a few weeks ago.

She reached up and felt the top of her head. It was still mildly tender from the blow. All of her other bruising had all healed, minus some of her larger ones, which had faded to a nice shade of light yellow. She was relatively back to normal.

She went out to the patio to clear some more tables before the late evening rush arrived.

"Vera?"

She looked up and saw Aaron approaching with a few of his kickball friends.

Oh fuck.

"Hey Aaron," she said, trying to hide the annoyance from her voice.

"How's it going?" He asked.

"Kind of busy. We just had a rush."

"Cool. Would you mind bringing us a beer when you have a second? We'll be sitting out here," Aaron said, sitting down at the table Vera had cleared.

This motherfucker.

"Yeah, I'll see if Sam can get to you," she said, rolling her eyes.

Vera headed inside and placed the dirty bus-bin on the counter behind the bar.

"Want to go handle that table outside?" She asked him.

Sam craned his neck to look out the window.

"Why?"

"I know them, and I don't feel like dealing with them."

"Think of the tips, Vera." He winked.

"*You* think of the tips," she retorted playfully, tossing a dish towel at him.

"We don't do table service anyway. I'll go let them know that they have to order inside."

He walked outside and Vera saw him talking to Aaron through the window.

Ugh, I've kissed both of them. She thought to herself as she turned to unload a rack of fresh glasses and steins.

She turned around and found herself facing Aaron as he stood at the register to order. Sam was nowhere in sight.

Damn it, Sam.

She approached the bar. "What can I get going for you, Aaron?"

"Two of the hazy IPAs and two of the pilsners, please." He smiled at her softly.

Ugh.

She turned to pour his drinks, determined to carry all four back with two hands. She set them down on the counter with a wobble.

"Did you want to open a tab?" She asked him politely.

"Uh, yeah." He handed her his card and looked around nervously.

He cleared his throat and she looked up.

"Hey Vera, I'm sorry about the way that I acted toward you after kickball a few weeks ago. I'm really not proud of my behavior that night."

Vera was taken aback by his comment. She didn't expect to hear from him again at all, much less receive an apology. She wasn't sure what to say. Her brain wanted to say, *it's okay,* or *don't worry about it,* but it wasn't okay. It hurt her. He owed her that apology.

She cleared her throat in return. "Thank you for that."

"Yeah. Well, I owe it to you. If you're not doing anything tonight, I'd love to buy you a drink somewhere. I might head over to *Streets* later," he said.

Vera shrugged. "I don't know. Maybe. I'll let you know," she said, not really sure why she had ambiguously started to agree.

"Okay then, I'll see you around," he said, collecting the beer from the counter.

He carried all four without any trouble. Vera deduced that it was because his hands were larger than hers and he could get his fist around two handles at once. She rolled her eyes at how easy he made it look though.

Vera finished up her shift quickly, wanting to get out of there. At the end of her shift, she considered taking Aaron up on that drink. She wasn't sure why, self-sabotage perhaps since things appeared to be going well with Sam and potentially George. She texted her group chat with her roommates and said: *Going out for a drink after work, don't wait up.* As soon as she sent her text to them though, she thought better of it and decided that she had better go home.

She collected her cash tips from Sam and said goodnight, driving home quickly to crawl into bed and watch a movie.

When she arrived home, Vera, pockets bursting with bills from the tip bucket, decided that she should deposit it to her checking account before she lost the money. She had a nasty habit of accidentally washing her jeans with her tips in the pockets. She chuckled at her own stupidity, remembering the last time she had washed a hundred-dollar bill and ruined it completely. *Never again*, she vowed.

She was able to snag a parking spot in her lot and didn't want to move her car, so she decided to walk. It was a beautiful night. She had some reservations about walking, for safety concerns, but the bank was just around the corner, and it was only 8:50 p.m.

She fastened her keys between her knuckles, just in case, and walked toward the bank. The streets were relatively empty, and Vera began to regret her decision to walk due to lack of foot traffic. She pushed the thought from her mind and approached the ATM on the side of the building.

She made quick, decisive moves. Entering her pin, checking her surroundings, depositing her cash, responding to the prompt on the screen, and then withdrawing her card and replacing it in her wallet.

Piece of cake.

She smiled and started to turn away from the ATM to head home.

Without warning, Vera heard a crack and a *pop*.

Her vision blurred at the edges. It wasn't until seconds later that pain radiated throughout her body.

"Oh, fuck…," she mumbled, disoriented.

It was a feeling she had felt only once before, when the cash register had come down on her head with enough force that she saw stars.

The world rocked off kilter and she took a step, trying to steady herself. She felt the arms of another person -who seemed to appear out of this air- around her, catching her, so that she didn't fall.

Thank you, she thought.

Her vision became filtered with black and gray snow, like the screen of an old TV when the channels were out. She imagined someone adjusting the *bunny ears* in her mind to repair the image. As her brain accepted a sense of security in the grasp of someone who had protected her from hitting the concrete, darkness overtook her heavy eyes and she collapsed.

CHAPTER 41

VERA

H*er head pounded hard. She lifted herself to her feet and looked around. Everything was tinted with a red hue. The air smelled of clay.*

Oh, not this again.

There was a crash and Vera's head rang. She was alone in a red room filled with red adobe powder. She took careful steps toward the door and peeked out. The air was thick and heavy. It felt as if gravity was compressing her.

She took deep unsatisfying breaths. Her chest felt heavy. A voice boomed in the distance and made her jump, frightened. A cacophony of sounds rattled through the air; pots and pans banging, ceramic breaking, bricks crumbling. It sounded as though the building was about to collapse.

She stepped into the open area, still tinted red, and saw that she was in a factory. A conveyor belt rolled along, covered in vases, mugs, bowls, and other clay vessels. Each one approaching the end of the line and crashing to the floor with a loud crack.

The sounds overwhelmed her senses. She looked at her hands and saw small red droplets appear from her fingertips. They were drops of blood. The red arose from her skin as if her very pores were sweating it out. She was speckled with blood, like a child covered in chicken pox.

They began to appear more rapidly, covering her, closing in any gaps of skin that were visible still. She could taste the blood- it tasted sweet. Her body was wet, and she was drowning.

Vera awoke with such force that she sat straight up and hit her head.

"Fuck!" She shouted as her skull collided with something hard. Her head pounded, she brought a hand to it.

The headache is real outside of the nightmare.

She wiped sweat from her forehead. The feeling of dampness from her dream was real too. She was soaked in sweat. She checked her watch to see what her blood sugar was reading on her monitor. 275. The high blood sugar was real too.

Ugh, fucking great, she thought sarcastically.

She knew it would be high. The nightmare she had just woken up from was one she experienced as a child when she was getting progressively more and more sick before she was diagnosed with type one.

She had the nightmare up until the point that she didn't know if she was awake or asleep because she had developed such a bad fever and was taken to the hospital. Her glucose was so dangerously high that she was rushed into the ER, given insulin, and put into a bed. She was later told that her glucose levels were reading as high as 750mg/dL.

Vera rubbed her forehead and looked at what she had struck herself on. She was sitting on a bathroom floor in front of a sink. She tried to help herself to her feet, using the toilet for support.

Where am I?

The room swayed as she stood and she lost her balance into the wall next to her. She gripped at it for assistance and failing to find anything to hold onto she slid down the torn floral wallpaper and back down to the floor.

Vera watched a cockroach crawl across the floor toward the bathtub. She crawled over to the tub as well and looked inside.

Oh, please don't let this be a SAW trap.

Vera's mind flashed to the worst corners of her mind. All of the horror movies she had seen: *Jigsaw, the Texas Chainsaw Massacre, Hostel,* and so on.

The bathtub was empty. She shifted her back to the wall again and tilted her head to it with a soft thud. She let her eyes adjust and searched the floor for her purse. No purse.

No insulin. That's not good. Maybe if I'm lucky, the diabetes will kill me before whoever is keeping me in their bathroom has a chance.

Vera exhaled roughly, trying to keep herself from having a panic attack. The more she thought about her situation, the worse she felt. Her eyes stung with fearful tears, and eventually she succumbed to the wave of sobs that overwhelmed her.

CHAPTER 42
GEORGE

It was Tuesday afternoon on campus. George checked his phone and frowned at the screen. Vera had not texted him back. He set his phone on the table and reached for a slice of combination pizza, tuning back into the conversation.

"Mr. Jones is out to get me, I swear it," Alex said, chewing and wagging his pizza slice at the group. "He never calls on me in class and then he gives me shit grades for participation in lecture."

Alison rolled her eyes. "Come on, Alex. Can you really expect him to like you with the way you behave?"

"Shut up Allie, nobody's talking to you."

"Well, I'm the only one responding to your stories, *dipshit.* The guys don't care about your complaints. Do you guys?"

"No," Phil said, without looking up from his textbook.

"No, not really Alex," George said, shaking his head.

"Fuck you guys." Alex laughed. "Jones is out to get me."

Alison shook her head and chucked.

"Hey Alison?" George asked.

"Hmm?" She responded, sipping from her fountain drink.

"Have you heard from Vera?"

"Why?" She grinned.

"I'm just wondering."

"You like her, don't you?" She teased.

"Are you and that chick, Vera... *an item?*" Alex said, feigning interest and excitement.

"Fuck off Alex." George rolled his eyes.

"She's hot, Georgie. Let me know if you're an item or else I might just make a move."

"Alex, stop." Alison snickered. She turned her attention to George. "I haven't heard from her, no."

"Hmm...," George sighed, picking up his phone again to check for a message.

"I didn't even know you guys talked like that." Alison laughed.

"I mean, we don't really, but we were in the middle of a conversation last night and she just stopped responding out of nowhere." George mumbled.

"Aw poor George got his feelings hurt," Alex said, reaching for another slice.

"Alex, I'm going to fucking hit you if you don't knock it off," George snapped.

"Yeah, that is unlike her. Usually, she'll politely tell me to stop texting her and that she's going to go to bed. She was raised right." Alison laughed. "She's polite over text."

Alison shrugged and continued, "Maybe her phone died and she lost the charger. Or maybe she dropped it in the toilet."

"Maybe she doesn't like you and doesn't know how to tell you yet." Alex grinned.

"I swear, why do we hang out with him?" George asked Alison.

She shook her head. Philip swatted at Alex without looking up from his notes. Alex dodged him with a chuckle.

"I'll shoot Vera a text right now and see if she responds,"

Alison said, taking her phone out from her bag and typing out a message.

"And now we wait," She said as she set her cell on the table next to George's.

"And now we wait." Alex smiled, chewing his slice.

George rolled his eyes.

CHAPTER 43

VERA

Vera opened her eyes slowly. As her vision came into focus, she saw that she was staring at the bathroom floor, her cheek pressed against the dirty tile. She had fallen back asleep. She blinked a few times to clear her vision and pushed herself up with her hands.

Fuck, it wasn't a dream.

Vera looked around the strange bathroom. She reached up to the door handle and tried to turn the knob. It was locked. She scooted her back to the door and brought her knees to her chest, sitting in front of it like a door stop as she assessed her surroundings.

She was in a bathroom, but it looked old and unkempt, like it was not used often, if at all. She had not tried to flush the toilet yet for fear of making noise, but she had decided that she would need to use it soon to relieve herself. Her high blood sugar was winning the battle against her bladder, and she really had to pee. She had also not tried the sink, but assumed that if she was still in Sacramento, the water would be fine to drink because she drank tap water at home.

As long as it doesn't come out brown or something…

She heard the voice of a man, muffled, coming through the wall. Someone else was home. Vera's heart raced. She squeezed her eyes shut and held her back against the door as hard as she could, pushing her feet against the base of the sink to wedge herself in place.

She heard the door handle being unlocked and looked up to see it turning.

He's coming in.

She held her ground, keeping herself tense with her knees locked as she tried to hold the door shut. She heard the man grunt as the door wouldn't budge open. He banged on the door.

"Open the fucking door!" He yelled.

Tears streamed down Vera's face as she held her position. He banged harder. She felt her knees begin to scream with pain as she extended them tightly against the sink, trying to hold him back.

She felt him throw his weight into the door, and she lost grip of her position. She fell against the wall and the door opened hard against her, banging her between the wooden door and the wall. She felt her head rattle and heard him come toppling into the bathroom.

She screamed and kicked her legs, trying to keep him from coming toward her. He grabbed her by the neck and lifted her up, then slammed her head into the wall, knocking her unconscious again.

The man assessed Vera, as she lay unconscious on the floor. What to do with her? He still had not decided. He lifted her body and dropped her into the empty bathtub with a thud. He exited the bathroom, closing the door behind him.

CHAPTER 44

GINA

A nother day in the office. Gina yawned into her laptop screen.

It's worth it. You're helping people.

She heard a gentle knock at her door and turned to face the sound. It was Elijah.

"Damn Gina." He chuckled. "Did you sleep at all last night?"

She rolled her eyes. "Yes. I got about three hours in, thanks."

"I'm sorry." He snickered. "I'm mostly playing. You don't look terrible. You do look a little tired though."

"Ugh, well it's early."

"Gina!" Elijah objected. "Girl, it's three-thirty. Pull yourself together."

Gina looked at her watch. *Damn, where did the day go?*

"Do you need something, Elijah?" She groaned.

"Not really. I just wanted to stop by. I haven't seen much of you today."

"I've been locked away in my office, trying to get through the y day on a few hours of sleep and a lot of coffee."

"Well, you could use another cup babe. You look like you're about to fall asleep at your desk. Want me to grab you one?" He asked with a snicker.

"I would love that. Thanks Elijah."

He smiled and turned to leave.

Gina stood and stretched her back. She had not seen any of her clients yet today. She only had one scheduled for after lunch today and that was Martin Alvarez, *Marty*, who didn't show. It gave her time to catch up on her notes, but she worried that he didn't call to cancel.

She tried not to get too worked up about things she had no control over, but having a depressed patient not show was always worrisome. However, he did not generally experience suicidal ideations from what she knew of him.

She tried to focus on what she could control. Gina had dinner plans with an old friend.

Just a few more hours, she told herself, resisting the urge to just grab her keys from her desk and head for the door now.

Elijah returned with a cup of coffee for her shortly after their talk and she accepted it gratefully. The coffee helped bring some of her energy back, but not her focus.

She tapped her pen anxiously as she finished up with her notes, checking the clock so often that she had to put a post-it over the time on her laptop in order to maintain her focus. That seemed to help. Time moves faster when you are less aware of its passing.

Finally, as if timed perfectly, Gina finished her notes and charting right as the clock struck 5:30 p.m. She shot out of her chair as if it had spontaneously caught fire and headed for the door, excited to see her friend.

———

Gina walked into the restaurant and looked around. She saw a hand wave from a table in the back corner and smiled, heading over.

"Hi Gina!" The woman grinned, standing to give her a tight hug.

"Hi Charlotte." She smiled widely.

"How have you been? I miss you. We should see each other more often."

Gina rolled her eyes. "You're the one who is always working crazy hours. I work a nine-to-five job."

Charlotte sat down and opened a menu. "Fair enough."

"What is this place?" Gina asked.

"It's my favorite Thai place in midtown."

"What's good here?"

"Gina, literally everything." Charlotte held the menu to her chest with affection. Gina laughed.

"I'm serious! I was here with my sister like a week or so ago and, I shit you not, someone collapsed right over there," she pointed. "I had to get up, give them CPR, and when I was finished, I sat right back down and finished my curry. I've been craving it ever since."

"Char, what? First of all, you're sick and I know someone who you should talk to but secondly, someone collapsed over there??"

"Yeah. It was actually really scary. I am downplaying it a lot. It was the first time I have ever had to do CPR outside of work. But he lived. So… I'm sorry if I ruined your appetite. I forget that other people who are not in medicine can be kind of faint of heart." Charlotte chucked.

"I don't even know how to respond to that," Gina said, opening her menu.

A server approached and they ordered their dishes. Today Charlotte went with chicken Pad Thai and Gina ordered the duck special. Charlotte played with her long hair while Gina unfolded her napkin onto her lap.

"So really," Charlotte asked, "How have you been? What's new?"

"Work has been hard." Gina sighed. "But I had a really good day yesterday and that reminded me of what I like about my job."

"I hear that." Charlotte rolled her eyes softly.

"Has work been hard for you too?"

"Yeah, without even getting into all of the murders and stuff that have been going on, we are just really short staffed. It's frustrating because I chose a specialty and I have been needing to divide my time between Urology and the emergency room because we just don't have enough hands."

"Can they even ask you to do that?" Gina asked, sipping from the water that had arrived at the table.

"I don't know. They are though. They just keep saying that we are in *crisis mode* and that they're working on a long-term solution."

Shortly after the waters arrived, their server walked out with their steaming plates of food.

"Thank you," they said to him in unison.

"That was fast," Gina mouthed to Charlotte in surprise.

"How was work today?" Charlotte asked.

"Slow actually," Gina commented. "One of my patients no-call-no-showed me."

"Is that a bad sign?" Charlotte asked, stirring her noodles to cool them down and let out some of the steam.

Gina considered the question. "Possibly. But I doubt it."

"Hmm," Charlotte responded softly.

"How's your sister?" Gina asked, breaking her chopsticks apart. "I haven't seen Vera in years."

"She's okay, I think. I saw her the other day and we went to the farmer's market together. She has kind of been getting back into dating." Charlotte exhaled a deep breath and looked up at Gina. "She found a body about a week ago though."

Gina's eyes went wide. "A victim from the murders?"

Charlotte nodded.

"Wow. That's heavy. Is she okay?"

"I think so. She's acting like she's okay. But I also found out from my mom the other day that she was attacked at the pub she works at a few weeks ago while she was closing. Someone came in and roughed her up and robbed the place." Charlotte took a bite of her noodles.

"Oh my god."

Charlotte nodded. "Yeah. She didn't tell me. I don't think she wants me to talk to her about it. I'm not really sure what to do with this information."

"Is she seeing a therapist or anything about this?"

"Not as far as I'm aware."

"Wow Charlotte, she's got a lot going on right now."

"Yes, she does," Charlotte said, looking out the window. "Yes, she does…"

CHAPTER 45
UNKNOWN

The man sat on a park bench thinking about his situation. He had that woman at home, locked in the bathroom unconscious. He watched Duke run up and down the grass field, chasing the squirrels again.

What are you going to do if you catch that squirrel, Duke? He wondered. *What am I going to do with this woman? Do I just kill her?*

The man pinched the bridge of his nose, feeling a migraine coming on. *Perhaps this was a mistake. She probably has a family, people who would look for her. This might have been a major fuck up.*

The man stretched his neck and looked over at Duke. He continued to run through the park. He yawned and closed his eyes, letting his mind wander.

He thought about an incident from the other night… He was feeling anxious about his encounter. His last victim had said something strange to him. He rolled his neck again and allowed his mind to take him back to the interaction.

He was stalking the way he liked to. Looking for the perfect vagrant in the streets. He saw someone leaned against a wall on the outskirts of Midtown. A drunk as it appeared. A filthy, homeless drunk.

Perfect.

The man approached the drunk casually, checking his surroundings first.

He must be a homeless veteran, the man thought as he sauntered over.

The man was on a pair of crutches, although he was so drunk that he was supporting most of his weight on the wall. As the man approached the homeless vet, he fumbled with his crutches and lost his balance, sliding down the wall and onto his butt.

"Bah!" He grunted in defeat. Then he looked at his prosthetic leg and started to cry fat, sloppy, drunken tears.

Pathetic. The man rolled his eyes as he approached from the shadows.

"Evening, sir," he said in a silky voice.

"Huh?" The vet looked up at him, disoriented.

"Can I help you up?"

"*Getawayfrom meyou*… you… go on. Get." He slurred.

The man sighed frustratedly.

"*Lookatme. Ima* mess." The homeless man cried. "I try, I try, and it isn't enough. I try and *itisntenough.*"

He wiped his face with his knuckle. The homeless man only had three fingers.

The man felt his face twist with disgust.

I should put this mongrel out of his misery. I'd be doing us both a favor.

The man began to feel anxious buzzing in his stomach. His throat became dry. He needed to do this now. The beast was awake. He couldn't look at this man for another second.

He reached for his hand to help the vet up. The homeless man batted him away, shouting.

"I said *leavemebe!*"

The man snatched his wrist and pulled him to his feet with one hand, with the other he flicked open the blade of his pocketknife.

The homeless man resisted but eventually his drunken, disabled body cooperated, swaying his weight toward the man just the way he had hoped. The vet collapsed against the man, sobbing, and the man drove his blade roughly into his abdomen.

He in took a sharp breath and wailed. The man brought his hand to his victim's mouth and backed him up into the wall, stabbing him franticly while holding him by the face to keep him quiet.

Blood seeped from his wounds and down his legs. It trickled steadily from his abdomen and coated the prosthetic leg in blood, dribbling onto the pavement like little red rain drops.

The man pulled back his arm and jabbed his victim once more with a hard, forceful stab, twisting the knife against his body and feeling his fist squish against the vet's bloody abdomen.

He withdrew his blade and released his victim all at once, allowing him to topple to the ground with a thud. He stood over his victim as he continued to bleed into the street, gasping and gurgling. The vet wiped his eyes and looked up at him.

"You...," He sobbed. "I know you!"

The man took a step back, alarmed.

"I- I've seen you before..."

The man turned to leave but thought that he had better finish the job if his victim did in fact recognize him.

He turned to deliver a final blow to his victim and slit his throat, but the vet grabbed him by his collar before he had a chance and pulled him close.

"I know you," he hissed. "I know your face, I've seen your face."

The man looked at him intensely, his eyes darkened.

"*Marty* never forgets a face."

The man smiled, eyes narrow, and drew his blade to Marty's throat.

"You'll have to take it to your grave then." He spat as he dragged the knife across his neck, severing what was left of their conversation.

The man stood and left Marty's body in the shadows.

He snapped back to reality, glancing over at Duke. He should head back. Duke looked tired and they had to walk. He didn't want to think about this issue with his last victim. He wanted to go home and decide what to do with the girl. He was getting sloppy if his last victim did in fact know who he was. He couldn't afford anyone to know who he was. He would have to end the girl. It was time.

The man stood and called the dog over, turning to head back to where he had stored Vera.

CHAPTER 46

VERA

Vera was in a boat. It rocked gently in the open ocean. All around her was water that she couldn't drink, and she was parched.

She cupped her hands, deciding that any water was good water, knowing it was a mistake. More than anything, it was to soothe her throat. She drank from her hands, over and over, coughing hard from the salt. She couldn't stop. She drank until her stomach was full of saltwater and then, she threw it all back up.

She searched the boat for something to alleviate her intense thirst. It was like nothing she had experienced before.

Vera crawled along the floor of the tiny boat.

"Agh!" She yelped.

She lifted her hand and saw that she had hooked herself with a fishing lure. A single drop of dark blood appeared. She licked it, not wanting to waste any moisture from her body. It was sweet, like jam.

She looked into the deep ocean, her blood had drawn sharks that now circled the boat.

———

Vera's eyes fluttered open.

Oh god… my head…

She brought her hands to her throbbing head.

I need to get out of here. Another blow to the head may kill me… she thought, knowing very little about head trauma.

She was laying in an empty bathtub. She attempted to get to her feet. Her body ached. She stood in the bathtub and took a careful step over the edge, using the wall to keep herself steady. Gently, she stretched her back, taking in a sharp breath with the pain.

She looked around the bathroom, hoping to find something to defend herself, anything. Nothing looked helpful, although the towel rack caught her eye. She wiggled it, trying to see if she could pry it from the wall. It wouldn't budge.

She took a painful breath and listened for movement outside of the bathroom. She placed her ear against the door softly. It was silent. She tried the doorknob again and to her surprise, it twisted, and the door opened a crack.

She leaned her neck forward and put her eye to the crack to look out, holding her breath. The door led to a hallway with laminate floors. The walls were an off white, although it did not look intentional, it looked as though they were dirty from years of neglect. There were no photos, frames, or decorations in the hall.

She pushed the door open. It gave a soft creak and Vera froze, fearful that the sound would alert the attacker of her presence. She waited. *Nothing.*

She took a careful step out into the hallway and listened. *Nothing.* Her mouth felt as though it were full cotton and her head pounded. She needed water. Vera checked her watch to see what her blood sugar was reading. *369. Fuck.*

She was dehydrating from her high blood sugar. Her head pounded from the abuse, and dehydration from her illness. She tried to swallow but felt that she didn't have enough saliva in her mouth to accommodate. Her tongue rubbed the roof of her mouth like sandpaper.

She tiptoed down the hallway, looking for a way out. The house was structured strangely, as if it were a very old model. Everything was so closed off, nothing like the big open floor plans that were so popular now.

A door to her right led into an enclosed kitchen. She checked her surroundings and decided that her need for water outweighed her fear. She approached the kitchen sink and tilted her head under the faucet, pouring water right into her mouth. She closed her eyes and drank for what felt like an eternity. Her stomach was full of water, but her throat ached for more. It wasn't enough.

Vera shut off the sink and looked around the kitchen. It was empty. She opened a drawer, looking for a knife, scissors, anything she could use to defend herself if the man came back. *Nothing.*

She glanced around. There was a window over the sink that had been boarded up from the outside. There was no refrigerator, just a vacant space waiting for one.

Where am I?

Vera exited the kitchen and stepped back into the hallway.

For a moment, she thought about returning to the bathroom, solely because it felt familiar and she was scared. She fought the urge and continued down the hall.

The next door, on her left, led to a small bedroom. The room had a window that had been boarded up from the outside as well. There was a twin bed frame against the wall with no mattress. Vera swallowed hard. She peaked further in and saw that there was a closet with sliding doors that had no clothing in it. She turned to leave.

The hall ended in a large space that Vera figured would have been the living room if it had contained any furniture. She appeared to be in an abandoned house.

In her peripheral vision, a bag caught her eye. It was her purse, laying in the middle of the floor. She approached it tentatively and zipped it open. Inside, she found her rose pink pouch that contained her insulin and syringes. She released an audible sigh of relief and lifted the bottle. It was empty, she had used the last of her insulin at Mosaic while she was working.

Tears of frustration streamed down her face. She was so angry with herself for not having more insulin stocked.

But I should have been home. I had more at home.

Vera steadied herself.

I have to get home, she thought.

She heard the screech of a screen gate opening to the front door and the sound of keys clattering together.

Fuck fuck fuck!

Panicked, Vera ran into the hall, not sure which way to go. She heard the front door open and dove into the closest room she could find. The bedroom. She stepped into the closet and slid the door shut as quietly as she could.

Vera pressed her back to the wall inside of the closet, trying to make herself small. She wanted to disappear, phase through the wall like a ghost and float out of the house all together.

She heard shuffling around as he walked in. She heard him stop in the hallway.

"Fuck!" His voice rang, muffled through the walls.

He had seen the open bathroom door.

Vera heard him rushing down the hall and then stomping around the house looking for her.

He's going to find me. Vera's eyes welled with tears.

Breathe, she reminded herself. She took a silent, shaky breath.

She reached into her purse and withdrew two syringes from her rose-colored medical supply bag. She removed the caps and closed them in her fist. It wasn't much, but it would be better than nothing if it came down to it.

A small crack in the closet let in a strip of light, just enough to illuminate Vera's surroundings. Her eyes darted around the small space, looking for something to help her.

Her eyes fell onto a strange shape.

What in the world?

Vera reached down to a small slab of wood against the wall of the closet, near the floor. It looked slightly different than the surrounding wood. She slid it gently to the left and it opened into a crawl space.

Can I get out through here? She wondered.

She crouched down to see if she could fit into the space, but it was too dark in the closet to see.

Dark. Oh no.

The light strip from the closet crack had been eclipsed. Vera was so distracted by the potential of an escape that she had not heard the man enter the room. He was here.

Vera released a soft breath and rose to her feet, clutching the syringes in her fist. She prepared for the inevitable.

The closet door slid open roughly and the man reached in and grabbed her, yanking her out of the space and tossing her into the bedroom wall with a hard *thud*. Vera screamed.

He advanced and reached out to grab her again. With the syringes in hand, Vera swung her arm wide and hit him hard in the neck with the needles of both empty syringes. He jumped, startled by the pain and shouted in surprise.

Vera took advantage of his reaction and dove back into the closet, through the hole in the wall, and tucked herself into the crawlspace. On her hands and knees, she crawled as far back as she could go before reaching a dead end.

The closet crawl space was an odd extension of the house that may have once been used for storage. It looked like the closet could be extended if they were to knock out a wall and add flooring.

She heard the man barrel into the closet, trying to find her, but he was too large to get himself inside of the crawl space.

"Get the fuck out of there!" He boomed.

Vera felt around in the dark, looking for another way to go. She felt a crack in the adjacent wall and tugged at the boards. As they came loose, she discovered a deeper crawl space, one that dove underneath the house. She squeezed through the small opening and into the deep space.

Immediately, her feet hit a dirt floor. She heard her captor shouting through the walls as she pressed forward. The space became very narrow and she was forced to drag herself under the house, flat as if she were snaking her way through barbed wire in a bootcamp. The ceiling became low and tight.

Her skin crawled with the feeling of passing through spider-webs and the thought of their makers, but her adrenaline surged as she pushed on. She could see a small amount of light ahead. It had a red glow, like the taillight of a car.

When she reached the edge of the house, Vera squeezed herself up and out. She was quickly overcome by the feeling that she was suffocating.

What's happening??

The world around her was a vibrant red and blue. She felt as though she had been thrown into a large pillowcase and she didn't have enough air.

Disoriented, she struggled under the weight of the colorful sheet, like a fish trapped in a net. She fell forward and toppled out of the mess and onto the pavement.

Vera looked up, breathless, at what had attacked her. The house that she had escaped from was coated in a red and blue fumigation sheet to block the view of it from the other houses in the area. Vera looked around. She bet that everyone in the neighborhood was under the impression that this house was abandoned.

The neighboring houses were small, and some were more over and more worn than others, but all of them looked relatively nice. Vera stood and stumbled backward, ready to run. The sound of a train startled her, she nearly jumped out of her skin. Vera looked up at where the sound may have come from realized that she was still in Sacramento. She guessed that she was somewhere near East Sac.

Vera ran into the street.

Elvas. I know this street.

She *was* in East Sacramento. She knew someone who lived over here. She could go to them for help.

Elvas Avenue was backed up against a small hill at which the train tracks ran on. Vera crossed the street and climbed the hill quickly, tripping and scraping her hands and knees as she moved through the rocks and trees. She wasn't sure where the man was and wanted to move as fast as possible.

The rattle of the approaching train echoed in the night sky and it sounded its horn loudly. Vera was almost at the top of the hill. She couldn't wait for the train to pass, if it were long, the man might find her, and she would never escape.

At the top of the tracks, Vera saw the light of the train approaching. She darted across the tracks quickly and stumbled once across, falling and rolling down the dirty hill as the train roared passed, just missing her.

Vera toppled through plants and stopped rolling only when her limp body violently struck a tree. She wrapped around it as her abdomen hit the trunk hard. She laid there for a minute, trying to process her pain and fear.

Keep going, she willed herself.

Vera got to her feet and limped through the neighborhood. She thought that she should scream, yell for help, but she wasn't sure that she could even speak at the moment. Her vision blurred her and her depth perception wavered in and out. The high blood sugar was making her feel incredibly ill.

To Vera's surprise, she had managed to keep hold of her small purse. She reached inside and pulled out her cell phone. It was not only dead, but completely broken. The screen was shattered.

Of course, she thought.

Vera dragged her battered body through the streets of the

suburbs. She had toppled into a neighborhood called *River Park*. It was a very nice neighborhood with a lot of families. It ran against the Sacramento River and homed a wonderful public access point called *Paradise Beach*. East Sacramento in general was a rather affluent area. She couldn't understand how she had been held captive on such a nice side of town.

The house she was headed to was deep in the labyrinth of neighborhood streets. She had been there only once to pick her friend up for an event they had gone to together months ago.

When she finally saw the white trim of the house and the manicured lawn, Vera felt her muscles scream in agony as they started to relax for the first time in hours.

She had always wanted to live in River Park but had never been lucky enough to find a rental space that she could afford. Some people just have better timing with these things.

Vera pounded hard on the door.

"Sam! Sam!" She gasped. "It's Vera!"

She heard the door unlock.

"Vera?" Sam rubbed his eyes, waking up. She had no idea what time it was.

"Please help me," she whispered as she began to collapse.

"Oh fuck, Vera!" He opened the screen and reached for her, bringing her into the house.

"What happened to you?" He scooped Vera up in his arms and carried her to his couch.

Vera struggled to find her voice.

"I was kidnapped. I think it was the Midtown Murderer. We have to call the police. He held me in a place on *Elvas*, a house that looks like it is under fumigation." She coughed, hard, trying to get her throat to cooperate with the words she was forcing out.

Sam stood to get her some water.

"Are you hurt?" He asked, returning with a glass.

"I don't know. I need to get home and take some insulin though, my blood sugar is really high. I feel terrible."

Vera heard the clicking of nails on laminate floor and looked up to see a black and white dog.

"I didn't know you had a dog," she said after draining the glass of water.

"Oh yeah. This is Duke."

CHAPTER 47

UNKNOWN

After freeing himself from the life he was living with his father in that dreadful house, the boy hitched rides from town to town. He did this for years.

At first, he struggled. It wasn't anything like the movies. He wasn't sure how to feed himself. He ate out of trash cans. He ate leftovers that he found on park benches. He would walk into fast food restaurants and take food from the pickup counter before the rightful customer got to it. He would steal from grocery stores occasionally. Sometimes he would break into houses.

If he got lucky and nobody was home in a house he had entered, he would sleep inside, close to the door so that he could make an escape. He had only been caught once and he ran so fast when he heard the family calling the police that he thought his legs might break. Most times though, he would make himself a meal and leave.

When winter came, he was in trouble. He was in California,

but it was still so cold. He tried his luck in homeless shelters. They were horrifying. He was astounded by the conditions. For one thing, it was no place to be if you wanted to be clean from drugs. People would do drugs openly, and nobody would stop them. The boy did not have a desire to engage in such behavior. He always felt that he was above that.

The theft in the shelters was bad as well. People ravaged each other. Anytime anything was left out in the open, unattended, it was taken. People were beaten and robbed in their sleep. The boy didn't feel safe.

Once, he awoke to the sound of screams, and saw that the woman who had laid down next to him had been assaulted and robbed. She died next to him. He decided at that point that the streets were better than the shelter.

The boy set back out into the streets, sleeping on benches, joining communities under the freeway entrances, whatever he had to do. For a long time, his blood lust lay dormant. He did not have a desire to kill again, only to stay alive.

One summer, he snuck into a campsite and made friends with *normal* children who didn't think he was any different. They invited him to camp with their group. He dragged his ratty sleeping bag over and laid out under the stars with his new friends.

One friend in particular, said that they should meet again. They planned that when his family came back in a month, the boy would come back too so that they could camp together.

Every day that led up to that point, the boy went to sleep thinking about his friend and the fun that they would have together at the campsite. He hoped silently that his friend would show up and it was not a lie.

When the time finally came, the boy washed himself in a river nearby and waited in the same spot where he had met his friend. When his friend showed up again, the boy knew that his life was going to change for the better.

The day that the boy's friend returned to the campground to see him was the best day of his life. It changed his future forever. The boy's friend was from Sacramento, visiting Lake Berryessa on a family vacation.

The boy's new friend was ten years old. The boy was twelve. The boy's friend had some other children with him. He said that they were his family, although none of them looked the same. The boy's friend said that family doesn't have to look the same or even have the same blood, sometimes family just means taking care of each other. The boy's friend was named Samuel.

Samuel and the boy spent all week together. He invited the boy to camp with his family, and the boy had never felt love like this before. He was treated kindly and fed. The family told stories at bedtime and they camped under the stars.

Samuel taught the boy how to throw a football and the boy showed Samuel his pocketknife that he got from living in the shelter. They used it to sharpen sticks together. Samuel was a Boy Scout and knew how to do cool camping tricks like tie knots and go fishing. He taught the boy how to do outdoorsy things.

Samuel told the boy that he wished he could live outside every day and camp forever. The boy told Samuel that he did live outside every day and that he would give anything to trade places with him. He told Samuel about how hard it was some days.

Late one evening, Samuel told his parents about the boy and how he lived outside. His parents brought the boy to the campfire and sat him down for a talk. The boy told them about how he had no parents and no home. They were very empathetic. They asked the boy if he would like to live with them and let them take care of him. They asked him if he would like to be a part of their family. They adopted children who needed help. That was why Samuel had so many brothers and sisters. They took the boy in, and now, he had a home. *Now he had a brother.*

CHAPTER 48

GINA

Gina drove home after dinner with Charlotte feeling giddy. She laughed in the car on the way home, remembering their conversations and the jokes that they had shared. Gina loved Charlotte and wished that they had spent more time together, but Char could be so busy.

Gina noticed that Char wasn't drinking either. She didn't say anything, but she suspected that there might be a reason for that. Charlotte loved her beer, especially with dinner. They always got a beer or a cocktail together when they went out to catch up. Gina smiled to herself.

She'll tell me when she's ready.

Gina and Charlotte had been friends since they were children. They were neighbors. They went to the same elementary school, middle school, and high school. Gina was Charlotte's maid of honor in her wedding. She liked Charlotte's husband Conner, she thought he was kind.

When Gina graduated with her PhD, Charlotte ordered a cake in the shape of Gina's head for her party. Gina was so embarrassed, but Charlotte was so proud of her friend's accomplishment. When Charlotte graduated from her physician assistant program with UC Davis, Gina pulled the same head-cake gag and she had never seen Charlotte so happy.

They were roommates after college and for weeks they would sit on the couch on Sunday's and drink wine in their graduate attire. Charlotte in her white coat and Gina in her Tudor bonnet.

Once Charlotte got married and started working, they saw much less of each other, but some love never dies. Charlotte was Gina's best friend.

She turned down her block and opened the garage door, stopping hard at the edge of her driveway.

Gina stared wide-eyed at the silhouette of a man. She took out her phone to call 911 but thought that she should first talk to him and give him a chance to leave.

"Howard," Gina said, gently as she opened her door. "What are you doing here?"

Howard stood at the end of her driveway, shaking his head.

"I've been waiting for you."

"I see that."

"I need to talk to you."

"Howard, this is not appropriate. You need to leave, or I am going to call the police."

"Dr. Garcia, you are in danger." He begged.

"Howard, I can't do this right now. I am trying to give you a chance here. I don't want to call the police, but this is completely inappropriate. You cannot come to my home like this. Ever. Do you understand me? How did you find out where I live?"

"I followed you."

Well fuck.

"Dr. Garcia…," He continued. "May I come in?"

Gina stood behind her driver door, car still running, trying to figure out the best way to handle her situation. Howard began to approach her.

Damn it, Howard. Damn you for putting me in this position. She thought to herself as she pulled out her phone and dialed 911.

"Howard, stop right there. I am calling the police. I will stand here and talk to you until they arrive but only if you take ten steps back and stay there," She said, sternly.

"Dr. Garcia…," He started.

"Hello, yes, I need the police," Gina said into her phone. She gave them her address and a vague but urgent description of her situation.

"Howard, I am not playing around. Back up."

He took a few steps back and stared at her.

They stood in silence.

"Dr. Garcia?" He asked after a moment.

"Yes?" She said nervously.

"You live here- don't you?"

She thought that was obvious. He said had he followed her home. She wasn't sure she could lie in this situation now, or what good it would do, but she didn't want him knowing where her house was. She remained silent. It was all that she could think to do.

"I thought so," he said, turning and looking up at the grand home. Her lack of response was a response in itself.

Gina had a beautiful house, she knew that she was very lucky.

"I saw the man in the purple windbreaker in this neighborhood. I think he lives around here. Is he a patient of yours? Maybe he found you like I did. Have you considered this?"

Gina's heart began to race.

"I think he is dangerous."

Gina cleared her throat. "Why do you think this?"

"I just know."

"Do you know who the man in the purple windbreaker is?"

"No…," his voice trailed off.

Gina's mind struck her like lightning. She had been wondering for weeks if the man in the purple jacket was a delusion. Now she wondered if Howard was using a subconscious defense mechanism to block out this character from his reality.

The mind will do incredible things to protect itself. Gina wondered, fearfully, if *he* was the man in the purple jacket. And if so, what would that mean?

"Howard, did the man in the purple jacket hurt somebody?" She asked, gently.

"I think so. I haven't seen him do it, but I think so." He nodded. "I don't like him. I don't trust him. And I've seen him follow me."

"Howard, were you in my home last week?" She asked, her voice shaking now.

"I had to warn you. I'm here again, to warn you."

"Did you break into my home?" Tears streamed down her face.

"Of course not, Dr. Garcia. That was the man in the purple windbreaker. But I came here to warn you, and I am here again now." He took a step toward her.

"Howard, stay right there." She commanded.

He stopped and stared at her.

"You're not safe…," he continued.

Gina's mind raced. How long had he been following her like this? Had he been inside of her house?

His conscious mind had fractured and was protecting itself from all of the violent crimes that he had committed. Was he the Midtown Murderer?

Gina knew she shouldn't ask but she couldn't stop herself, she wasn't a therapist right now. She was a frightened human being, and she was being confronted by a potentially violent man. Alone. At night.

"Howard, are you the man in the purple windbreaker?"

He looked as though she had slapped him, and she immediately regretted her decision to speak.

"Am I- Am I the man? Dr. Garcia have you listened to a fucking *word* I've said?" His voice shook.

Oh no, what have I done...

"Am *I* THE MAN?" He shouted.

"Howard..."

"I'm not the man! I'm not the man! I am not the man in the windbreaker! I'm not!" He was panicking.

This was not the way to approach this situation. His mind was unraveling, refusing to let him accept something so big.

"Dr. Garcia! I'm *NOT* the man in the windbreaker!" He took two more steps toward her, yelling.

Gina took a quick step back and caught her high heel in a crack in the pavement. She fell backward and scrambled to get to her feet. As soon as she fell, Howard rushed toward her.

"Howard! No!" She shouted.

He stopped as he heard sirens approaching. Soon his face was illuminated by alternating shades of red and blue light.

Howard looked at her and shook his head.

Gina helped herself to her feet as law enforcement approached him quickly and escorted him off of her property. After placing him in the back of the car, they took Gina's statement.

Over the officer's shoulder, she watched him. He stared out at her from the window of the police car. He didn't blink. He mouthed to her very clearly *purple windbreaker.*

Inside, Gina took a minute to collect herself. She tossed her heels angrily at the couch and reached for her red wine from the bar cart. She held the bottle in her hands and stared at it, then shook her head. *No.*

Gina went to the lower shelf and poured herself a glass of whisky from Matt's collection. It burned her throat as she sipped it, but the aftertaste was just what she needed. It warmed her mouth and made her tongue feel thick with sharp heat. She decided to add a splash of water and some orange. It was just slightly too strong for her on its own.

She pulled her phone out to call Matteo and ask when he would be home. She didn't want to be alone. It went straight to voicemail.

He must be working late tonight.

Gina carried her shoes upstairs and tossed them into her closet. She stripped from her clothes and ran herself a bath. She sat on the edge of the tub with her whisky and watched the bubbles swirl in as she added soap to the running water.

She took another sip from her glass and let it warm her mouth. She shivered, wanting to be submerged in warmth and feel safe.

When the tub was full, she lit a few candles, dimmed the overhead light, and put some music on before crawling into the tub. *Debussy's Rêverie* poured from her small speaker as she slipped below the surface of the water in her deep master bathtub.

She rolled her neck back and let the warmth of the water relax her aching muscles. She took another sip of her whisky. The taste was growing on her. It was like drinking a flame, a campfire.

She watched the candles around her flicker and cast dancing shadows along her bathroom walls. She felt as if she were surrounded by warmth and light. She closed her eyes and let the flames move behind her eyelids. Behind her eyelids she watched the changing shades and colors of her perceived darkness as her fingers gently played with the bubbles.

Once she was too warm to bear it, she stood, dizzy from the whisky and heat, and removed herself from the tub. Gina dried herself and walked into the bedroom, wrapped in a soft towel. She went into her closet, looking for something to wear. Matt had not responded to her yet and she missed him.

She walked out of her closet and went to open his, thinking she would wear one of his big t-shirts and sit on the couch until he got home. She picked out a soft green one and pulled it over her naked body.

Gina brushed back her shaggy, wet hair and headed toward the stairs. Out of the corner of her eye, she saw that she had left Matteo's closet doors open and went back to close them. She reached for the handle and stopped cold. A piece of purple fabric poked out from the back of his closet, tucked away behind dozens of other hanging shirts.

She reached out and touched it with her fingertips. The fabric was light and crinkled with her touch. She swallowed hard and unhooked the hanger from the bar. Gina stood in her room, alone, clutching a purple windbreaker.

CHAPTER 49

VERA

Sam stepped away to call the police and Vera drew her knees to her chest on the couch. She felt anxious, edgy, and tired.

Duke approached the couch and sniffed at Vera's toes on the edge of the cushion. She sat in a ball with her knees drawn to her chest and her arms around them. Duke gave her toes a timid lick. She reached out and patted his head.

Sam walked back into the room.

"Are they on their way?" Vera asked.

"Yeah, they're on their way," Sam said, nodding.

Vera put her chin against her knees.

"What time is it?" She asked.

"Just after ten o'clock," he said softly.

"Would you drive me home after I speak to the police?"

"Of course Ver." He said, taking her hand.

She smiled.

"Hey Sam, can I use your restroom?" She asked.

"Yeah, it's just down the hall."

Vera stood, letting go of his hand, and made her way to the bathroom slowly. Everything ached.

She shut the door gently behind her and looked in the mirror. She tried to focus her eyes, but her vision blurred in and out. She needed to get home and take some insulin, urgently. She checked her watch to read her blood sugar levels again. 425. Between the stress, adrenaline, and lack of insulin, her blood glucose levels were climbing sky high.

Vera splashed some water on her face.

There was a hard knock at the front door. She heard Sam open it and there was muffled talking outside. The dog barked.

"Hey Duke," a voice said. She didn't recognize it as Sam.

Vera cracked the door so that she could listen.

"What the fuck is wrong with you?" Sam whispered angrily.

"What?"

"Do you have any fucking idea what you've done? I know this one! She's my friend. You fucked up."

"I told you I wanted to try something new," the man hissed.

"You stick to fucking homeless people! That was the deal! That's what we agreed on! You don't kidnap people with fucking families and ties to the community! Someone is going to come looking for her!"

"They won't find her."

"Matthew, do you have any idea what fucking position you put me in?" Sam said, raising his voice.

"My name isn't *Matthew*," the man snapped.

"Yes, it is! Matt this is insane!"

"My name is *Matteo*!" The man shouted.

"Your name is Matthew, and you are a fucking street rat! You're no better than the trash you are out there chopping into pieces at night or whatever you are doing! Clean up your mess Matt."

Vera heard the man strike Sam with a loud slap.

"We're in this together," he hissed.

"Just get her out of my house," Sam said sharply.

Vera closed the door quietly. And bit her lip hard to fight back her tears. *No more crying.*

There was a small shower window in Sam's bathroom. Vera locked the door handle and opened the window as quietly as she could. She thought that she could fit through it if she squeezed. With her feet on the edges of the bathtub, she hoisted herself up and into the window. Her shoulders were a tight fit, but she got them through. She felt the windowsill digging into her abdomen as her weight hung on the edge while she lifted from her feet. She wiggled herself through and with a final shove, she made it.

She gasped sharply as she felt her glucose monitor rip out of her skin as it caught on the edge of the window when her stomach passed through. She has just changed it the other day.

"Fuck!" She yelped, and then clapped her hands to her mouth.

"Vera?" She heard Sam calling from inside.

"Vera." He jiggled the door handle.

"Vera, open up, the cops are here they want to talk to you."

"Vera!" He kicked at the door.

Vera got to her feet and started to run. She heard shouting from inside the house as she tore out of the neighborhood toward the river. She ran up the levy and onto the paved bike path, breathing hard.

"Vera!" She heard Sam calling her name outside, looking for her.

Vera pushed her legs, willing them to carry her to somewhere she could hide. Her mind raced, she wasn't thinking clearly, she was moving and that was it. Any distance that she could put between herself and Sam was a good thing.

"Vera! Where are you?" The voices weren't far behind her.

They were definitely on the bike path now too. She dove into the trees and hid behind a bush, taking a moment to catch her breath.

She had no phone, no purse, no weapons, no insulin, and no way to read her blood sugars with the glucose monitor detached from her skin. She felt dizzy and disoriented. And *thirsty*.

She waited and listened, feeling her adrenaline fade and eyelids droop with exhaustion.

Just one more minute in the bush, she said to herself, knowing she had to move again soon before they found her.

"Vera?" Sam's voice was close. Her adrenaline resurfaced as she heard him say her name, making her hairs stand on end.

Vera took a deep breath and darted through the bushes, running back up to the trail, thinking that being in a public space was her best bet. She ran toward the road and onto the bridge that connected East Sac and Sacramento State to the other side of town, *The Guy West Bridge*. A pedestrian path ran along one side of the bridge, separate from the road that cars crossed on. She stood on the path, taking a moment to catch her breath.

"Stop running, Vera," Sam said.

She looked up and saw him standing about forty feet to her left, blocking her path. The bike path was narrow, and he had a wide arm span. He would grab her if she tried to run past him. Reflexively, tears began to stream down her face as she turned right and saw the man who had attacked her standing closer to her than Sam was on her other side.

He looked at her, his eyes glinted with chaos and hunger as he took a step forward. With her head on a swivel, Vera saw Sam begin to approach on her left.

Fuck fuck fuck. I can't outrun them.

She steeled herself and lifted her weight with her arms on the rail of the bridge, looking down at the river. The black water twinkled as stars and moonlight reflected off of its dark surface. For a moment, she looked up at the moon, and everything seemed still. A soft breeze blew through her hair.

Please don't let me die.

Her instincts held her back, but as she saw the men growing closer, she knew what she had to do. Sam looked at her, eyes full of sorrow, and shook his head in a warning. In her peripheral vision, Vera saw the other man growing closer. Vera choked on her tears and tried to remember to breathe.

Fuck fuck fuck.

The man on her right broke into a run, and she threw herself off the bridge.

CHAPTER 50
MATTHEW DE LONG

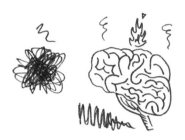

Matthew hated his name. He hated where he came from. He hated his origin story. His mother was nonexistent in his life. She had died shortly after giving birth to his sister. However it was not the birth that killed her. It was cancer. The same cancer that his sister developed years later.

Their father resented them because he didn't feel he was equipped to handle children on his own and because he felt that they looked like their mother. He drank to cope. Eventually he started to use drugs because he was unable to escape his own nightmares.

He started beating his children shortly after their mother passed because he had nowhere else to direct his anger. His daughter submitted to the violence and after receiving her cancer diagnosis, her will to fight was already so low that she didn't stand a chance against the disease. She was a victim of learned helplessness.

After she died too, Matthew was broken beyond repair. He was a shell of the boy that he used to be. He learned to process his anger through violence as well. His father resorted to beating the violence out of him, thinking that would work.

When Matthew finally snapped and killed his father, he felt that he could leave his family name on the front porch the day he walked out. Matthew DeLong died in that house with his family. He had no name now.

When he met Samuel, everything changed. He felt whole again, almost like a new child. They were brothers. And he loved his family. His new mom and pop were Italian, *Dellucci*. Matthew was completely infatuated with their culture and the idea of having a family that traced back to another country. Generations of love all connected to one name. And now it was his. He changed his name to Matteo because it was better suited to the family. He was Matteo Dellucci, and nobody could tell him otherwise.

He had always been Matteo Dellucci. He knew that once he was taken in by a loving family. He had always belonged with them.

They had money and they gave him a proper education. Matteo went to college and traveled abroad. He got a job and he lived a normal life. Almost.

Matt still had a darkness that was unkempt. It was a tangled, matted mess inside of him. A force so great that he knew it couldn't be tamed. He was still angry. Matthew DeLong was smothered by layers and layers of Matteo Dellucci, but he would resurface now and again.

He beat his girlfriends when they tried to leave him. He got into bar fights over stupid bets. He couldn't play sports, because he got into too many fights with the opposing team. He would see red, *blood red*, and there was no other option in his mind other than violence.

However, nothing, *nothing*, stoked the fire within him like the homeless population. It was a reminder of his previous life. A reminder of his undesirable past. He wanted to bury it. He wanted to murder it. If he could kill Matthew DeLong, he would. So, in the face of every vagrant that he mutilated, that he beat, that he murdered- he saw himself, and it gave him great joy to watch the light go out of Matthew DeLong's eyes.

CHAPTER 51

VERA

Vera hit the water hard, her skin slapping it and stinging sharply as she sank down into the river, knocking the breath out of her in a swarm of bubbles that rushed to the surface.

What did I just do???

Vera resurfaced, panicked, gasping for air. She was a terrible swimmer, but she could tread water and she knew better than to fight the flow of the river. She was terrified, nonetheless.

What was swimming below her? How deep was the water? What was sitting at the bottom?

Vera knew that the river was generally an undesirable place to be submerged. People would play at the river, tan in the sun, drink beers, and throw sticks for their dogs, but the river itself was filthy. Most people didn't actually swim in it.

She had heard stories of there being broken glass and needles at the bottom, lodged in the dirt. She knew of homeless camps along the riverbanks and had heard rumors that they relieved themselves straight into the water. The river flowed, and the current was strong, so she was thankful that it was not stagnant water with that in mind.

The river was also a hot spot for fishing. People would go to the more open parts of the river in boats and pull massive fish out of the water. She had seen seals from the bay that had somehow made their way into the American and Sacramento rivers. She knew that it commonly held salmon and bass, but what else?

The water was black under the night sky and her mind took her to horrible places with the thought of being dragged under by some beast as the current whisked her downstream.

"Agh!" Vera cried out, taking in a mouthful of water as she felt herself smack against something hard and slimy, probably a tree that had fallen into the river and become submerged deep in the mud.

She struggled to keep her head above water as the river carried her back the direction she had just ran.

Jumping off the bridge?! What a terrible idea!

Vera could have sworn that the river flowed the other way and would carry her away from East Sac. She thought it would take her past Sac State and into the *Carmichael* area up the road. *So stupid!*

She gurgled and started trying to swim diagonally with the current, hoping to get herself to some piece of land with the momentum of the river as it carried her past the start of Paradise Beach, in the opposite direction she thought.

Something creeped against her skin under the water and she cried out, swallowing more of the river. She thrashed her body trying to get away, but it clung tightly to her, and Vera realized that she had become tangled in fishing line. She could see a river access point up ahead and swam hard for the beach with the limited range of motion she still had while being wrapped in the line. She felt a sharp pain in her leg and knew that she had been stabbed by the attached fishing hook.

She coughed and gasped, struggling to make it to the shore. It was so far away.

I'm not going to make it.

Her arms grew tired, her muscles began to lock up, and her body was tired of fighting. Tired of what it had been through. *Tired.* She wanted to rest.

With a few more strong attempts, Vera pushed herself toward the upcoming beach, but the current was too strong due to the incredibly rainy winter they had. The water levels were the highest they had been in years. She choked on the black water and franticly tried to keep her head above the surface as splashes filled her nose and mouth.

I'm going to die out here... Vera thought, horrified.

Again, she felt something brush against her. It felt hard as it bumped into her and her whole body jumped in terror. Whatever it was, it was big. She tried to push herself away from it but felt something smack against her other side and catch the fishing line that she was wrapped in. She felt a hard yank of the hook caught under her skin.

Vera cried out in pain and batted her arms around, trying to keep distance between herself and whatever was near her. She felt something rough against her hand, much closer than she had expected, and realized that she was caught between two floating logs. Immediately, she clung to the larger one for support, hoping to get her head out of the water and rest her tired legs.

The log twisted and rolled under her weight, and she sunk back into the water. She resurfaced in a panic and saw the log floating away from her. Vera swam hard to get it and felt the hook under her skin rip out, as the line had caught the log that was moving faster than she was.

"Aghhh!" Vera gurgled in the water. Pain and fear dragged her down and made her heavy as the logs flowed forward, escaping her grip.

Keep going. She willed herself.

In one last ditch effort, she thrust herself forward and caught the large log. She draped her arms over it, setting her chin on the wood, and let herself breathe for a moment as the black river carried her roughly under the moonlit sky.

Long minutes passed and Vera felt her eyes weigh heavily on her. She was exhausted and cold. The river was illuminated solely by the moon and she strained her eyes to keep track of her surroundings. The darkness was disorienting. She had been floating for too long though, she knew that. She clung to the log, afraid to push away from her safety, but she knew that she had to find her way to shore.

I'll just close my eyes for a moment… she thought, laying her cheek against the bark and imagining she was in her bed. A splash of water on her face scared her back to reality after a minute and she nearly lost her grip.

Fuck, stay awake Vera…

She squinted her eyes against the darkness as she passed under another bridge. She thought she saw another beach up ahead.

This is it, I have to make it to this beach or I'll die out here…

Everything in Vera's body told her to freeze and hold onto the log for dear life, but she knew she had to make a break for the beach. She squeezed her eyes shut and tried to count herself down to let go.

One, two… thr-

Something very large swam against her leg quickly. That one was alive. It wasn't a log. It wasn't a plant. It was unmistakably a creature of the river passing against her. It swam deeply below her and sent chills throughout her entire body as she felt it brush against her again.

Reflexively, she tore away from the log and thrashed, trying to scare it away. She twisted her body and kicked her legs, swallowing water, and fearfully throwing herself toward the beach. As soon her she was a few feet from the log, she felt the weight of her body drag her down. She had not been swimming for a while now and without the support from the log, she forgot how much effort she had exerted to stay above the surface of the river.

Vera choked and gasped, feeling her muscles lock up, rejecting her attempts to swim. She felt her arms collapsing as the weight of her legs pulled her down, deep into the river. She gave herself another pitiful few strokes before giving up. Again, water began to fill her nose and mouth. She coughed but couldn't bring herself to fight anymore. Vera closed her eyes as her head sank below the surface of the water.

She sank for a moment, feeling bubbles escape her lips and rise to the surface as her hair cascaded around her, suspended by the flowing water.

After another moment of fearful sinking Vera felt her feet drag along the bottom of the river and opened her eyes in the blackness. She tried to stand, realizing that she had made it to a much shallower point. She stood with a great deal of effort and was relieved to realize how much progress toward the beach she had made. Standing on her toes, she was just tall enough to keep her head above water. She fought the current with her steps, walking slowly and with purpose through the water, before collapsing on the shore when she finally made it to an ankle deep level.

She dragged her body forward until her face was out of the water.

I did it, she thought to herself. *I did it.*

Vera laid in the muddy sand, face down, and let herself become a victim to sleep.

CHAPTER 52

GEORGE

Alex turned onto the midtown grid after exiting the McDonald's drive through. George unwrapped his Egg McMuffin excitedly.

"You'd better not make a mess of my car dude," Alex scolded.

George rolled his eyes, looking around at the trash covered floor. "Really, dude?"

"Really!" Alex laughed.

George picked up a crumpled Taco Bell wrapper from the floor of Alex's 1991 Honda Accord.

"Taco Bell only huh?"

"Shut up," Alex retorted.

"You know you drive a *beater*, right?" George teased.

"This baby has been there for all my important milestones man. I lost my virginity in this car," Alex said, wide eyed.

George slurped his drive-through orange juice through the straw. "What? Last week with that chick from Benny's party? Was that your first time?" George snickered sarcastically.

Alex shoved him and grinned. "Yeah right man. I'm a fuckin' expert. Maybe in time I'll tell you my secret tricks."

George coughed hard and laughed. "That's the last thing I want. Don't tell me about your sex life Alex."

Alex smiled. "Pass me a hash brown."

They drove down 28th Street toward the *Sutter's Landing* river access point all the way at the end. After a few minutes, Alex pulled up the road and smiled at the empty parking lot.

"I love getting here in the mornings when there is nobody around."

George looked out the window at the soft navy sky as the sun struggled to come up. They pulled into a parking spot next to the community skate park that shared the access point. The dark warehouse had an ominous presence this early in the morning without the bustle of teenagers skating and loitering about.

As George rolled up his window, he took in a deep breath of morning air, catching a whiff of marijuana from the skatepark, and thinking that someone must have been sleeping in there and had woken up for a morning bowl.

Alex looked over at George.

"Bro, last time I was here, I swear I caught a fish this big." He gestured with his entire arm span.

They looked at each other and snickered.

"You're stupid, dude." George laughed as he got out of the car once they had parked. He reached into the back seat for his fishing pole and stuffed the last bite of McMuffin in his mouth.

Alex reached for his pole and tackle box from the back as well and locked the car. They walked out toward the path that led to the beach. George stopped abruptly when Alex jumped.

"Oh!" Alex shouted. "The beer!"

"Keep your voice down Alex," George laughed. "It's early. You'll scare the fish."

"Can't fish without beer Georgie!" Alex rushed back to the car and returned with a small cooler full of *Coors Light*.

Alex caught up to George and they walked toward the beach together. Alex led the way to his "secret spot" and George followed. The sun rose softly in the sky, turning it a cool periwinkle with a touch of pink in the distance. The river was calm and still, perfect for fishing.

They walked across the bike trail, down a dirt path, and into a beach clearing. Alex led them down the beach to the right for another hundred feet and stopped.

"Right… about…. here!" Alex said, smiling and turning to George. "What do you think?"

"It looks like all be spots we just passed Alex, and it's not really a secret spot." George laughed.

"No, this one has places to sit down, see." He gestured to the stumps that were pulled from the brush and out toward the beach. "I pulled all of these stumps out. They're *my* stump chairs."

George sat down on one of the stumps and fiddled with his fishing line, preparing his hook for when he cast out.

"Oh yeah, not bad, good back support," he teased.

Alex rolled his eyes. "Hater."

Once George was ready, he stood and cast his line by the river's edge. It was a brisk morning. He leaned his head back and let the breeze kiss his face.

"Toss me a beer?" He said to Alex after a few minutes.

They stood quietly, drinking their beers and listening to the birds wake up and begin their morning songs.

"Do you have class today?" George mumbled after a stretch of silence.

"Yeah, I have one after lunch. I'll probably go home and shower first," Alex replied softly.

George looked out at the soft flow of the current and thought about his conversation with Vera about skipping rocks. He hadn't had a single bite yet, so he reeled in his line and walked into the trees to picked up a soft, flat stone.

Once he found the perfect rock, he flicked his wrist and sent the stone skimming across the surface of the river. *One, two, three, four, clunk* and it sank.

"Dude! What the hell! You're scaring the fish away!"

George chucked and skipped another.

"Oh my god. Fuckin' stop. Are we fishing or not?"

"Alright, alright," George said, putting his hands up and reaching for his fishing pole to cast out again.

Alex scoffed. "Good luck now, there aren't any fish left in this spot after you tossed a bunch of rocks at them. They're probably all over there now," he said pointing.

George shook his head and drained his beer, reaching for another.

"I'm gonna go take a piss," Alex said, bringing in his line and leaning his fishing pole against one of the tree stumps.

George watched him walk down the shore to the right and into the trees. He turned back to the water and exhaled a calm breath.

He felt a little nudge on his line.

Oh?

Another soft nudge.

"Come on you little bastard…," George mumbled to himself.

He felt a quick tug and watched his line drag out.

"Yes! Oh, *fish on!*" He laughed excitedly, snapping back his pole to set the hook and reel in his catch.

"Fuck!" He heard Alex shout from the trees.

"George! GEORGE! Get the fuck over here! George!"

"Shit!" George said, fumbling with his line.

"One sec! I've got a bite!"

"George get the fuck over here NOW!" Alex yelled.

"Damn it," George said, reeling in his line quickly.

"GEORGE!" Alex wailed.

"Shit." He said, pulling in his line. "Oh nice!" he said, lifting a decent sized bass out of the water. He unhooked the fish's pierced cheek with his pliers and tossed him back into the river quickly.

"You lucked out today, you little shit," he muttered to the fish as he jogged down the beach to find Alex.

He made his way into the trees in the direction Alex had gone and fumbled through the plants.

"Alex? Where are you?"

"Over here!" He called out.

George followed toward his voice and saw through the trees that he was at the edge of the river crouched over something.

"What is that?" George asked.

"Some chick. I think she's dead…" Alex mumbled. "We have to call somebody."

George approached the body carefully. He noted the stringy mess of dark hair, matted with dirt and mud.

"Do you think she drowned?" He asked.

"It looks like it…" Alex said, picking up a stick and using it to prod the body.

"Alex, cut it out, that's a fucking real person."

She groaned slightly when he jabbed at her.

"Oh my god, she's alive!" Alex said, wide eyed.

George stepped closer and gently rolled her over.

"Oh fuck. Alex, it's Vera!" He shouted. "It's Vera! Get your phone! Call an ambulance! Vera, can you hear me, what happened to you?" George yelled, panicked.

Alex went pale.

"Alex! Call an ambulance!"

George lifted Vera off the beach in his arms and carried her back the way that they came. She was limp and pale, dead weight in his arms.

"You know what, fuck the ambulance, come on, let's drive her to the hospital. Get your keys," George commanded.

Alex went off running and George carried Vera up the trail and into the parking lot.

"You're okay, Ver," George whispered. "You're going to be okay."

CHAPTER 53

GINA

Gina sat on her bedroom floor, stunned by what she had discovered. The purple windbreaker was a delusion of her client's manic, psychotic, state. He couldn't be real. But what did it mean if Matteo had a purple windbreaker? It didn't mean anything. It couldn't.

She held it at arm's length, assessing it. It really was more of a purple jacket anyway, not a windbreaker. She tilted her head, as if maybe if she could get a look at it from another angle, she would understand.

The sun shone through the curtains of her bedroom, and she realized it was morning. Where was Matteo anyway? Charlotte never liked Matteo. She said that he seemed *shady*. Gina was in love with him though, absolutely head over heels, so Charlotte was supportive.

Some nights, he didn't come home though, and Gina had recently been suspecting that he might be cheating on her. He was a nutritionist for Christ's sake. Why would he need to work so late? Gina felt sick to her stomach.

He was cheating on her. He had to be. He wasn't stalking her clients in the night and hurting people. He was a bad boyfriend.

She stood and went into his closet, tearing his clothing out by the handfuls and throwing them into piles on the floor. She searched for some kind of evidence to his affair. A thong, a naked photo, a condom wrapper, a long strand of hair, lipstick on a shirt collar, anything that might help explain what was happening. *Nothing.*

She stood, breathing heavily over a pile of Matteo's clothing, tears streaming down her face. Howard Young suffered from schizotypal personality disorder and a touch of bipolar. He made connections that weren't there. He must have seen Matteo in this purple jacket at her work or something and created a narrative that wasn't real, like his story about broken glass and cups. She tried to steady her breathing.

Get a hold of yourself Gina.

She closed her eyes and pressed her tongue to the roof of her mouth, trying to stop her tears from falling.

Get a hold of yourself.

She went back to the purple jacket and dug through the pockets. She found a receipt from a Motel 6.

Perfect. So, he is a lousy cheating piece of shit.

She held it in her hands, examining it, looking for a date. She turned it over and gasped, dropping it and watching it flutter to the floor like a moth with a broken wing. There was a red smear on the back of the paper. Was it blood?

She thought back to the news stories she had seen.

Didn't they find a body by the Motel 6? Or was that somewhere else…? There have been so many.

No, it was absurd. Gina would know if Matt was a murderer.

She was a psychologist for *fucksake*. She chewed at her nails, unsure what to do.

Unsure who or what to believe.

She heard the front door open and keys clatter on the counter.

Matteo was home.

CHAPTER 54

CHARLOTTE

C harlotte had pulled a shift from hell in the emergency room. She was on call and ended up being paged in to help the ER after midnight. She absolutely was livid. Charlotte resented having to spend so much time in a section of the hospital that was generally not hers; however, the hospital was in crisis mode since the discovery of a serial murderer.

With every new person brought in, there was a palpable tension that they might have been a victim of the killer, although they had not seen another victim at their site since the homeless woman who had her nose broken.

Charlotte was finally finished with her night, as the sun was coming up, of course. *Ugh*. She couldn't wait to get home and crawl into bed. It was 6:30 in the morning.

She walked through the ER with her bag and headed for the door when a man rushed in with a battered young woman in his arms. He hurried past Charlotte and into the emergency room.

"Please, someone help me," he begged.

Charlotte let her curiosity get the better of her and went to find someone to assist them with their incoming trauma.

She was not five feet away when it all came together, and she felt the room spin as she caught a better look at the patient.

"V-Vera?" She felt her vision blur. "Oh no…," She was going down. The adrenaline, lack of sleep, and shock sent Charlotte to the floor.

"What the hell?!" Alex shouted, walking in behind George as Charlotte hit the floor in front of them. "Can we get some help here? What kind of hospital is this?"

Dr. Jones rushed over and checked to see if Charlotte had hit her head. He called two young medical assistants to the scene and asked them to handle getting her to a chair.

He turned to George as he stood helplessly, holding Vera.

"What is this? What happened?" Dr. Jones asked roughly.

"We found her at the river at *Sutter's Landing*. We thought she had drowned but it looks like she is alive. I'm not sure what happened, but we know her. We just found her this morning," Alex said quickly.

"Okay, what is her name?" Dr. Jones asked, waving over a stretcher for them to set her down.

"Her name is Vera Miller."

"We've got it from here boys. Thank you," Dr. Jones said, taking Vera away.

Alex looked over at the woman who had fainted. She was sitting upright in a chair, drinking from a cup water with two young women in scrubs.

"What was that about?" Alex mumbled to George.

She looked over and caught George's eye, standing and approaching them suddenly.

"What happened?" She asked Alex.

"We don't know, we just found her." He replied, defensive.

"Found her? Found her where?" Charlotte's eyes were wide with fear.

"At the river. She was washed up on shore. Do you know her?" George asked.

"That's my sister," Charlotte said, tears streaming down her face.

CHAPTER 55

SAM

The first time Sam became acutely aware of Matthew's dark tendencies was when he was fourteen and Matt was sixteen. It was Halloween and they had watched a horror movie together. The killer stabbed his victim in a murderous rage and then decapitated him and Matt said, "That doesn't look like it would be that hard to do, I bet I could do it." But they were just kids and Sam tried not to think too much of it.

He had sisters, but Matt was his only brother. He loved him more than anything. He would do anything for him. He had such a desire to emulate him, but he became aware that they had some different interests- particularly when it came to violence.

Sam had never been in a fight. Matt was so angry all the time that he would pick fights with strangers at random. Sam watched his brother throw fits like this and he knew that Matt had a kind of fire in him that couldn't be tamed. It would burn everyone and everything in its path.

When Matt went away to school as an adult, Sam thought that he had put his violence to rest. He went to Italy and seemed so happy. Sam went out to visit him once, when Matt was twenty-two and Sam was twenty. They went out one night while they were in *Gallipoli*. Sam and Matt were hitting it off with some Italian twins that they had met at a club, and they went back to the girl's place together.

Sam was kissing his girl, Cecilia, on the balcony when they heard a piercing scream. Sam and Cecelia ran inside to see Matt standing over the other twin, Lucia. Lucia was on the floor crying and bleeding from her nose. Cecilia shoved Matt and cursed at him in Italian, kicking the both of them out of their house so that she could tend to Lucia.

It looked as though Matt had struck her, hard, but Sam never got the story. Matt laughed when Sam asked what had happened and said that she had fallen.

It was on that same trip that Matt met his current girlfriend, Gina. Something in him changed in the moment they met. He seemed to soften; it really appeared to be love at first sight for him. By the end of Gina's trip, Matt was ready to come home because he couldn't stand the thought of being without her. Although Sam suspected it was because he had grown attached enough that he had claimed her as his and was already becoming possessive. Sam knew his brother's heart. He knew he didn't want her to *get away*.

Matt started keeping Sam at arm's length once they returned to the states and he and Gina moved in together. Truly, Sam didn't mind. Matt always supported Sam and they had made a pact to take care of each other and support one another no matter what the circumstance, no matter what the cost. By the time they had made that pact, Sam thought that Matt was rounding out his sharp edges. Gina seemed to be good for him, although Sam really had never formally met her. Matt kept her separate entirely.

They built their individual lives in Sacramento. Although, slowly but surely, Sam saw Matthew resurfacing beneath Matteo. He saw that he was growing restless, feeling his dark blood boil under his skin and his need to satiate his malevolent appetite.

They went out for drinks one night. They always drank whisky together, *Pendleton*, and on this particular night, Matt was feeling extremely pent up. When they left the bar that night, they walked home, knowing that neither of them could drive. Matt saw a man sleeping behind a dumpster in an alley and he looked to Sam and laughed. "Watch this," he said, and then he proceeded to beat the man to death.

Sam was shocked to see it in front of his face, but not all in all surprised that he had finally broken like this. He tried to stop him, but something in him held him back. He froze like a deer in the headlights. He loved his brother. His insane, evil, psychologically twisted brother. Matt told Sam that the guy was just a homeless man and that nobody would even know he was gone. It made sense at the time and Sam fell victim to protecting his brother.

It became like a game. The stakes were high; it was like gambling. They would get creative, strategize, try to find the best places for him to hunt, and in new and creative ways. Sam dehumanized the victims to cope, and Matt was so disconnected from empathy that Sam didn't think his brother ever saw them as human to begin with.

One day, Matt brought home a dog, but he told Sam that Gina was allergic. He asked Sam if the dog could live with him, and Sam accepted. How could he say no? Matt was his brother.

When the killings got bad in midtown and he had a name cultivated for him, *The Midtown Murderer*. Sam worried that things might be falling apart, but when they didn't, he began to think that maybe his brother really was invincible.

Matt had a good job, and he was charismatic. He had a lot of money in savings and he helped Sam buy a home in East Sacramento, on *Elvas*. It was a fixer-upper for sure. A real piece of work that sold for very little, considering the neighborhood. Sam had been renting in River Park for a few years and couldn't wait to own the home on Elvas. Matt told Sam that it would be his once it was finished, as long as he could come stay the night and hang out when he wanted to.

It wasn't until Vera showed up on his doorstep that he realized Matt had been using it as a crash point when he hunted his victims. Many nights, Matt would sleep over at Sam's place, or rinse off after he had attacked someone, but recently he had not been coming over as often, other than to drop off Duke after his walks. Sam wondered if Matt had been staying at the house on Elvas.

Overall, Sam minded his own business. He got a job at Mosaic and continued his education in school. He made friends, and became involved with a girl, *Vera*. Matt had no idea that the victim he had picked up at the ATM was someone that Sam was invested in. But Sam knew where his loyalties belonged. As quickly as he developed feelings for Vera, he shut them down. His brother needed him now, and she knew too much.

CHAPTER 56

MATT

Matteo climbed the stairs to his bedroom quietly, so as not to wake Gina too early before work. He knew that she had a late start today and thought that he might be able to slip into bed without her noticing that he had been gone all night. He didn't have a good story under his belt for defense. He really didn't expect to be out late like he was.

He stopped at a mirror in the hall and examined his neck. Two small puncture wounds were clearly visible from when Vera had stuck him with those needles. He ran his fingers over them. Hopefully she wouldn't notice.

As he rounded the corner at the top of the stairs, he noted that the light to their bedroom was on. He opened the door gently and saw Gina sitting on the floor surrounded by piles and piles of his clothing, all torn out from the closet. It looked like their room had been hit by a hurricane.

"Gina, what the hell happened?"

Gina didn't move. She looked at the piles of clothing and stood up; she had been crying.

Shit, what did she find? What did I do now?

Matteo ran his hands through his hair angrily.

"Gina. What happened?" He pushed. He was frustrated. He wanted to go to sleep. This was the last fucking thing he needed right now. His prey had escaped earlier, and Sam was mad at him; he couldn't deal with Gina too.

"Why didn't you come home last night?" She asked finally.

"I was working late."

"Oh yeah? Did you sleep at the fucking office? You're a nutritionist, Matteo, not a goddamn surgeon. Where were you?"

"I was out."

"Yeah, I know that. Where. Were. You." She hissed.

"I *said* I was out." He snapped.

Gina ran her hands through her hair. "Are you sleeping with someone else?" She asked.

Oh my god. Are you kidding me right now? Matt thought to himself. He was a lot of things, but he was not an adulterous man. He would never cheat on Gina.

"Gina, what the fuck? No. Of course not. What is your problem?" He yelled at her. He was *really* angry now.

"What the hell is this?!" Gina said, holding a piece of paper out to him. "It's a receipt for a Motel 6! Is this fucking lipstick on the back? Tell me you're sleeping with someone else, Matt, because I don't know what else to think." She began pacing the room.

Matt felt his heart sink. *It's blood.*

"I mean what else? Huh? Are you the Midtown Murderer or something?" Gina said, sarcastically, throwing her hands up. "Because it's either lipstick or blood. It had better be fucking lipstick, Matteo," She said breathlessly, begging and in denial.

Matt was at a loss for words. Gina stopped pacing and looked at him.

"Matteo?"

He stared at her, his eyes wide.

"Matteo?" Her voice shook as she took a step away from him.

How dare she accuse him of so many things. Look at the life they had. Look at what he has done for her. Look at all that he continues to do. She would come at him and accuse him of *cheating* on her? After everything they had been through? After everything he had been through? Family is the most important thing of all. Gina was his family. Maybe she didn't deserve to be. Maybe she was rotten after all. All he had was Sam and that's all he would ever need.

He looked at her and smiled, a sickening, violent smile.

"Matt, tell me this is lipstick…," Gina begged.

He took a step toward her.

"It's lipstick," he said sweetly, maintaining his gruesome grin.

Gina swallowed hard. "It isn't…, is it?"

Matt looked down at the floor and chucked softly to himself.

"Oh, baby, look at the mess you've made."

He smiled up at her again.

Gina was shaking like a leaf. She folded up the receipt and slipped it into the pocket of her sweatpants. Matt watched her do it and his face hardened.

"Gina. Give me the receipt."

Her eyes darted around the room, looking for a way out.

"Give me the receipt. I'm not going to ask you again." Matt held out his hand.

Gina took a deep breath, unsure what she was going to do, and darted for the door. Matt shook his head.

Looks like we'll be doing this the hard way.

He turned through the doorway to follow her out and grabbed her by the back of her shirt, catching her by surprise. She gagged as her crew neck caught her throat hard. Gina swung an arm out and hit him hard with an elbow to the face.

He released her shirt but gave her a hard shove and she went toppling down the stairs. She hit the wall at the bottom with a hard thud.

"GIVE ME THAT RECEIPT GINA!" He bellowed from the top of the staircase.

"*Fuck you* Matteo!" She shouted through her tears.

He started down the stairs and Gina stood to run.

"Oh my god," Matteo mumbled to himself frustratedly.

He skipped the last few steps and rushed into the kitchen, he grabbed Gina by the back of the neck and tossed her hard into the wall. A framed photo of the two of them fell and broke on the ground. Gina sobbed.

"Give me that receipt," he snarled at her, picking her up by her shirt and holding her against the wall.

"No!" She cried out. "I'm going to the police!"

He slapped her hard across the face and she wailed. He let go of her shirt and wound up to hit her again, swinging his arm with such momentum that it sent her toppling to the ground after striking her.

Gina fell into the pile of broken glass from the picture frame and began to bleed. Tears streamed down her face. She picked up a shard of broken glass and backed up into a corner.

"Stay back!" She said, her voice shaking.

He lunged for her and Gina took a swipe, cutting his cheek deeply with the blade of glass. Blood poured down his face in dark streaks. His eyes went wild, frenzied, hungry, like a predator ready to move in for the kill.

He lunged for her again and she took another swipe, this time getting his abdomen through his shirt. She rolled through the glass and tried to go between his legs to escape but he came down on top of her and Gina was crushed beneath his weight.

He brought his fists down hard, raining blows. He heard her nose break and felt the bones crack against his hand. He laughed a wicked laugh.

"Who are you???" Gina cried, blood filling her mouth.

He stood and kicked her. She curled into a ball to protect herself and Matteo turned to the kitchen, reaching for their knife block.

Gina saw it coming but couldn't move. Paralyzed by fear and the pain of broken bones, she laid on the kitchen floor, helpless, waiting for it all to end.

He turned back toward her, holding a long knife from their block. It was beautiful, a housewarming gift from her father. She had always loved those knives. Gina closed her eyes.

This is it. Please let it be quick. She thought to herself.

A loud crack startled her, and she looked up, gasping in surprise.

Howard Young was standing in her kitchen with them. He had swung a bottle of Pendleton that was on the counter from the night before and broken it over Matteo's head.

Whisky poured onto the floor and ran down Matt's body as he lost his balance and fell forward. His knife clattered to the floor and slid under the refrigerator. Howard approached him nervously and struck him once more with his fist, knocking him unconscious.

Gina looked up at him, stunned.

"What the *hell* are you doing here?" She asked him.

"The- the man with the purple…" He trailed off, exacerbated, "I told you that you were in danger."

Gina smiled gently through her tears. "You were right."

"I was right," he repeated to himself. "I was right…"

"Howard, *please*, call 911 before he wakes up."

Howard withdrew his cell from his pocket and dialed.

Gina scanned her surroundings wondering how he had gotten inside. The front door was wide open. Matteo must have left it unlocked when he got home.

Howard crouched on the ground next to Gina.

"I'm sorry that I called the police on you yesterday," Gina said, thankful that he had returned and saved her life.

"They removed me from the property and gave me a ride home."

"I am going to transfer your care to a colleague, Howard. I am so grateful, and I owe my life to you, but this relationship has become inappropriate. I'm sorry."

He shook his head. "I understand. I'm glad you are okay, Dr. Garcia."

She smiled through her pain. They sat in silence, listening for the sound of the approaching sirens.

CHAPTER 57

VERA

Vera opened her eyes slowly to the sound of beeping monitors and muffled voices. The first thing she noted was the bittersweet smell of *Acqua di Gio*. She smiled to herself. *I'm haunted by the ghosts of boyfriends past...*

She blinked the sleep from her eyes and waited for them to adjust. Charlotte's husband Conner sat in a chair next to her, reading a book. She turned her head toward him.

"That any good?" She mumbled.

Conner set his book down and looked over at her with a gentle, sleepy smile.

"You're awake," he said.

"I'm awake," Vera echoed with a mumble.

He looked down at his book. "*Stephen King*," he said, patting it affectionately. "All of his work is good."

Vera turned her head to face the ceiling.

"You haven't seen enough horror yet?" She muttered.

"It's my escape from reality. Although I think your situation is more twisted than what is happening in the first few pages of this story. I'm sorry; I'll put it away."

Vera looked at him sadly. She didn't mean to direct her anger at him. She liked Conner and it was comforting to her that he wanted to be here.

Vera lifted a hand to scratch her nose, she examined her hand, noticing an IV as she did so.

"What happened?" She asked Conner, hoping that she hadn't scared the conversation out of him.

"Do you remember the attack?" He asked.

"Yeah, I don't remember how I ended up here though."

"Well, the police want to take a report, but it sounds like you were found on a riverbank by a couple of guys. You were pretty banged up. The doctor said that you have four cracked ribs. Your blood sugar was 590 by the time they got you in, so they've given you some insulin. You've been through a lot."

"Where is Charlotte?" Vera asked sadly, wanting to see her sister.

"She went home to take a shower. I told her I would stay with you. She had been here since late last night; she was on call. She was actually here when you were brought in. Char was a mess when she saw you like that. It took a long time for me to convince her to take a break and go home to recover for an hour or so. I'm sure you know she is pregnant... I'm just trying to look out for her. She was so worked up," Conner said apologetically, as if he were thinking now that he had said it out loud, that he should have let her stay.

"No, it's okay. I understand. I know how she can be," Vera reassured him.

She meant it, too. Charlotte was a tiger sister. She was fiercely loyal. Vera was actually surprised that Conner had convinced her to go home at all.

"I'm glad you are okay," he said, reaching out a hand to her. She took it and smiled.

"I'm going to run to the cafeteria and get some coffee. Is that alright? Do you want anything?"

Vera shook her head. "I'm okay. Go ahead though. Thanks for asking."

Conner stood to leave. "Be right back," he said, with a warm smile as he turned out of the door.

Vera's whole body ached. She closed her eyes and allowed a single tear to roll down her cheek. Her mind flashed to the cold, dark river as she thrashed around, against the current. She opened her eyes and tried to focus on something else.

She could hear a steady drip from the leaky hospital sink in her bathroom and was brought back to the moment when she woke up on the tile floor of that disgusting, dilapidated house.

Vera squeezed her eyes shut and tried to breathe through her anxiety.

"Hello Vera." She opened her eyes, hoping that she had misheard that voice.

Sam stood in front of her. He closed the door with a soft click. Vera reached for her call button, but he lunged for her bed and got to it first, pulling the remote away from her reach. He sat down on the end of her bed.

"I want you to know that I wasn't in on your kidnapping. I had real feelings for you. I thought that this relationship might have had a shot at becoming something. I am so angry with my brother for putting me in this position."

"Your brother?" Vera choked out. Her throat was still raw.

"Yeah. Didn't know I had a brother, did you?" He smiled sadly.

"He's the Midtown Murderer, isn't he?"

"Yeah, unfortunately. But he's family and I love him."

"Sam, you need to go to the police. Do the right thing."

Sam was quiet for a moment. Vera thought that he might actually be considering it. After another quiet moment, he looked at her and stood.

"Oh, I intend to," Sam said, picking up a pillow from the side chair that Conner had been sitting in.

"Sam…," Vera pleaded.

"You know way too much, Vera," Sam said, walking toward her with the pillow held up to smother her.

"Vera, how are we feeling?" The door opened roughly, and Dr. Jones stepped into the room, looking down at his clipboard.

Sam dropped the pillow and shot Vera a vengeful, panicked glance before bolting out of the room. He shoulder-checked Dr. Jones as he left, knocking him off balance and into the wall.

"HEY!" Dr. Jones shouted, following Sam into the hall. He turned back to Vera. "What was that about?" He snapped angrily.

"That's one of the men who attacked me, Dr. Jones," Vera croaked. "Get help, please."

With wide, alert eyes, Dr. Jones darted out into the hallway to call a code and get security.

"Lock down the hospital." Vera heard him say from outside of her door.

CHAPTER 58

SAM

Sam raced down the hall, skidding around a corner and crashing into a cluster of nurses who were standing around a counter. One woman fell to her feet, the other yelled at him and told him to stop running.

Things began to happen very quickly. The hospital was on lock down and he had no idea what he was going to do. Sam had not thought his plan through at all. He just went into this blindly protecting Matteo, because that is what Matteo would do for him. They were brothers. They had each other's backs no matter the circumstances.

Sam turned down a quiet hallway and tried several door handles until he found one that would unlock. He looked around. He was in a small cafeteria. He was surprised to see it empty. Or almost empty... As he released a breath of relief thinking that he was alone, he saw a man step around a corner holding a paper cup of coffee.

Be cool…, Sam told himself.

Conner walked up to him slowly, sipping his coffee.

"I heard the hospital is on lock down. Any idea what happened?" He asked Sam.

Sam composed himself silently. "Uh, yeah, I don't know. I'm here visiting my grandpa…," he lied.

"Oh, I'm sorry to hear that. Is he okay?"

"Yeah, uh, hip replacement or something like that. He just got out of surgery."

"Hmm." Conner nodded suspiciously. He looked around.

"Well, I'm sure he had a great doctor. I work here myself. I am an orthopedic surgeon for the hospital." He paused to blow on his hot coffee to cool it, and then continued.

"I specialize in hip replacements actually. That and amputations. Pretty much all surgeries related. I didn't realize we had any hip replacements scheduled today. I usually work with one other surgeon who does them, but she is on maternity leave. So… I would have been the one to do that surgery. I've done a few knees this week, but no hips. And none today." Conner sipped his coffee, eyeing Sam.

"I know you," Conner continued, pointing with one finger lifted from the rim his paper cup. "Where do I know you from?"

Sam shook his head.

"Do you work at that pub with Vera?"

Sam shook his head again.

Conner watched him, putting pieces together in his mind. If he was right, and this was one of the men responsible for Vera's attack, he should do something. If he was wrong, and this was a friend of Vera's visiting a family member and he confronted him physically, that would be assault, and he could lose his job and medical license if he were charged.

Sam shifted nervously and looked around the room, it was empty.

Conner shook his finger at him softly and nodded his head. "You're the guy, aren't you?"

"What guy?" Sam asked, playing dumb.

"Why are you *really* here?" Conner asked.

Sam cleared his throat, thinking fast. "Vera and I are dating. She wanted to keep it a secret. I was trying to sneak in and see her without running into anyone. We work together, you know? We want to keep in low key. I was just hoping to see her. I'm so worried about her."

Conner nodded slowly.

"You came to visit Vera, huh?" He asked.

"Yeah. I just stopped in to check on her."

There was a pause and they looked at each other thoughtfully. Sam thought that Conner might be buying it. Conner's eyes hardened and he released a breath.

"How did you know she was here?" Conner asked sharply.

Shit.

Sam swung a fist at Conner, hoping to catch him by surprise across the jaw, but Conner had seen it coming and dodged it quickly.

Conner flicked his wrist and tossed hot coffee onto Sam in a rapid splash. Steam rose from Sam's skin and he screamed.

Conner took advantage of his distraction and dove at Sam, tackling him by the waist, sending them both onto the floor. Conner rolled onto Sam and put his knees into his back, pinning him still.

"Hey! Can I get some help in here!" He shouted as loudly as he could. "Security!" He yelled.

Sam struggled beneath him, thrashing and kicking. Conner was much larger than Sam and had him trapped.

Not without a fight, Sam thought to himself angrily.

His hand was pinned to his side, but he could reach into his pocket. He pulled a small Swiss Army knife from his jeans and swayed, trying to rock Conner's weight.

Conner resisted him and continued to call for help.

Come on, Sam, Matt would be able to do it. He willed himself.

With all of his strength, he bucked one last time, sending Conner slightly off balance, which was just enough to let up on his weight. Sam rolled his position so that he was facing up and when Conner came back on top of him Sam dug the blade of his knife into Conner's thigh.

Conner howled in pain and surprise. Sam pulled the knife back out and Conner's wound gushed with blood.

"Fuck!" Conner cried out fearfully, holding pressure to his wound to try to stop the bleeding. He toppled over, off of Sam and onto the floor. Sam stood to run, but Matt's voice echoed in his head.

Finish the job.

Sam took a step toward Conner, knife raised over his head, ready to deliver another blow, when security burst through the door to the small cafeteria, running quickly upon seeing the scene.

Startled, Sam dropped the knife and turned to run. Security tackled him in an instant swoop and held him down as the police followed in suit.

Conner was assessed quickly, and hospital staff poured in when called upon to tend to one of their own.

"Dr. Kowalski!" One of the nurses called out, rushing to his side. "Get help!" She called to the others.

Lightheaded from the blood loss, Conner looked over at Sam as he struggled. They locked eyes. Conner lifted a shaky, blood covered hand and gave him a middle finger as the police lifted Sam to his feet, escorting him out in handcuffs.

CHAPTER 59

VERA

News broke about the arrest of the Midtown Murderer and spread like wildfire. The city released an almost audible sigh of relief as locals felt safer leaving the house.

Vera's wounds took some time to heal, but she left the hospital shortly after her blood glucose levels stabilized and she was properly rehydrated. The following Monday, she returned to work for her usual shift.

Mosaic Brew Pub took a huge emotional hit during this time. The arrest of Sam, a well-liked employee, for being an accomplice to the murders in midtown upset their regular customers significantly. Many people did not want to bring their business to Mosaic any longer.

The owners did their best to distance themselves from these crimes and released a public statement that they were not affiliated with, nor do they support, the actions of their former employee.

Sam's name was dragged through the mud in the eyes of the community. Nevertheless, a new body of curious customers with dark taste began to frequent the pub as if it were a haunted house.

"The Midtown Murderer worked here...," they would whisper, misinformed.

"No, his accomplice worked here."

"I hear they murdered someone together in the brew house."

The rumors spread and Mosaic suffered for it. The pub had seen tough days, but they were resilient. Through perseverance, they would survive the wave of media attention, and people would move on to the next big story after that. There was always something else.

Vera stood behind the bar, wiping the counter where their regular Marty used to sit. After learning of his very tragic death, she spoke to the owners about getting a plaque made in his memory to put above the bar. They were enthusiastic about the idea, for a chance to honor a good man's memory and to help soften the blow that the murders had on their image. The community liked Marty. He was a wonderful man who had been through hell. He was a fighter. Vera liked to think that he had at least gone down with some fire.

She pushed her bangs out of her face and took a seat on a stool behind the bar. It had been a slow day. She poured herself a short beer from the tap and took a refreshing sip. It was a new hazy IPA. Vera's mind flashed to the day she came in after her car was side swiped at school and Sam had offered her their new Hazy that was on tap at the time.

"You know I don't like that shit Sam...," she had laughed.

She pictured his wink in her mind as he turned to pour her one anyway. She shuddered. She was so confused by her relationship with Sam and felt so betrayed by him. She had nightmares about him now, kissing her, and then trying to smother her with a pillow.

As well as other equally vivid dreams of waking up on the

bathroom floor in that filthy house. The faucet of the sink would be running, pouring cold, dark river water into the room- flooding the bathroom with the Sacramento River as she tried to tread water, unable to escape. She would gasp for air, treading as the room filled up to the ceiling, until she sank to the floor. She would always wake up in a cold sweat. She found herself washing her sheets several times a week.

Vera looked down at the hazy in her hand and set it back on the counter. It turned out better than the one that Sam had her taste those few weeks back, but she still preferred something with more bite. A West Coast IPA or a Pale Ale. Marty would have liked the new hazy though. And it would have fucked his blood sugar up, too. Vera felt a tear prickle in the corner of her eye for their lost regular. She wiped it away quickly as she saw a customer approach in her peripheral vision.

"Hey Ver," George said softly as she turned around.

"Oh, hey George." She smiled.

"How are you doing?"

Vera looked around, the pub was empty. She sighed.

"I'm okay. About as well as you would expect, I think."

He pulled out a stool and took a seat at the bar.

"Beer?" Vera asked.

"Sure. Surprise me," he said. His tone was playful but gentle, as though he didn't want to disturb the silent pub and wanted to be conscientious of her mood.

She turned and poured them each a Pale Ale. She poured herself a half pint since she was working but poured a full stein for George. She set his beer on the counter.

"What is it?" He asked.

"You tell me." She smiled.

He rolled his eyes playfully and took a sip, leaving a mustache of foam resting on his upper lip for a moment before wiping it with the back of his hand.

"It's kind of hoppy. Is it a West Coast?"

"Close. It is our Pale Ale. It's a little milder than the West Coast," Vera said, sipping hers.

"I like it," he responded after another drink.

They sat quietly for a moment and enjoyed a comfortable, beer-drinking-silence.

"You know, I didn't come for the beer," George said.

"I know." Vera smiled softly.

The weight of that hung between them in their silence. It was unspoken, but there was something there. Although Vera wasn't ready to address it yet. And George could tell, he would wait.

"You know, I think you saved my life George."

He lowered the stein from his lips and shook his head.

"Dr. Jones saved your life. I just carried you off the riverbank," George said seriously.

"I did have to let my fish go to rescue you though. But you're a much better catch," he added to lighten the mood.

Vera chucked at his cheesy joke.

"Well, thank you." She smiled.

"You're welcome," He replied softly, lifting his beer again.

"Cheers, Vera."

"Cheers, George."

They finished the rest of their beers in silence.

CHAPTER 60
ELIJAH

Elijah mixed some cream into his coffee and walked out of the break room. It had been a long weekend. He and Daniel had gone to Monterey to spend some alone time together, out of Sacramento, and away from the violence. On Thursday last week, a news story broke that the Midtown Murderer had been caught but they were refusing to publicize a name or photo of him in attempt to reduce glamorizing his crimes.

It was agreed that giving murderers the spotlight was the wrong message to be sending to people. He was off the street, and that was the end of the news. The very next day, however, the name of an accomplice had been leaked by a hospital staff member who was present during his Wednesday arrest, and the city buzzed with this information. Still, Elijah and Daniel wanted to get away from it all. It was just too heavy.

Elijah yawned and sat down at his desk, wishing he were still in Monterey instead of preparing to see his first client of the day. She was referred by Gina. The client was a friend of hers whom she could not see herself because it would be an inappropriate conflict of interest. That and the fact that Gina had taken a leave of absence to recover from some sudden personal turmoil that she didn't want to go into with Elijah. He understood. *We all have our own skeletons in our closets.*

Last week, she had called out of work due to a family emergency and never returned after that. She said that something traumatic had happened and she needed time to process it, but she wasn't sure how long she would be out. She implied that she may never come back.

Gina transferred her client Howard Young to Elijah, and he was fine with that since he had helped consult on this case anyway. She referred her diabetic client, Martin Alvarez, to Lucy Williams, another psychologist and Certified Diabetes Educator that worked in their practice, although it was discovered shortly after the referral had gone through that Mr. Alvarez lost his life to the Midtown Murderer.

Elijah was shocked to find that out and suspected that this may be, at least part of the reason, that Gina had left. He was sure that even if it was not the reason, this was not contributing well to her personal issues. Gina's last client, Mark Langdon, refused to return to therapy after finding out that Dr. Garcia was taking leave, so they let him go.

Elijah finished his coffee and stood to retrieve his new client from the waiting area and bring her back to his office. She was a young woman, twenty-three years old, who was recovering from a trauma. Gina alluded that she might have some PTSD, but who could say without seeing her for an assessment.

She had a young face, dark hair and long bangs that framed

her tanned cheeks. She didn't smile as she sat in the waiting room. She looked nervous, like clients often did on their first day in. Gina had mentioned that this referral had no prior experience with therapy.

He gestured for her to follow him, and she walked slowly down the hallway with her hands clasped in front of her. She took a seat on the edge of his soft green couch and looked around.

"Good morning," he said softly.

"Good morning," she replied.

"Do you prefer Vera or Miss Miller?" He asked.

"Vera is fine," she said, rubbing her hands on her jeans.

"So, Vera, tell me your story. What brings you in?" Elijah asked gently.

She released a soft breath and smiled sadly.

"*Where do I begin?*"

AFTERWORD FROM THE AUTHOR

I have wanted to write about diabetes for years. I thought I would write it as non-fiction. I dreamed about giving a Ted Talk, detailing what should be changed and how living with diabetes is so much more than just balancing blood sugar levels like one would balance a checkbook. It's complex, exhausting, and emotional. It is a full-time job.

34 million Americans have diabetes, that is 1 in 10 people. I would be willing to bet that you have diabetes, or that you know someone in your family or friend group who does. 1.9 million of those diabetics have type 1 diabetes. The population is significantly less vast than type 2 diabetes but a huge number still.

If I am being optimistic, I would judge that of those 34 million people struggling to deal with their diabetes, and those 1.9 million people who can directly relate to type 1 diabetes, at least half of them can read. So, I figured maybe I could get my message across and connect to people this way. Maybe I could reach people without diabetes, too. People who like to read and people who like thrillers. My hope is to spread awareness. To show readers that we are among you, living normal lives, with added daily decisions and frustrations.

Most of the experiences that Vera goes through in her regular diabetic life are based on things that I have experienced myself. A lot of them are things that have actually happened to me. The plot of the thriller is fiction, I confess. But Vera's daily diabetic life is *very* close to my own, and possibly to yours too, if you are type 1 as well.

I see you. And I empathize with your struggles.

Made in the USA
Las Vegas, NV
02 March 2024